...ll Your Brother

...Heath's unique sense of twisted fun
...ld be his best thriller yet. It's brilliant
from start to finish, boasting an irresistible premise and shocking
twists all the way through. It's fiendish in its cleverness and
startling in its originality. Don't miss it.'
GABRIEL BERGMOSER, author of *The Hunted*

'Forget the plot twist, Jack Heath's books are pure
twist from start to finish.'
SARAH BAILEY, author of *The Housemate*

'Jack Heath's latest thriller is like *Survivor* on steroids . . .
but with real intelligence and a ton of heart. *Kill Your Brother*
is rural noir at its hottest, grittiest and most claustrophobic . . .
and its most exciting.'
GREG WOODLAND, author of *The Night Whistler*

'Keep *Kill Your Brother* with your passport and children, because
if the house catches fire, you'll fight to take it with you.'
PAUL CLEAVE, author of *The Cleaner*

'Jack Heath's new novel, *Kill Your Brother*, is compelling
from its chilling title to the gripping finish. Evil flies
out from where you least expect.'
JOHN M. GREEN, author of *Nowhere Man*

'*Kill Your Brother* is a pacy, tense thriller with memorable characters
and an unpredictable mystery at its core. I gulped the entire thing
down in a single sitting and you'll want to do the same!'
SAM HAWKE, author of *City of Lies*

'A complex and claustrophobic thriller with a hell of a conundrum
at its core, and a truly twisted series of developments along the way.'
ALAN BAXTER, author of *Bound*

'Heath's characters grab you by the throat and drag you
with them—every fight, every defeat, every hope.'
SULARI GENTILL, author of *Shanghai Secrets*

KILL YOUR BROTHER

JACK HEATH

ALLEN&UNWIN

SYDNEY・MELBOURNE・AUCKLAND・LONDON

This edition published in 2023
First published in 2021

Allen & Unwin
Cammeraygal Country
83 Alexander Street
Crows Nest NSW 2065
Australia
Phone: (61 2) 8425 0100
Email: info@allenandunwin.com
Web: www.allenandunwin.com

Allen & Unwin acknowledges the Traditional Owners of the Country on which we live and work. We pay our respects to all Aboriginal and Torres Strait Islander Elders, past and present.

A catalogue record for this book is available from the National Library of Australia

ISBN 978 1 76106 955 0

Set in Sabon LT by Midland Typesetters, Australia
Printed and bound in Australia by the Opus Group

10 9 8 7 6 5 4 3 2 1

The paper in this book is FSC® certified. FSC® promotes environmentally responsible, socially beneficial and economically viable management of the world's forests.

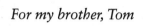

For my brother, Tom

AUTHOR'S NOTE

This book is based on the Audible Original *Kill Your Brother*. It has been expanded and revised for print and digital publication. Both versions of the story contain scenes that some readers may find disturbing. The book is unsuitable for children and some adults.

If somebody whispered to me, 'You can have your pick',
If kind fortune came to woo me, when the gold was thick,
I would still, by hill and hollow, round the world away,
Stirring deeds of contest follow, till I'm bent and grey.

—Grantland Rice

PROLOGUE

'I think we got off on the wrong foot,' the woman says.

Elise keeps her voice even. 'Right.'

'Are you hungry?' The woman's hair is steely grey, her arms muscled from years of labour, her right shoulder bruised from the butt of a rifle. But she sounds gentle, like someone's aunt. The illusion is completed by a sleeveless linen shirt with mother-of-pearl buttons, and the plate of homemade biscuits she's put on the antique coffee table.

'I'm fine,' Elise says.

The woman slides the plate towards her anyway. The biscuits are topped with raspberry jam and sprinkled with coconut, but their sweetness might be hiding a more dangerous ingredient. Elise grips the arms of the recliner, her fingertips gouging the overstuffed fabric, so she won't be tempted to take one.

'You poor thing.' The woman is looking at the puncture wounds on Elise's hands.

'They don't hurt,' she lies.

'Here.' The woman crosses the living room and opens a lacquered pine cupboard.

Her back is turned. Should Elise run? But she's still weak from the tranquilliser—and it's already too late. The woman is coming back, taking Betadine and bandages from a plastic box.

'Really, I'm okay.' Elise needs antibiotics, not antiseptic. The woman ignores her, kneeling and dabbing the stinging fluid on the scratches, then winding stretchy bandages around her knuckles and wrists.

The woman's fingers are cold, talon-like. Elise can smell Lady Grey tea on her breath.

Soon Elise's knuckles are trussed up. She looks like a kickboxer about to step into the ring.

'There. All better?' The woman sounds as though she's talking to a toddler.

Elise nods.

'I don't want you to be uncomfortable,' the woman presses. 'No more than is necessary.'

'Thanks.'

The woman puts the first-aid box back in the cupboard and settles into the couch opposite. 'So,' she says, 'we have a problem. I hope we can solve it together.'

Elise doesn't trust herself to speak.

The woman continues: 'There's an American term: beef. It means to take issue with something someone has done. Or something someone else has done—a "beef" can be inherited. You've heard of that?'

'I guess so,' Elise says cautiously. It's almost funny. She's on a sheep farm, but the sheep are long gone, and the farmer is explaining the concept of having a beef.

'Have we met before?' the woman asks suddenly, frowning.

Elise's pulse goes into overdrive. 'I, uh, saw you following me. I wouldn't say we met.'

'But before that?'

'No, I don't think so.'

The woman gives Elise a thoughtful look. Elise has dyed her hair red and cut it short, and there's a phoenix tattoo on her neck—has she changed enough?

Finally the woman leans back against the couch. 'Hmm. Just a moment of déjà vu.'

Elise holds her gaze. 'Must be.'

'Anyway, I have no problem with you. My beef is with *him.*' The woman jerks her head towards the back of the house.

'What did he do to you?' Elise tries to sound as though she doesn't care one way or the other.

'To me? Nothing at all.' The woman clears her throat. 'The point is, I can't let you go. Because you know he's here.'

Elise licks her lips. 'I won't tell anyone about—'

'Don't insult me,' the woman snaps. For a second, the friendly aunt disappears, replaced by something hard and sharp. Her deep-set eyes darken in her leathery face. Then the warmth is back. 'So I find myself in a pickle—that's a good expression, too.'

A grandfather clock ticks softly in the corner.

'When I captured him, I made sure no one would come looking, or I thought I had.' The woman gives Elise a grudging nod. 'But I made no such preparations with you. People must be wondering where you are.'

Elise doubts this. She's unemployed. She has no friends left. Anyone who notices her disappearance will be pleased about it. No help is coming.

'I think I have a solution.' The woman stands up again. There's a little cardboard box on the mantel. The woman opens it, and produces a knife.

Elise tries to leap out of the armchair. The woman lunges at the same moment. Elise makes it only halfway up before the woman shoves her back down and pins her against the upholstery, crushing her shoulder. She's terrifyingly strong. Elise has no hope of overpowering her. Not with the sedative still swimming through her veins.

The knife trembles in the woman's grip. It's a short blade, just big enough to slice an apple. Through clenched teeth, she says, 'Hear me out.'

Elise swallows, her heart thumping in her ears. 'Okay. I'm listening.'

The woman releases her. Puts the knife on the coffee table next to the biscuits, raises her open palms. 'Here's my proposal. I'll let you go. And you won't tell the police where you've been.'

'Deal,' Elise says quickly.

'I'm not finished.' The woman picks up a biscuit. 'You won't tell anyone—because if you do, you'll be arrested for murder.'

Sickly dread fills up Elise's guts. 'Murder?'

'That's right. I promise I'll set you free.' The woman takes a bite, chews, swallows, and brushes some coconut off her lip. 'All you have to do,' she says, 'is kill him.'

CHAPTER 1

The studio looks like a mechanic's office—white-painted brick, an unmarked metal door, murky stains on the driveway. It's tucked between a takeaway shop and a tile display showroom in the industrial outskirts of Canberra. Given the prices Aiden Deere charges for his paintings, Elise had expected something a bit fancier. A fountain, maybe. A sign, at least.

Despite the wintry morning breeze, she unzips her puffer jacket. Tugs her tank top down. She's not above showing some cleavage, if that's what it takes. She breathes in and out, rehearsing the line in her head. Raps her knuckles against the door. Waits.

No one comes.

After a minute, Elise's composure slips. He hasn't even opened the door yet, and already things aren't going to plan. She's screwed up somehow, like always.

She knocks again, louder. When she presses her ear to the door, she hears the whirring of an extractor fan.

There's a small window to the right. Darkness inside. Elise makes binoculars out of her hands and presses them against the dirty glass. The studio is cavernous, with stacks of wooden frames in one corner and cans of paint in another. A huge orange canvas is veined with abstract smears of white and yellow. On a battered desk, a laptop is glowing.

Elise looks around. The only visible car is a white Holden Barina, parked forty or fifty metres away. A popular model: the third one she's seen today. The driver is facing the feed store on the other side of the street.

Satisfied that she's not being observed, Elise feels her way around the window frame. The hinges are visible, so it must open outwards. But there's nothing to grab. No way to pull it. She rummages in her bag for something she can use to lever it open.

Something moves behind the glass, and she stifles a yelp. Someone has been standing in front of the canvas this whole time, camouflaged by his paint-splattered overalls. A straight razor drips in one gloved hand. Goggles and an air filter cover his face. He's looking right at her.

Heart pounding, Elise knocks on the glass, like she wasn't trying to break in. The man seems to get bigger as he approaches. The studio floor is elevated above the ground, but even so, he's at least two metres tall and as wide as a removalist or a wrestler.

He fiddles with a hidden latch, then pushes the window open a crack. 'Yes?'

'No one answered the door,' Elise says.

'I'm working.' The man gestures at his canvas with the razor, flicking some paint off the blade.

Elise is no art critic. In high school, her visual arts teacher gently asked her if she was colour blind—twice. But to her, the painting doesn't look great. Just smudges in various shades of orange. Maybe it's not going well. Maybe that's why the painter looks pissed off.

'Can I come in?' she asks, waiting to see if he recognises her from the news.

'Who are you?'

She exhales, relieved. 'My name's Tina Thatcher—I'm a private investigator.' The lie sounds natural. The two-hour drive from Warrigal gave her plenty of time to practise.

She opens her wallet. An image search showed her what a real private investigator's licence looked like, but after she inserted her own photo, her printer didn't replicate the colours properly. Her red hair came out pink, and the frames of her glasses look grey instead of black. At least the painter is observing the fake licence through dirty glass.

'"Commercial and private enquiry agent",' he reads. 'What do you want?'

'You're not in any trouble,' she says, as though she's in a position to make some. 'I just wanted to ask some questions about one of your clients.'

'My clients?' The artist looks wary.

'The people who buy your paintings. They're all commissioned, right? I could have waited until my business partner was back in town, but I thought it might be simpler to just drop in for a quick chat.'

He stares at her for a long moment, his eyes inscrutable behind the goggles. She tries to look impatient rather than nervous.

'Come in,' the artist says finally, and shuts the window.

A moment later, the metal door opens. The artist has removed his mask and goggles. He's about forty, with a heavy brow and a shaved skull. Meaty forearms. One ear crumpled from a long-ago punch. She had pictured a moustache, a beret, a smock, a palette. Not this overalled neanderthal who would look more at home onstage with Midnight Oil than in an art studio.

'That's quite a door,' Elise says, as she walks through. It's tall and thick, with an impressive deadbolt on the inside.

'Can't be too careful.' He gives her a pointed look. 'Paint is expensive.'

Strange that he cited the cost of his supplies rather than the value of his art. His pieces sell for thousands of dollars, sometimes tens of thousands. A thief could make a handsome profit listing them on the dark web, alongside drugs, guns and other unsavoury things.

'I'm Tina, by the way.'

'You already said that.'

She'll have to be more direct. 'You're Aiden Deere, right?'

His grunt could be a yes or a no.

The studio isn't as dark as it looked through the window. Downlights illuminate certain spots on certain walls, though no finished paintings are on display. Acrylic fumes fill the air. The floor is sealed concrete, speckled with a rainbow of old droplets, like a cake covered in hundreds and thousands.

'Drink?' he asks. Generous, since he just caught her trying to break in.

The etiquette would be to accept, but not anything that costs money or takes effort to prepare. She should ask for a glass of water.

'I'll have a beer,' Elise says instead.

It's eleven o'clock on a Monday, and she can feel him judging her. But he takes a bottle of Hahn Light out of a minifridge under a workbench. He cracks it and hands it to her. The glass isn't cold—Elise doesn't think the fridge is running. She sips anyway, lets the bubbles fizz on her tongue.

How long has it been? She couldn't drink while she was training, or while she was on call. And after she lost her job, she couldn't afford it.

The artist doesn't take anything out of the fridge for himself. He tosses a cigarette into his mouth instead, then flicks open a gold lighter with a crossed swords logo. His eyes gleam in the flame, watching her.

Avoiding his gaze, Elise turns to the canvas. The seething mess of orange. 'This is good.'

'You like it?' Deere—or the man she assumes is Deere—doesn't sound convinced.

'Yeah. It's got so much ...' She waves a hand around. '... you know, texture. What is it?'

'It's an old woman in a wheelchair. Can't you see her?'

Elise studies the swirls and splats. To her it resembles a roaring fire, though if she tilts her head, she thinks she can see a person in the flames. But when she looks back at Deere, he smirks. He's messing with her.

'Who's it for?' she asks.

'Can't tell you. The buyer may choose to announce it when she takes possession, or she may not. I can't compromise the privacy of my customers. So, whoever you're here to ask me about—'

'A high school PE teacher from Warrigal. Callum Glyk. G-L-Y-K.' Elise can't tell if Deere recognises the name. 'It might be pronounced Gleek, or Glike.'

She's laying it on a little thick, but Deere doesn't look suspicious.

'I can't tell you anything.' He blows some smoke from the corner of his mouth.

'You must remember him. The painting he bought from you was light grey, with green splodgy bits.'

She found the canvas leaning against the wall in Callum's garage, still bubble-wrapped, the torn box not far away. As though something had happened to him before he'd had the chance to hang it.

'"Green splodgy bits",' Deere repeats drily.

He's not taking her seriously. She injects some more authority into her voice. 'I'm investigating his death.'

'He's dead?' Deere looks surprised.

'You didn't know?'

'I don't keep track of buyers after the transaction is completed.'

'So he *was* a client.' Elise takes a victory sip from the bottle. 'Tell me how you met him.'

'I didn't. I hardly ever meet the buyers.'

'Callum never showed any interest in art. You expect me to believe he paid thousands of dollars to commission something like this—' she gestures at the half-finished nonsense painting '—from someone he'd never met?'

'I work through an agent.'

'Yeah, that's what it says on your website. But your agent doesn't appear to represent any other artists.'

10

Deere says nothing. Tension fills the air, crowding out the paint fumes.

'It's a good strategy,' Elise continues. 'People don't try to screw you if you have an agent. And customers trust you to deliver, if they think the agent won't release the funds until you do. On the phone, I'm guessing your agent sounds a lot like you.'

Deere's right eye twitches. 'You said Callum didn't care about art. According to who?'

'People that knew him,' Elise says cautiously. 'Friends, family.'

'The family hired you?' She can see the cogs turning. 'Because the police don't think his death is suspicious.'

Elise opens her mouth, then shuts it.

'Let me guess.' Deere rubs the back of his stubbly head. 'He was found hanging from the rafters, or with a gut full of pills, and the family doesn't want to believe that he—'

'It's not like that. He just vanished.'

'Vanished?'

'He left work one day, told his colleagues he'd see them tomorrow, then never came back. When the police searched his house, his stuff was there, but he wasn't.'

'What makes you think he's dead? He might have just abandoned his job and gone on a holiday.'

'He hasn't touched any of his accounts. He hasn't contacted his father, or his sister.' It's this last part that makes her so certain. Callum used to text Elise all the time. 'One of the last things he did before he disappeared was transfer seven thousand dollars to your account.'

That's a lie. Callum paid the money in February, almost four months before he vanished. But Elise has run down every other lead. This is her last hope.

'You think I somehow conned him into buying a painting,' Deere says slowly, 'and then what? Slit his throat?' He holds up the razor.

Elise is suddenly conscious of the space between them, and how quiet the studio is. The walls are thick, the windows double-glazed. If she screamed, would anyone hear her? Probably not.

Deere takes a step towards her. He's huge, like a golem.

She reaches into the back pocket of her jeans with one hand, gripping the can of pepper spray. She bought it years ago and has never used it. Will it work? What if there's an extra tab she needs to pull to activate it?

But Deere comes at her with something she can't fight: pity. 'I wish I could help you.' He takes a business card out of his pocket. He looks tired. 'But I'm just a guy who makes paintings. I never met the man you're looking for. And, as you correctly guessed, that means my agent never met him either.'

'You must know something.' Elise wishes it didn't sound like a plea.

Deere gives her the card. 'For if you turn up any other clues.'

He's trying to get rid of her. The card is black on both sides, but when Elise tilts it, an embossed phone number shines in the light.

'Is there a number I can contact you on?' he asks.

'No.' She keeps her phone switched off. No matter how many times she changes her number, people always find the new one.

There's no table. Elise puts the bottle on the concrete floor so she won't be tempted to finish it. The last thing she needs is a drink driving charge.

'Thanks for your time,' she says.

'No worries,' Deere replies.

She can feel his gaze on her back as she walks out.

CHAPTER 2

Elise can't face the long drive back to Warrigal. Even walking to her Suzuki Swift feels like too much. She goes to the takeaway shop next door instead and plonks into one of the spindly metal chairs out the front.

When she and Callum were kids, one of the houses they lived in backed onto dense bushland, with anthills and wombat holes and gum boughs thick enough to climb on. They played hide-and-seek out there for hours. He was always better at it, always guessing where she was immediately, and then patiently explaining how he'd known she would choose the spot behind this log, or in that ditch.

It was fun until it wasn't. One evening she was doing really well—she'd been hiding up a eucalyptus tree for ages. Then, just as the sun crawled behind the horizon, she had the sudden feeling she was alone. Callum wasn't going to emerge from the shrubbery. He was gone.

She has that same sensation now. But this time, she won't wander back to the house and find him playing *Halo* on the couch. This time she's lost him for good.

'Are you going to order something?' A girl with acne and a nose stud has emerged from the shop. 'Otherwise you can't sit here.'

Elise forces a smile. 'Right. I'll have a fish fillet and two dollars of chips.' She's allowed to eat whatever she wants for lunch, these days.

'We don't do chips that way anymore. You want Small, Medium or Large?'

'Small, then.'

'That's three fifty.'

'Okay.'

'Plus five for the fish.'

'Fine.'

The girl sighs, annoyed at having to do her job. She tears a ticket off a pad, as though there are other customers. 'You're order eighteen,' she says, and disappears back into the shop.

Elise has never liked teenage girls. Even when she was one, the others avoided her, sensing she was different long before she knew for herself. At the peak of her career, she was invited back to her old school to give a speech. Slumped on their plastic chairs, the students glared at her when she made jokes and laughed at her when she tried to be serious. No one asks her to make speeches anymore, and she's glad. She doesn't know how her brother survived as a teacher there—

But of course, he didn't. Maybe it was one of his students who killed him.

The Barina is still parked on the other side of the street. The driver—white, forties, greying hair mostly hidden by a floppy sunhat—keeps her head turned towards the feed store, as though waiting for someone. Except the store looks closed. And if the woman were actually waiting, she'd be reading a book or fiddling with her phone. Instead, she's just staring through her sunglasses at the store. The angle makes it hard for Elise to see her face clearly.

Maybe that's the point.

Elise thinks about the three white Holden Barinas she's seen today. It could have been the same one each time, following her since she left her house.

The hairs on her arms stand up. Even as she tells herself she's being paranoid, the woman glances over, sees her watching and quickly turns back to the feed store.

Elise stands up and walks towards the Barina. 'Excuse me.'

The woman starts her engine.

'Hey!' Elise breaks into a jog. 'I need to talk to you.'

The handbrake crunches, and the car launches forward. Elise runs after it.

Once upon a time she could have kept up with a car doing thirty-five, at least for a while. Her friends would sometimes get in a ute and drive away without her, just to watch her close the distance. She'd pound the asphalt then throw herself into the tray, laughing.

Not today. She almost gets close enough to knock on the rear windscreen, but the Barina keeps accelerating, and soon it's well out of reach. It zooms away, bitumen crackling under the wheels, leaving Elise bent over and wheezing. She's not the athlete she used to be.

She squints at the numberplate as the car disappears around a corner. *YMK4-something-something*. She makes it into a song in her head, to help her remember. *YMK4-something-something.*

It's not so suspicious to drive away when a stranger crosses the street towards you, yelling. But the more Elise thinks about it, the more certain she is that the car has been following her all day.

She's used to being stared at. But this woman pursued her the whole way from Warrigal to Canberra and didn't even stick around to have a go at her. Who is she?

Elise walks back to her Suzuki, wondering what to do next. A real private investigator would know. She'll hire one, if Dad comes through with the money.

'Hey.'

She turns. The teenager is holding a paper parcel, already going transparent from the oil inside.

'Order eighteen,' she says, like a challenge.

'Oh. Thanks.' Elise reaches for the parcel.

The girl withholds it. 'Ten dollars.'

'You said eight fifty.'

'Plus GST.'

Elise is pretty sure that eight dollars fifty plus ten per cent doesn't equal ten dollars. 'In that case, I don't want it.'

'You can't just not take it.'

'I don't have ten dollars.' Elise wishes this was more of an exaggeration. She starts walking back to the car.

The girl follows. 'I know who you are. I'll call the cops on you.'

Elise flinches. The dye job, the glasses and the tattoo fool most people, but not everyone. She can't think of a clever retort, so she climbs into her car and slams the door.

As Elise starts the engine, the girl flings the parcel at the driver's side window. It explodes against the glass, a shower of overcooked chips. Elise drives away, refusing even to look in the rear-view mirror.

CHAPTER 3

The front window of her house is smashed.

Elise kills the engine but stays in the driver's seat, studying the damage through the windscreen. She's had her tyres stabbed and her emails hacked, and seen her name scrawled on toilet walls, but this is new. Big triangles of glass remain in the bottom of the frame, so it's unlikely anyone has climbed into the house.

Unlikely. Not impossible.

She raises the hood of her jacket to protect her ears from the cold wind, climbs out of the car and approaches the broken window. Even on a sunny day like today, it's dark inside. She always keeps the curtains drawn.

'This is the police. Come out with your hands up.' She makes her voice deeper, more commanding. Channelling Kiara, who always sounded like she was in charge, whether she was threatening to arrest a group of angry drunks or ordering Elise to get out of bed.

Silence.

'The building is surrounded,' Elise adds. 'You have ten seconds to comply.'

She counts to ten. Then fifteen. No sound from inside the house.

Elise gets out her phone and switches it on, ignoring the twenty-one missed calls. She uses the flashlight app to shine a light through the gap between the curtains. A starscape of broken glass glitters on the living-room floor. No sign of a brick. Whoever did this came right up to the window, maybe with a cricket bat.

She unlocks the front door and flicks on the lights. Trapped flies flit around inside the fittings. Her withering plants, her dusty trophy cabinet, the framed photo of her and Callum, the boxes Dad dumped here after Mum died— nothing looks like it's been touched. But there are muddy footprints on the floor.

A chill crawls up her spine. Instinctively, she reaches for her phone to call Callum. Then she remembers that he's gone. He will never come to her rescue again.

She crouches next to the mud. It's not like on those crime shows, where the tread is as clear as a barcode. She can barely tell they are footprints, let alone the size or style of shoe.

Elise creeps from room to room, turning on lights. There's no one under her single bed. No one hiding in her closet among the cargo pants and old running jackets. No one behind the shower curtain in the bathtub, or crouched next to the washing machine in the kitchen. Nothing appears to have been stolen—not even her laptop, which is only half-hidden by a dressing-gown on the couch.

Whoever was here, they're gone. It looks like the intruder

smashed the window, climbed in, had a look around, then left. Why?

Maybe just to rattle Elise. To remind her that she'll never be forgiven.

Guppy is scratching at the back door, his wet little nose pressed right up against the glass. Elise slides it open. The Scotty dog runs in, sniffing around her feet.

'Bloody useless guard dog you are,' she grumbles. He probably hid as soon as he heard the intruder approaching. The doorbell usually leaves him cowering in the closet. But she's relieved to see him.

Guppy flops onto his back expectantly. Elise scratches his tummy, then gently palpates it, checking his organs. She's always worried someone will poison him.

As a kid, she never really liked animals. She and Callum kept blue-tongue lizards as pets, but she didn't spend much time with them. When one turned up dead in the backyard, shredded by a cat or a fox, Elise cried but got over it quickly.

As an adult, though, she likes animals more than people. She found Guppy wandering the streets without a collar. The vet suspected she had stolen him but couldn't prove it, and after confirming there was no microchip, he was forced to let her adopt him.

Guppy doesn't know about Elise's past, and if he did, he wouldn't care. He's just happy to be with her.

The dog waits for her to finish examining him, then runs over to the refrigerator, barking. He jumps, his claws scratching the fridge door.

'Hold your horses,' Elise says. 'I'll get you some afternoon tea in a second.'

She grabs a broom and sweeps the broken glass into a corner, then bags it up and puts it in the bin. Her landlord will be pissed off. Last time it was graffiti on her front door, which Elise covered with cheap paint. The time before that it was dog shit in her letterbox, easily removed. But windows are expensive.

Guppy barks again, snuffling around the bottom of the fridge. The muddy footprints are clustered in that area.

There's a dark smudge on the handle of the fridge door.

Elise's skin erupts into goosebumps. She listens to the humming of the fridge for a moment. What's in there?

She doesn't want to call the police. They're sick of hearing about Callum, and as for the vandalism and harassment, they've implied that she brought it on herself. If someone kills her, they'll investigate. Until then, she's on her own.

Elise swallows her unease and approaches the fridge. She wraps one finger around the handle, careful to avoid the smudge. 'Back,' she tells Guppy.

He whimpers, but hurries away and hops up onto the ratty couch.

Elise opens the door, and recoils. The fridge is stuffed with dozens of used sanitary pads. Pink stains are all over the shelves, the egg carton, the milk bottle and the bread, as though the intruder dabbed the soiled cotton all over them. Most of the pads are old, the blood dark brown. Someone, or several someones, must have planned this for a while.

The light inside the fridge is broken, so Elise doesn't notice the message right away. When she does, she has to bend down to read it, her head right in the toxic cloud. The whole mess smells like the bins behind the local butcher's. She covers her mouth with the inside of her elbow.

The message is scrawled on the back wall of the fridge in permanent marker:

Enjoy—you fucking VAMPIRE

CHAPTER 4

'Yes?'

Hearing Kiara's voice brings both pain and relief, like squeezing a pimple. Elise can picture her at her desk, drumming her painted nails on the tabletop, her long hair stuffed into the police cap that she never takes off between nine and five. She even wore it in bed, one time. Making up for her reluctance to use the handcuffs.

'It's me,' Elise says, redundantly. Her name would have appeared on Kiara's phone. 'How are you?'

'I'm fine. What can I do for you?' There's no background noise. A teenage boy went missing in early May and it's still in the news, even though Callum's disappearance is more recent. Kiara's three colleagues might all be out looking for the boy.

Elise gets up off the lumpy mattress. She can't talk on the phone lying down. It's like her mouth only works when her feet are moving.

'I want to, uh, report a crime.'

Elise waits for Kiara to tell her to dial triple-O instead of calling her personal mobile. Instead, Kiara's voice softens a little. 'What's happened?'

'Uh . . .' Elise had intended to talk about the break-in, the footprints, the mess in the fridge. But the hint of mercy makes her clam up. She doesn't want Kiara to think she's pathetic. Someone who can't solve her own problems.

'Are you still there?' Kiara asks. 'Ms Glyk?'

Ms Glyk. The formality wakes her up, like getting dropped into a bathtub full of ice.

'Someone's been following me,' Elise blurts out. 'That's what I want to report.'

She hears Kiara tapping at a keyboard. 'Go on.'

'A woman. Forties. Driving a white Holden Barina. Registration YMK4-something-something.'

More tapping, as Kiara searches the motor vehicle registry. 'How many times have you seen the car?'

'Once for sure, and possibly two other times.'

'Once for sure.' Kiara doesn't sound impressed.

'She followed me the whole way to Canberra,' Elise insists.

'What were you doing in Canberra?'

'Just, you know. Chasing up a lead.'

Kiara sighs. 'Elise, you can't keep doing this.'

'Why? Are the police going to start doing their jobs?' Elise regrets this before she's even finished saying it.

'We *are* doing our jobs,' Kiara says sharply. 'We've circulated Callum's description to other departments throughout the state. We're trying to work out where he sourced the drugs. We're—'

'He didn't source them. They were planted in his house. And how will his description help you find his killer?'

'We've been over this, Elise.'

She's right. This conversation always ends with the same stand-off. Kiara has chosen not to believe her, and that's that.

Elise finds herself standing in front of the smashed window, staring at the patchwork of cardboard and packing tape where the glass used to be. 'So who owns the Barina?'

'I can't just give out contact details from the motor registry. You know that.'

'What if she broke into my house? Would you do something then?' There are surely too many pads in the fridge to be the work of one person. The Barina driver could have been involved. Maybe that was why she was following Elise—so she could warn her accomplice when Elise was on her way home.

'I'll have a chat with Mrs Hartnell. But *you* have to stay out of it. Okay?'

Hartnell. Not one of Kiara's three colleagues. Must be the driver.

'Okay,' Elise says.

'Anything else I can do for you?'

'No.' Elise takes a deep breath. 'Thanks, Kiara. I really appreciate it.'

The last sentence goes unheard. Kiara has already hung up.

Elise throws the phone at the couch. She's made plenty of mistakes. She doesn't beat herself up about most of them—other people are happy to do that for her. But the moment she screwed things up with Kiara is the one she keeps coming back to, the one that makes her wish she had a time machine.

She folds her body into a hamstring stretch. The pain sharpens her focus. Warrigal is a small town, and Hartnell isn't a common name. Maybe she can find the Barina driver before Kiara contacts her.

Anything else I can do for you?

Maybe Kiara gave her Hartnell's name out of sympathy—or just to get rid of her.

Elise can feel the tears coming, so she deepens the stretch. *Concentrate.* Breathe in, hold, release. A minute later, she straightens and grabs her laptop.

There are lots of Hartnells on social media. Hunched over the screen like a gargoyle, Elise scrolls past thousands of smiling faces, people dancing in clubs, drinking in restaurants, lounging in bikinis at the coast.

She's on edge, using social media again after all this time. The bright, friendly colours don't fool her anymore. The internet is like pond scum. It looks safe and solid, until you make a misstep. Then you fall right through, into all the misogyny under the surface.

After an hour of searching, Elise has only found one Hartnell in Warrigal with an identifiable profile picture, and it's the wrong one—a teenage girl with a pink pixie cut. The girl has grey-green eyes, chubby cheeks, and a goofy grin that doesn't seem to match her black clothes and lipstick. She's dressed like a goth, or an emo, or whatever kids call that style these days.

Elise rubs her throbbing eyes. She should be wearing her glasses. When they were first prescribed, she only wore them at home, too embarrassed to be seen in them outside. She didn't look like herself. Now she *only* wears them outside, as a disguise. Putting them on at home makes her feel like she's hiding.

She gives up on social media and tries the digital archive of *The Warrigal Times*. The same girl pops up. This time it's an article about her funeral.

Elise feels a pang of shock. Goofy-grin girl died on 14 February. Maybe the relatives don't know how to take the girl's social media profile down. Or they're leaving it up so other people can post farewell messages.

Her name was Moon Hartnell, and she was fifteen. The article doesn't say how she died. In a hopeless little town like Warrigal, that usually means suicide. The plague quietly consuming rural Australia.

There's a photo of the funeral. People are forcing smiles for the camera. Half-smiles, so as not to insult the dead girl. No one is crying, but a few people have been. Tissues clenched in the hands of the men, smeared makeup on the women.

And there she is—the Barina driver.

She's standing a bit away from the rest of the group. Maybe she wasn't directly related to Moon. No redness around her eyes. She's wearing a dark blue blazer with a lily at the lapel. Her flat stare gives Elise a chill. It's as though the woman can see her through the photo.

Clockwise from left. Elise reads the list of names and finally gets to the woman: *Stephanie Hartnell.* Once Elise knows the name, she feels like she can see it in the woman's face. Those lines around her mouth, the ruthlessly pulled-back hair, her square jaw—she looks like a Stephanie.

The handwriting in Elise's fridge looked vaguely familiar, with long descenders, and a distinctive circle above the J instead of a dot. But this woman is a total stranger.

'Why were you following me?' Elise mutters. The people who target her usually have a sense of superiority about them, but also a laziness—they don't pursue her very far. Stephanie tailed her the whole way to Canberra. Would she have done that if she was just a lookout for the fridge-stuffer?

Elise goes to the White Pages website and scrolls through the Hartnells. There it is—*Hartnell, S & V*. A phone number and a street address. Stephanie may not even know her address is online. Elise didn't, until vandals started finding her house.

She cracks her knuckles, feeling vindicated. She's been hassled by so many strangers that it's enormously satisfying to identify one of them, especially when she started with only two thirds of a licence plate. Maybe she could become a real private investigator.

Glaring at Stephanie's picture, she picks up her phone and punches in the number. Then she changes her mind, remembering how Stephanie drove away when Elise tried to confront her.

She taps the address into the Maps app. It's a forty-five-minute drive. Looks like a big property, a farm maybe.

She checks her watch. Almost four. She should go right now, before Kiara has the chance to contact Stephanie.

Elise gives her tank top a sniff. It's still okay. She shrugs into the puffer jacket and pulls the track pants back up her legs. She puts her glasses on and immediately feels like someone else. Invisible and invincible.

She won't be gone long, so she decides to leave the dog inside. She fills a plastic bowl with dry biscuits and puts it on the floor.

Guppy looks unimpressed. He'd rather be eating the bloody pads from the fridge.

'I'll be back soon,' Elise promises, and grabs her keys.

CHAPTER 5

The *check-engine* light has been on for a week, but the Suzuki starts. Elise mutters a prayer of thanks to the car gods, and heads for the highway.

She's almost there when her phone dings. Probably an angry stranger, but she prods the screen, just in case.

Elise. I'm not giving you any more money. Dad.

The text is just like him: efficient and short. Elise has loomed over her father since she was sixteen. After she was exposed, Dad accused Mum of having had an affair. 'She can't be my kid,' he snarled. 'She's a foot taller than me!' Never mind that she had his sandy hair, his dimples, his pointed chin. Callum was much more likely to be a changeling, with his dark fringe, high cheekbones and angled brows.

Elise hits the call button. Maybe she can change his mind. But the phone rings and rings, then cuts out, like always. She punches the steering wheel.

It had been painful, asking Dad for money. Knowing he wouldn't answer the door of his townhouse, she made an appointment at his practice under a false name and sat in the waiting room, surrounded by the very old and the very young. Avoiding eye contact with them all, she started searching through a stack of ancient magazines—and was alarmed to see herself on one of the covers, clad in a sports crop top and holding an Australian flag. She quickly buried it at the bottom of the pile.

When Dad came out of his office and saw her, his smile froze on his face, making him look like his photograph on the sign out front. She watched him argue with himself for a moment and ultimately decide not to make a scene.

'Come through, *Jane*,' he said.

Dad's office in Canberra was smaller than the one he'd had in Warrigal. Windowless. Butcher's paper was spread over a narrow bed, as though he was running some kind of Sweeney Todd operation. One wall was decorated with thankyou cards from grateful patients, who must not have spent as much time with him as Elise had.

Dad closed the door. 'Are you sick?'

Elise said, 'Yes,' knowing he would kick her out immediately if the answer was no.

Dad sat down on his desk rather than his chair. His hairy knuckles went white as he gripped the edge. 'Symptoms?'

Elise looked around. 'Nice office. You like it here?' She was trying to be nice, but it came out sounding sarcastic.

'It's fine. My patients tend to have actual illnesses.' Dad fixed her with a glare. 'Things I can treat. They're not just here to interrogate me about you.'

'I'm sorry you had to move,' Elise said, even though moving was her father's favourite thing. They had lived in three different towns before they settled in Warrigal. Every time Elise was on the verge of making a friend at school, Dad would wrench the whole family away.

'You're not sick,' Dad said. 'And I doubt you can pay for this appointment. So . . .'

'I have anxiety,' Elise said. 'My brother is missing.'

Dad clenched his jaw, making his cheeks inflate. 'If there's an actual cause, it's not anxiety.'

'I hope you're not that blunt with your other patients.'

'Elise—'

'I've found a private investigator. He looks really good. For $275 per hour, he says he can—'

'You want to hire someone to tell us what we already know?'

Elise stuffed her fists into her pockets. 'We *don't* know, Dad.'

Dad sank into his chair. 'Every day someone walks through that door and lies to me. They'll say they have a sore back, or a toothache, and they'll ask for opiates. I can tell their pain is fake, because I'm a stranger. Their families can't. It's easy to fool someone you know. More opportunities to bullshit them. More chances to learn their blind spots.'

He glowered at her as he said this. Even though she'd never lied to him, not directly.

'Callum wasn't on drugs,' Elise said.

'Let it go, Elise.'

I can't, she wanted to scream. *How can you?*

Instead, she said, 'The PI told me a case like this can usually be wrapped up in five hours. That's only $1375. You're a doctor. You can afford it.'

'I'm a doctor who spent all his money on his daughter's—'

'Please, Dad.' She swallowed. 'No one else is looking for him.'

Dad was silent for a long time. Then he said, 'I'll consider it.'

She knew he was lying. He had already decided, but she couldn't tell which way. He clearly wanted her to stew for a while, but was it so she would be extra grateful when he said yes? Or so she would be even more devastated when he said no? She thanked him and left, her chest tight.

Now she wants to shout at him, but unlike her, he's somehow figured out how to switch off voicemail.

She throws the phone onto the passenger seat. How like Dad, to hate his daughter so much that he would abandon his son. She can't think of anyone else as bitter as him—

Then suddenly she can, and she knows why the handwriting in the fridge looked familiar.

She does a U-turn on the deserted road, her fists tight around the steering wheel, her jaw sore from clenching. This will only take a minute.

———

Elise crosses the bridge, startling some birds. They flap down to the banks of the Murrumbidgee River. She takes a right turn onto Victoria Street and holds her breath as she enters the town centre. There's a Woolworths, a discount chemist, the King George pub, a Turkish pizza place, a dentist's surgery that she has never seen anyone go into, and the hairdresser's where she's sure they once cut her fringe crooked on purpose. She turns right again at St Barnabas' Church, driving past the statue that represents all the Australians who died in the Great War, and

34

the sign that's supposed to say Cook Street but has been vandalised again. A poster is taped to a light pole: HAVE YOU SEEN ZACH? Here's Coffee Guru, the karate dojo, the Vietnamese bakery owned by Kiara's mother, a place that used to be a video rental store and is still vacant, a tattoo parlour, and the emergency vet, which Elise often thinks is the saddest place in the world. Here's the local burger place that folded when the McDonald's opened, and there's the McDonald's that closed its doors soon after. She rolls past the public high school where Callum taught PE, until he vanished.

Elise turns off Cook Street and exhales. She's made it from one side of Warrigal to the other on a single breath.

Soon she's driving past a row of small houses on big blocks. The paint is fresh, the gutters clean, the lawns trimmed with nail-clipper precision. The occupants are making the best of things.

A man in a bomber jacket is walking his kelpie. He's elderly, which is typical of Warrigal. No one ever moves here, and the young people usually flee when they turn eighteen. Now that most of the residents are too old to have children, the school is slowly shrinking, and the town is in a death spiral. Elise would leave too, except that if she does, she'll never find out what happened to Callum. It would feel like abandoning him.

The man sees Elise, and stops. His hard eyes, mostly buried in the folds of his wrinkled face, follow her as she drives past. It's a long time since she's been on this side of the river, but apparently not long enough.

She drives down a few different streets before finding the house. It hasn't changed much. White walls, grey roof—it has the feel of a chiropractor's office rather than someone's home.

Elise parks in front of the driveway, blocking it. She gets out of the car and walks right across the garden, trampling the daisies on her way to the front door. Ignoring the doorbell, she thumps the wood with her fist.

'I'm coming,' a voice shouts. Elise hears hurried footsteps on a laminate floor. Then the door swings open.

Anushka is only twenty-nine, but she already has puffiness around her eyes, sun-damaged skin, a sagging pelican-neck. She's wearing washing-up gloves and a lime-green apron. The hallway behind her is scattered with Duplo and crayons, but there are no sounds of children.

'Elise Glyk,' she says. 'This is a surprise.'

'Is it?'

The silence drags out.

'I thought I'd check how you were feeling,' Elise says. 'Puffy? A bit tired? Sore tits? Want me to warm up a heat pack for you?'

Anushka looks smug instead of affronted, confirming Elise's hunch about who was responsible for the mess in her fridge. 'I don't know what you're talking about.'

'Bullshit. Did Stephanie Hartnell help you out, or is she menopausal?'

'Huh?' This time, Anushka's confusion seems genuine.

'You know who I'm talking about.'

Anushka changes the subject. 'It's funny—I was just thinking about you. About how pleased I was, when I heard you were going to the Gold Coast. We were all so happy for you.' She peels off a washing-up glove with a wet snap. 'This was before, obviously.'

Anushka might be lying, or she might genuinely remember herself as a supportive friend rather than a jealous bitch. Elise decides she doesn't care which.

'I've had enough.' She stuffs her hands into the pockets of her jacket. 'You and all your friends need to knock it off.'

'*You've* had enough?' Anushka gestures at the front yard, her outfit, the hall behind her. It all looks fine to Elise, but apparently not to Anushka. 'Do you know where I'd be right now, if I got the opportunities you did?'

'Right here, probably.' No one knows better than Elise how little money most athletes make. It can barely be called a career.

'*Here* would be a completely different place. This town would be known for something other than liars and cheats. You didn't just steal *my* dream, you—'

'I didn't steal anything from you. I made it onto the team because I was faster.'

'By a quarter of a second. Which is about how long it took to prove you didn't belong there.'

If she wants Elise to feel ashamed, she's out of luck. Elise's well of shame ran dry years ago. 'If you or your friends come near my house or my dog again, I'll call the police.'

'I still don't know what you're on about. But if I did, I'd point out that you and your junkie brother aren't popular with the police. Or with anyone, come to think of it.'

The rage bubbles up. Elise takes her fists out of her pockets. 'My brother isn't—'

'Whatever.' Anushka closes the door.

Elise turns to face the front yard again, glaring at the grass. She wants to break a window or kick over the letterbox, but she gets the feeling that's what Anushka wants. An excuse to play the victim some more, to tell everyone in town what a monster Elise is all over again.

She makes do with spitting on the flowers as she walks back to the car.

CHAPTER 6

A sombre voice on the radio is talking about the missing teenage boy, so Elise switches to a music station as she drives towards Stephanie Hartnell's address. The songs get older and older as she drives—Bachelor Girl followed by Silverchair followed by Jimmy Barnes—as if she's heading not just into the bush but into the past. Eventually the signal fuzzes out completely, leaving Elise to her thoughts.

Anushka didn't recognise Stephanie Hartnell's name. If Stephanie wasn't acting as her lookout, why did she follow Elise all the way to Canberra?

Elise squints into the setting sun. The road is long and straight, soft-shouldered, with paddocks on either side. Trucks use it to bypass the town. From time to time she sees a single stunted tree, half a dozen cows clustered around it like kids sharing a cigarette. The land sometimes floods, judging by the white depth markers every two kilometres, but you wouldn't know it to look at the dead grass and the dusty asphalt. It's midwinter, and there may not be any rain until spring.

Soon she's off the bypass and onto a narrower road, rougher under the tyres. The paddocks are replaced by scrub, and Elise can see denser bush in the distance. The setting sun strobes through leafless branches.

A sign up ahead: HIDDEN DRIVEWAY. According to the GPS, this is it—a gravel trail to her left, snaking around nothing on a slight incline that could generously be called a hill. A house at the top, broad and flat, built when land was cheap. Brick walls, big windows. No sign of the Barina, but it could be in the double garage. The area around the house and the driveway has been cleared. The rest of the property seems to be bushland, fenced in with barbed wire.

Elise's Suzuki is distinctive, having been keyed over and over. If Stephanie sees her coming up the driveway, she might not answer the door. Elise goes past without turning. Another fence, perpendicular to the road, marks the edge of the property. She swerves off-road, too suddenly, the car bouncing on the dirt so hard that her teeth slam together, then she parks in a cluster of trees. Visible from the road, but only to someone paying close attention. The car will be here an hour at the most. There's a rotting FOR SALE sign up ahead—Stephanie's neighbours hopefully aren't around to notice the car on their land.

Her phone has no signal, so she leaves it in the charger cradle, locks the Suzuki with a cheery *chup, chup* and walks back towards Stephanie's property, breathing in eucalyptus and the stale smell of cow pats.

When Elise reaches the barbed-wire fence, she puts her hand on the top of a post and vaults over. A shoelace catches on the wire, and she lands hard on the opposite leg, almost twisting her ankle on the uneven ground. The indignity of a champion hurdler struggling to hop over a metre-high fence is not lost on her. Swearing, she untangles her shoe and crouches to tie it up. Her knees ache. There's not much cartilage left in them, these days.

Birds flutter away. A bee hums past her ear. No movement from the house on the hill.

Elise avoids the driveway, still not wanting to give Stephanie any warning. But it's hard to move quietly through the scrub—the shadows are growing, hiding dry leaves and noisy twigs. The terrain is strange. Some parts are dry and rocky, others knobbled with tree roots. At one point she passes a low mound of dirt, as though someone decided to build a veggie patch but couldn't get anything to grow. She wonders what kind of farm this was, if any.

When Elise is parallel with the house, she darts out of the scrub and climbs up onto the porch. It's dark inside, and there's no smoke from the chimney. The front door is frosted glass, protected by a security door. She rings the bell, which makes a pleasant arpeggio.

The echoes die away. No movement from within the house.

She rings the bell again and raps her knuckles on the security door. Nothing. Maybe Stephanie is out the back.

Elise circles around the house. There's a well-tended garden behind it, with roses, camellias and a pomegranate tree. A grapevine crawls over a pergola. There's a large, mossy boulder at the bottom of the path. Beyond that there's more cleared land, like maybe animals used to graze here, but right now nothing is green enough to eat. The ground is just dirt and old kangaroo shit.

No people anywhere.

Elise goes up the stairs onto the back veranda. The door is freshly painted, masking tape still stuck to the edges of the window. It's protected by a screen door with heavy-duty security mesh. Elise peers through. In the fading light she can see a galley kitchen, empty. A landline phone is mounted on the wall.

The cord has been sliced through.

Spiders of fear creep up the back of Elise's neck. She listens for a long moment. No voices or music from inside the house, and she's too far from the road to hear traffic. No bird or insect sounds, either. It's as though the world is holding its breath. Waiting to see what Elise will do.

It'll be dark, soon. But she has time for a quick look around.

She tries the handle. Locked. Who would bother to lock a door, way out here?

Someone up to no good, she thinks, choosing to ignore the irony. She sneaks across the veranda towards a window. She can see a living area—a fireplace, a fluffy white rug, two chairs on opposite sides of a coffee table. Everything is dusty and faded.

The flyscreen is on the outside, so the window must open inwards. Elise jams her car key into the seam and pops the screen out of its frame, then gives the glass a gentle push. It squeaks open.

Cringing at the noise, she crouches below the window. Seconds pass. A minute. Two. No one comes.

She rises, then climbs through the gap. The air is much warmer inside than out, like the heater was on recently. The house is well made. No creaking from the floor, no loose skirting boards. Big, double-glazed windows overlook the front and back of the property. Wet dishes sit on the drying rack. Stephanie hasn't been gone long. Maybe she's out to dinner.

There's a faintly bitter smell. It reminds Elise of an odour in one of the houses she lived in as a kid, where the source turned out to be a dead bird under her bed. It had apparently been trapped in the house somehow and starved. Maybe a rat has died inside Stephanie's walls.

Elise doesn't know what she's looking for. She had hoped it would be obvious once she was here. A journal on a writing desk, perhaps, open to an entry that explained why Stephanie was following her. A computer with an inbox on the screen, ready to be searched for Elise's name. But other than the sliced phone line, the house looks like that of an ordinary woman approaching middle age.

Elise explores. The kitchen is connected to the living area, then there's a small entryway with a coat hook and a shoe rack beside the front door. A hallway takes her past an office, a bathroom and two bedrooms to the garage, where she confirms there are no cars. Just a wheelbarrow, gumboots, some garden tools and several ten-litre bottles of water, hard plastic, the kind with little spouts on the front. There are also dozens of boxes of cornflakes. It looks like Stephanie is preparing for the end of the world.

One of the bedrooms has been turned into an office. There's a computer on a desk next to a lamp and a sheaf of papers. Elise turns on the computer, but it's password protected, so she shuts it down and looks at the papers. It's hard to see, and the desk lamp doesn't seem to have a switch. She reaches for her phone, but it's still in the car. She tries tapping the lamp, clapping, then gives up and just squints at the papers in the failing light.

She spends half an hour going through power bills, superannuation updates, and phone and internet statements. Stephanie is well-off. Her super fund balance leaves Elise sick with envy. When Elise was a paramedic, her salary was only $53K. Whatever Stephanie does for work, it's more profitable than saving lives.

No calls are listed in the two most recent phone statements, which makes Elise think the landline was cut a while ago. But an earlier statement features a change of address, and no calls are listed there, either. Maybe Stephanie only uses her mobile. Or maybe she just doesn't have any friends.

Elise finds two rifles in the closet. By law they should be in a locked box, but plenty of farmers leave them out, if they use them a lot. There's a tub of ammunition, and another tub filled with neat bundles of syringes, each with pink nylon fluff at one end. Tranquilliser darts.

Six years ago, activists invaded the town to prevent a kangaroo cull. They spent their nights trespassing and waving torches around so the hunters couldn't safely shoot, then switched off the lights and hid before any police turned up. The activists left only when the shire council agreed to stop the cull. Since then, locals tranquillise the male roos and cut their balls off instead of killing them. 'I'd rather be dead,' Callum joked at the time.

But there's no livestock here. No reason to worry about foxes or to protect the grass from roos. What is Stephanie planning to shoot?

Elise moves on to the bedrooms. The first one is full of moving boxes, all marked *M*. She opens a few. She finds a purple bedspread, some YA books, and some trophies shaped like theatre masks and calculators. Prizes for drama and maths. She finds a ukulele, a box of fine-tipped paintbrushes, and clothes that would fit a teenage girl. Black T-shirts with band names screen-printed on them, black pleather jackets with silver studs. The kinds of outfits worn by Moon Hartnell, the pink-haired girl whose funeral Stephanie attended.

The other bedroom must belong to Stephanie and her husband. A king-size bed, dressers on either side with reading lamps. The wardrobe is only half full. Jeans, loose shirts, plain bras and undies. Potpourri in little mesh sacks in each drawer. The clothes of a woman who's practical but still wants to smell nice.

The other half of the wardrobe holds only dust. But when Elise stands on the bed, she sees a leather belt up the back of the top shelf. Something a tall person could reach but might not see, especially if he was angrily stuffing clothes into a suitcase.

The story is starting to come together. Moon Hartnell commits suicide. Her parents move house, then split up. Now Stephanie lives here alone, with enough money from the divorce settlement that she doesn't need the farm to produce anything.

Elise opens the dressers but doesn't pay much attention to the earrings and antifungal creams inside. She's thinking. Could Stephanie Hartnell have been following her because she blames Elise for the breakdown of her marriage? It's not as much of a stretch as it should be. Elise seems to get the blame for anything and everything that goes wrong in Warrigal. She was supposed to put this town on the map, and instead she made it a national disgrace.

Maybe Stephanie's husband had a crush on her, or something. Plenty of people did, once upon a time. After she made the team, she was in newspapers and on TV.

But she doesn't want this to be about her—she wants it to be somehow about Callum. To give her some clue about what happened to him. Could he have been seeing Stephanie? He'd been working out, shaving every day, buying nice clothes. Elise suspected he was dating somebody, though he denied it. He was used to being seen around town with a sexy twenty-something on his arm. He might have been embarrassed to admit he was dating a woman in her forties.

There are no photos of Stephanie's husband. Actually, no photos of anybody. There aren't even any mirrors.

For some reason, this detail unsettles Elise. Her bad feelings about this place become impossible to ignore, and it's now too dark to keep searching without turning on some lights, which would be visible from the road. She creeps back the way she came, fighting the urge to run.

This was a mistake. She's breaking and entering, and for what? She's learned nothing useful.

When she reaches the living room, tyres grind up the driveway outside.

Elise drops to the floor just as headlights hit the front window. One second slower, and she would have been visible to the driver.

She listens for a moment, her face against the faded carpet. Brakes squeak outside. An engine idles and then dies, plunging the room into blackness.

Heart racing, Elise commando-crawls through the living room into the kitchen. Slowly, carefully, she climbs onto the bench and wriggles out of the window onto the back veranda. As she pulls the window closed behind her, she hears the car door thump, and footsteps crunch along the gravel towards the front porch.

The flyscreen is still detached. Proof that someone was here. And Stephanie would have no trouble proving who, if the house were dusted for prints.

Elise lifts up the flyscreen and holds it in place. Getting it into the frame won't be quiet. She has to time this perfectly.

Silence for one breath. Two. Then a key rattles in the front door.

Now! Elise shoves the flyscreen, feeling it pop into place just as the lock clicks. She creeps along the veranda to the stairs and down into the garden, where she breaks into a sprint. One last pink smudge of sun dissolves into the distant mountain range, leaving the ground a shapeless black mass. She ducks behind the boulder at the back of the garden, out of sight.

Crouching, she listens. She can faintly hear Stephanie moving around inside the house. Should Elise run into the trees, then creep through them to the car? Or is it safer to wait here until Stephanie goes to bed?

'Hello?'

Elise jolts. That voice didn't come from the house. It was closer. And it was male.

She peeks around the boulder. The garden is empty.

'Is someone there?' the voice says.

Elise turns around. The voice is alarmingly close, but she still can't see anybody.

It's like she's being haunted.

As she edges sideways, her foot lands on something hard and plastic. It looks like the access hatch for a septic tank. There's a little square of glass, maybe so the owner can check how full it is without opening it. The lid is padlocked shut. A wheel is fixed to the ground next to it, like part of a pulley system.

The unease is like a bowling ball in Elise's gut. Why would someone lock their septic tank? Are shit-thieves roaming the countryside?

No. Stephanie is keeping something dangerous. Illegal.

This is bad. Get out of here.

She doesn't. Instead she bends over, peering down into the little window.

A face appears at the glass.

Elise scrambles backwards across the dirt, her heart pounding. *What the hell?*

'Let me out! Please!' The man's face is right there, but his voice comes from a few metres away, where a ventilation tube protrudes from the dirt. The disconnect is jarring.

Elise crawls back to the window for a better look. The man's face is sallow, bearded. His hair matted and dirty.

His bloodshot eyes widen. Blue lips parting.

'Leesy?' His voice is a hoarse whisper.

Elise's jaw drops. 'Callum?'

CHAPTER 7

Her first thought isn't that Callum is alive. Her first thought is that *she's* dead, too. That she stepped off the edge of the world and tumbled right down into the darkness of the afterlife. Finding Callum in a septic tank at the bottom of a farmhouse garden—it's too strange to be real.

His panicked breaths fog up the little window. 'How did you know I was here?' He sounds as though he can't believe it either, like he might be dreaming her.

Elise *didn't* know. She never expected this. She's unprepared. Her brother is alive. He's alive!

More noises from the house. A faint thump that might be a door slamming. Elise shifts sideways so the boulder is between her and the house, but doesn't break eye contact with Callum, feeling like he'll vanish again if she looks away.

'How did you get here?' she whispers, peering down at him.

His scabbed lips are trembling. 'Don't worry about that—do you have the key?'

Elise didn't see any keys while she was searching the house. She examines the padlock. It's big, with a fat head and a thick bar. It would take an angle grinder to cut through it.

But the lid is just plastic. 'Get back,' Elise says, standing up.

'That won't work,' Callum says.

Ignoring him, she stomps on the lid. There's no give—it's like kicking concrete. She tries a different spot, closer to the edge. There's a noisy thud, but her shoe doesn't leave a dent.

'Elise,' Callum says urgently, 'you have to find the key. She keeps one on her—'

'Who?' Elise is still catching up.

'The woman who lives here! There must be a spare, somewhere in the house.'

'I can't go back into the house. She just got home.'

'She just got . . .?' The remaining colour drains from Callum's face. 'You have to hide.'

'I can't leave you.' Elise has been looking for Callum for so long. She can't lose him again.

'She'll be here to check on me in a second. Go, now!'

Elise tears herself away from the little window and peeks around the boulder again. Lights are on inside the house now, pushing back the shadows. No sign of Stephanie yet.

Elise's mouth is dry. Her ears are ringing. She reaches for her phone, but she still doesn't have it. Her pepper spray is no protection against the rifles in the closet. All she can do is flee.

'I'll come back, okay?' she says.

'Just go,' Callum hisses.

Elise dashes towards the neighbour's property. She can jump the barbed-wire fence, while a forty-something woman like Stephanie probably can't. Once Elise is safely on the other side, she can make her way back to the car and call the police.

The fence is about two hundred metres away. Under ideal conditions Elise has run that distance in twenty-five seconds. But these conditions are not ideal—the ground is pitted and flaky. She can see the hazards in the twilight, but that doesn't mean they're easy to avoid.

The screen door bangs. Elise looks back. Stephanie is on the porch, dressed in black boots, khaki pants and a cardigan. She has a torch in one hand and a rifle slung over her shoulder. In person, she's tall, with a confident stride. Now that she's back on her own property, she doesn't look much like the nervous woman who spied on Elise from the cover of a Holden Barina.

Elise freezes, hoping not to draw Stephanie's gaze. Too late. The woman looks at her and does a double take, eyes widening with alarm before she swings the torch beam around, dazzling Elise.

Blinking frantically, Elise starts running again. Terror gives her an extra burst of speed. The fence is less than a hundred metres away now, but there's no cover, here or on the other side.

A sharp *pop* splits the night. Elise suppresses a scream. She's been yelled at, spat on, had her tyres slashed. But no one has ever fired a gun at her before. She's never felt this animal panic, her heart somersaulting in her chest.

Pop! The shot doesn't touch Elise, but she feels it whiz past, the vibration in the air like an electric shock.

She pelts towards the fence, zigzagging to make herself a harder target. She keeps her arms up as she runs, as though she can parry away a bullet.

Twenty metres to the fence. In the dark, Elise can't see the barbed wire stretched between the posts, but she knows it's there. Hopefully it's no higher than it was at the front of the property.

Gritting her teeth, she pushes for one last explosion of speed. Hurtles towards the fence. Comes in low, about to jump—

Pop! Something stabs her in the back, just behind her right shoulder blade.

The world flickers, strange colours swirling at the edges. The fence seems to grow, rising like a drawbridge in front of her. Her legs are turning to jelly.

She tries to make the jump anyway. But she clips one foot with the other, stumbles and falls. Tries to shield her face with her arms, but they are jelly, too. The last thing she sees is the barbed wire, all too visible now, rushing up to meet her.

CHAPTER 8

'New kid! Get over here.'

Elise turned to look, but didn't stop running. She couldn't, once she'd found her rhythm. She had to lose speed gradually, like a plane touching down on the runway.

'While we're young, mate.' The teacher wasn't young. Sagging cheeks, receding hairline. His polo shirt stretched by a pot belly, his shorts barely held up by his shrinking old-man bum.

'Sorry, Mr P.' Elise redirected her momentum, turning sideways and crossing the track in front of the other Year Sevens, who looked annoyed. But she wasn't exactly cutting them off, since they were so far behind.

Elise enjoyed their resentment. Bec might have been better at maths, and Lacey always knew the right answer in English class, but nobody ran better than her.

Mr Panagoulis didn't look happy, though. He jabbed a gnarled finger at his big red stopwatch. 'What do you call this?'

Elise checked the screen. 'Two minutes fifteen.'

'Don't be cheeky.'

'That's what it says.'

'And what should it say?'

Elise ran her tongue over her braces. 'Dunno. Something less than that?'

The teacher glanced up at the clouds, exasperated. 'Come with me.'

Still puffing in the cold, Elise followed him to the gums at the edge of the oval, out of earshot of the other students. But not out of sight—Elise stayed on this side of the ragged trunks. She was always careful like that.

She glanced back, checking that her big brother was watching. Callum was stretching beside the track with the other Year Tens, waiting for his turn to race. He flashed a smile, like she had nothing to worry about. He had her back, no matter what.

'Two fifteen isn't good enough,' Panagoulis said.

Elise's cheeks grew hot. 'It's faster than any of the others. Why aren't you picking on them?'

'Because they're doing their best.'

Elise's heart was still racing from the run. Her legs were weak. 'So am I.'

'Maybe you are right now, but what about at home? How often do you train? What's your diet like?' The teacher's watery eyes roamed over her body.

None of your business, she thought. 'It's fine.'

'I had this student, years ago. Ron. Played footy like I'd never seen. It wasn't just that he could kick and catch— he'd see the ball falling towards the grass, then jump the way it was about to bounce. I swear, it was as if he could see the future.'

This was an odd thing for Panagoulis to praise, since he only cared about the past. His stories sometimes went as far back as the Berlin Olympics.

'Uh-huh,' Elise said.

'Other kids always wanted him on their team. Not just on the pitch—off it, too. He got invited to parties. Girls adored him. Girls like you.'

Elise tried to picture that. Now that she was in Year Seven, all the other girls seemed to have lost interest in sport, preferring to focus on who should be excluded from what. Since then, Elise had mostly hung out with boys. But it was hard to imagine herself adoring one.

'Ron didn't practise,' Panagoulis continued. 'Why would he, when he was already popular, admired, and so on? After he graduated, I heard he tried out for the Magpies. Didn't make the team, though. He was the best here, but that didn't prepare him for going up against the best from all the other schools.'

A starting gun cracked. Callum's race. Elise looked over in time to see him launch into motion, easily overtaking the other Year Tens with his long stride.

From the sidelines, the other Year Sevens watched Elise suspiciously, clearly wondering why she was getting special attention. She'd only just moved to Warrigal. It was hard enough to make friends without her teachers making it harder.

Panagoulis inspected the bottom of his shoe, then scraped it against a tree trunk. 'You know what stops people from reaching their potential?'

The sooner Elise told him what he wanted to hear, the sooner this was over. 'Laziness?'

'Contentment. They decide they're happy where they are, and they stop practising.'

Elise bounced on her toes, keen to be back on the track. She wanted to practise right now, and this lecture was stopping her.

'You have to make a choice, Glyk,' Panagoulis continued. 'You can decide that being top dog at this school is good enough. Or you can get your priorities straight and start trying your best, not just here but at home, too. You're good, sure. But without some extra practice, you're never going to make the regionals.'

Panic flickered in Elise's chest. 'Regionals?'

'Sure. I'm thinking hurdles, since your jumping is almost as good as your running. It'll be hard, though. Other kids have been training for this since they were six.'

Elise had never thought about actually competing. She just liked running, the feel of it. While she was concentrating on putting one foot in front of the other, it seemed impossible to worry about anything else. Not Mum and Dad, and the cold silences around the dinner table. Not the other girls at school, who never let her into their little clubs. All that disappeared among the thudding of her shoes, the pounding of her heart, the sweat pouring into her eyes.

She realised Panagoulis was looking at her expectantly.

Elise nodded. 'Right.'

'Good. Now get back out there.' He made it sound like she had been the one holding him up. As she ran to the track, she could feel jealous stares on her neck. But when she turned to look, no one was facing her, and she wondered if she had imagined it.

'Don't mind them, Leesy.' Callum had finished his race and was leaning against a goalpost.

'I don't,' Elise said.

'Hmm.' Callum didn't seem out of breath, and his hair was stylishly dishevelled rather than smeared all over his forehead, like Elise's. He wasn't as fast as her but always managed to give the impression that he could be, if he tried.

Callum's good looks made him seem charming. People laughed and opened up to him, even when he asked questions that would get an ugly person punched. His chattiness and oddball sense of humour made him popular, but Elise could tell it was a performance, and she often found herself wondering what was really going on in his head.

'Mr P wants to send me to the regionals.' She tried to make it sound like it was no big deal.

Callum's mouth fell open. 'Really? That's huge!'

'Yeah, I guess.'

'Congrats.' He hugged her. Actions like that seemed to come naturally to him, while Elise would always hesitate for too long, make it weird somehow.

She slipped out of his grip. People were watching.

'I don't know if I'm good enough,' she said.

'You're good enough,' he said firmly. 'Can I help? We can train after school, or something.'

Callum may have been lazy, but he was dedicated to his family. When Dad had abruptly moved them all to Warrigal, Elise had moaned about leaving her friends behind. Callum hadn't, even though he had more friends to lose. He'd even had a girlfriend, Michaela, and he must have known he'd never see her again. Just before the move, Michaela had turned up on their doorstep, weeping. But Callum had endured the move in stoic silence. 'Dad needs this,' he'd said, when Elise brought it up.

She took a deep breath. 'Thanks, Cal,' she said.

Callum grinned, tapped the ash off an imaginary cigar, and affected an American accent. 'You and me against the world, baby girl.'

'Coach says I should try out for the regionals,' Elise said.

She hadn't expected her parents to be impressed, but she had hoped to surprise them at least. Dad just kept chewing his roast potatoes, while Mum sawed at her steak with a blunt knife.

'Wow, that's great!' Callum said, as though he hadn't heard this news already. Like he was trying to show them what a supportive parent would sound like, hypothetically.

Mum pointed at his elbows. He quickly lifted them off the table.

Dad swallowed. 'What would that involve?'

Elise's heart raced a little faster. 'Not much. Some training after school.'

'How often?'

'Three or four days a week.' It would probably be five.

'Hm.' Dad reloaded his fork and slowly pushed it into his mouth.

'I could help with that,' Callum offered. 'The training.'

Elise opened her mouth to point out that he'd already promised this, then shut it again when she remembered he was pretending he hadn't heard about the regionals. He'd always been a better liar than her.

'I don't know,' Mum said cautiously, and looked side-ways at Dad. She never looked at anyone straight on, always at an angle, like a pigeon.

Since this last move, Mum and Dad had mostly stopped talking to each other directly, and communicated via their children. Elise got the feeling that Mum didn't like Warrigal very much—not that she'd seemed happy in the last town, either.

'What about St John?' Dad asked.

Elise was a volunteer cadet for St John Ambulance. But they only called on her for big events, like the Easter Show and the annual mountain-bike race. 'I can do both.'

Dad sighed heavily. 'It could be harder than you think, sweetie.'

'For me, or for you?'

'Oi.' Dad pointed his fork at her. 'No cheek.'

Elise clamped her mouth shut.

'I don't know,' Mum said again.

'I can do it,' Elise said, annoyed. 'I'm the fastest in my year. Faster than most of the older students, too. If I trained, I could be the best in the state.'

She forced herself to meet Dad's eye as she said the words. They sounded so arrogant. But it was the truth.

'She's really good,' Callum put in. Elise was grateful for his support, even though, in a way, her parents' reluctance was his fault. They'd bought him a guitar, and he'd prac-tised for a few days, but then left it in his closet to gather dust. After that he'd wanted to do karate. He'd gone to a dojo once a week, then once a month, then misplaced his belt and never gone again.

Now it was Elise wanting to try things. But by squandering the chances he'd been given, Callum had taught Mum and Dad not to bet on their children's success.

'How much is this going to cost me?' Dad asked.

Elise wanted to ask what the point of coming here had been, if they still had to worry about money. They'd moved from a larger town, where Dad had been competing with several other GPs. Now he was the only doctor in a town full of old people. Wasn't their family rich? But that question wouldn't get her what she wanted, and she could tell he was nearly convinced. 'Not much.'

Finally, Dad nodded.

'Okay,' Mum said. 'You can try out. But we don't want you to get your hopes up.'

'I won't,' Elise lied. This morning, the regionals hadn't even been on her radar. But now she'd had to fight for them, she was determined to win.

CHAPTER 9

Elise's eyelids flutter open. There's cold concrete beneath her body and even colder drool smeared across her cheek. Her armpits are sore, and her buttocks. Her hands. Everything, actually.

For the few remaining young adults in Warrigal, waking up too drunk to know where they are is a typical Sunday. But for Elise, it only happened once. She'd just been sent home from the Gold Coast and had gone straight to Kingo's, not even dumping her gear at her house. Sculling one Vodka Cruiser after another. Hearing the whispers, feeling all those angry stares on the back of her neck. Someone eventually got in her face, and she didn't take it well. The last thing she remembered was telling the bartender to 'turn that fucking TV off'.

Then she woke up in the alley outside, her mouth gritty, her bag gone. Her legs were bruised, like someone had kicked her. It wasn't until she was vomiting into a recycling bin filled with bottles that she even realised where she was.

And when she reported the assault and the theft, she met Kiara. The police officer with a hard voice but kind eyes, who didn't seem to think Elise had deserved what she got, even though Elise privately felt like she did. Kiara wasn't interested in what had happened at the Games—she didn't seem to care about sport at all. She only cared that Elise needed help. She was sympathetic, and gentle, and she smelled good, and . . .

Elise wrinkles her nose. What is she smelling now? The bitter tang of body odour and piss.

'Elise?' Callum slowly comes into focus, leaning over her. 'Are you awake?'

He's wearing his nicest clothes—a V-neck shirt with a logo embroidered on the breast, dark chinos, leather shoes—but they're stained and frayed. His formerly thick, wavy hair is limp and dirty. His cheeks are hollow, and there are dark circles around his eyes.

'Cal?' Elise's mouth feels swollen and numb, like she's just had her wisdom teeth removed. She tries to sit up, but she's too dizzy. She slumps back down.

He's alive. She didn't dream it. But how?

There's something hard under her head. No, *on* her head. She feels her way across the carbon-fibre surface. She's wearing a bicycle helmet. What the hell?

'Take it easy,' Callum says. 'She shot you with an animal tranquilliser. Not sure what kind, but it's nasty. You'll have dizziness, headaches, sore muscles, chills . . .'

Elise unbuckles the helmet and tosses it aside. Her arms sting. They're covered with little puncture wounds from the barbed-wire fence. She touches her face and finds scratches there, too. She's lucky she didn't lose an eye.

'Where are we?'

Callum gestures around the room. It's too dark to make out much detail. But there's a little square window up above. Through it, she can see stars.

The horror is like glue hardening in her guts. 'No.'

Callum squeezes her shoulder. 'I'm sorry.'

'No!' Elise shakes him off and scrambles to her feet. She staggers unsteadily across the room and bumps into a concrete wall.

'Leesy, listen. You have to save your strength.'

Elise barely hears him through the fog of panic. She feels her way across the wall until she finds the metal rungs of a ladder. She grips them and tries to climb up towards the little window.

'Don't—you'll fall.'

Elise ignores him, hauling herself upwards. But the nausea overtakes her when she's only a couple of rungs up. The world spins. She slips backwards, arms windmilling.

Callum catches her. But he's not as strong as he used to be, and they both collapse onto the floor.

She squirms, trying to get back to the ladder. 'We have to get out!'

'The hatch is locked,' Callum wheezes. 'Just relax for a second.'

'Relax?' Insane laughter bubbles up Elise's throat. 'We're buried alive! No one knows we're here except the woman who shot me! Do you not get how completely screwed we are?'

She meets Callum's hollow-eyed stare. He does get it. 'There are two of us now. And only one of her. We'll think of something. But you have to calm down, okay?'

Elise sucks in a deep breath so she can shout at him some more. But the act of inhaling takes her nerves from a boil to a simmer. The trembling in her hands becomes less intense.

'Have a seat.' He drags over a shapeless object that is clearly not a seat.

She collapses onto the thing—it feels like a sheepskin rug. There's a tender lump next to her spine. Centre mass. Stephanie is a good shot.

Elise searches her pockets. Still no phone, and now her pepper spray, wallet and keys are missing, too. Her glasses are gone—maybe they fell off when she hit the fence.

'What day is it?' Callum asks.

She can't have been unconscious more than a couple of hours, or she'd be suffering from more than just dizziness and a headache. 'Tuesday, I guess. The twenty-first.'

She thinks of Guppy. She told him she'd be right back. He must be so scared.

'What month?' Callum rubs his eyes.

'July.'

'Jesus. How did you find me? Tell me everything.'

'You tell *me* everything. What the fuck happened to you? Who is that lady? Why—?'

She's interrupted by approaching footsteps above. Torchlight shines down through the window, creating a circle of light around Elise, like she's about to be abducted by a UFO. She scrambles out of the circle, blinking furiously.

The padlock rattles. The hatch creaks open. Elise is frozen, unsure whether to run towards the opening or back away. Before she can decide, something comes down through the hatch, taking shape as she squints against the torchlight. It's a wicker basket, dangling on a shoelace.

Elise suddenly understands why she woke up wearing a bike helmet. She must have been lowered through the hatch while she was unconscious, probably using that pulley she saw above. The soreness under her arms would be from the straps. The helmet protected her head.

The basket drops the last metre and lands with a hard rustle, the shoelace spiralling to the floor around it.

The hatch slams shut. The lock clicks. More footsteps, fading away.

Elise crawls over to the basket. It's full of little plastic bottles—face cream, hand cream, sanitiser. There's a hairbrush and a packet of wet wipes. Some sanitary pads, which bring back an unwelcome memory of her fridge. There are also some home-baked Anzac biscuits and a couple of apples.

Elise paws through the items. 'What the . . .?'

'Wow.' Callum crawls over. 'She never gives me this stuff. I guess she likes you.'

The words make Elise's skin crawl. 'Who is she?'

'I was going to ask you the same question.'

'You don't know?'

'All I know is that she's crazy,' Callum says. 'She grabbed me in broad daylight, in the car park behind Woolies. Put something over my face. Then I woke up here.'

It's hard to believe Callum was overpowered and carried here by a woman in her forties. She must be incredibly strong.

'The police never found your car,' Elise says.

'Stolen, I guess.' Callum crams a biscuit into his mouth. 'How'd you find me?'

Elise talks about texting him and getting no response, her calls going straight to voicemail. About visiting his home and finding him gone. Talking to his work and discovering he'd been missing for days. Calling the police, who searched the house and found both ecstasy and GHB, as well as Callum's phone, still on the charger.

He doesn't sound surprised. 'The drugs weren't mine.'

'I know that.' Elise has never seen her brother use drugs. He doesn't even drink.

'*She* put them there.' He points at the ceiling, as though referring to a vengeful god. 'She told me it would stop anyone from looking for me.'

'Well, she was wrong. There was only a little bit of ecstasy, but plenty of GHB, and the police said that proved intent to distribute. So they definitely looked for you, but gave up after a month. They thought you might have escaped overseas.'

'I wouldn't just leave you like that,' he says.

'That's what I told them, but they didn't believe me. After I hadn't heard from you in a few days, I got worried you might be dead. After a couple of weeks, I was sure of it.'

'Oh, Leesy.' He squeezes her hand.

'It's okay,' she says, like it was nothing. She doesn't tell him how every man between the ages of twenty and forty started to look like him. How she kept seeing him out of the corner of her eye, but when she turned there would be no one. How her heart leapt into her throat whenever the phone or doorbell rang, and the adrenaline crash afterwards would leave her unable to rise from the couch.

How she stopped hoping the knocks on the door would be Callum, and started worrying they were his killer.

'I'm just glad you're alive.' She changes the subject. 'Anyway. I got access to your bank account details and phone records.'

Callum frowns. 'How?'

'Kiara's colleagues had given up, but all the files were still on the police intranet. I borrowed her laptop and took a look at them.'

She doesn't tell him that Kiara caught her. Dumped her. Threatened to have her charged. That wound is still too raw.

'So I retraced your steps. Called everyone you called. Went everywhere you went. I told people I was a private investigator so they'd talk to me.'

Callum laughs, startled. 'You did what?'

'My name doesn't exactly open doors, these days.'

'Right.' The amusement dies on his face. 'Sorry.'

'So the biggest transaction was seven thousand dollars. You'd bought a painting from an artist in Canberra—'

He has been scrubbing his armpits with a wet wipe, but he stops when she says this.

'What?' she asks.

He goes back to scrubbing. 'It's nothing.'

'*What?*'

He sighs. 'The painting was supposed to be a birthday present for you.'

Elise is shocked. 'A seven-thousand-dollar birthday present?'

He looks embarrassed. 'Mum left me some things in her will. I didn't have the space, and I needed the money, so I sold them. Don't tell Dad, okay? But then I got a pay rise at school, and suddenly I didn't need the money after all. I knew you'd had a rough couple of years, so I just thought . . .' He trails off.

Despite everything, Elise is touched—but still confused. Why would he have thought she'd appreciate a painting?

And why *that* painting? Perhaps Aiden Deere was the number one ranked artist on a search engine or something, so Callum just assumed he was good. Elise would have much preferred to have the seven thousand dollars.

'Thank you,' she says anyway.

He shrugs. 'You're my little sister.'

'Well,' she says, 'I went to visit the painter.'

'Really? What was he like?'

'Uh . . .' She tries to think of a concise way to describe Aiden Deere. 'Big.'

Callum nods slowly, as though this is profound. 'What did he tell you?'

'Basically nothing. But a car followed me the whole way there, and I memorised the numberplate. Kiara gave me the owner's surname, then I found a photo of her on the internet, which gave me her full name. Then I found her in the White Pages, which gave me her address. I drove there, and she caught me.'

'And now you're here.'

'Now I'm here.' With no phone. With nobody looking for her. With no trail to follow, even if someone did look. When she's eventually reported missing, the police will assume that she has escaped overseas, like her brother.

She can hear their father's voice in her head: *You've really done it now, kiddo.*

CHAPTER 10

Soon the first fingers of daylight are probing the little window above, and Elise can see her prison.

The septic tank is maybe five metres long, four wide, about two point five in height. It's divided in half by a knee-high wall and a lowered section of the ceiling, probably to stop floating scum and settled sludge flowing from one side to the other. There's no sludge now—the floor is dry and dusty. But it still smells like shit, especially near the stack of buckets in the corner, which Elise guesses are makeshift toilets. At least they have lids. The floor is littered with cornflake boxes and ten-litre water bottles, all empty.

It looks like Stephanie was using the tank for storage even before Callum arrived. Dozens of bags of fertiliser are stacked against the walls—probably flammable, kept underground in case of bushfires. Elise now realises the 'sheepskin rug' she's been sitting on is a pile of woollen fleeces, maybe too misshapen to sell. There's a second pile under Callum.

'Did Kiara know you were coming here?' he asks.

'No.'

'Did you tell anyone else?'

'Yeah. My dog.'

A defeated silence. Poor Guppy. What will happen to him if she doesn't come home?

'Kiara might figure it out though, right?' Callum presses.

'Maybe.' But Elise thinks he's clutching at straws. Kiara will call Stephanie and tell her to stop following Elise. Stephanie will say she doesn't know what Kiara is talking about. Kiara will probably believe her and leave an annoyed voicemail for Elise. That will be the end of it.

Callum is scratching under his shirt. 'If Kiara came out here, she'd see your Suzuki.'

'I parked on the neighbour's property, behind some trees.' Kiara might miss the driveway and have to turn around. If she did, she could notice the Suzuki. But she wouldn't snoop around the property—she'd knock on Stephanie's front door and ask her some questions. Stephanie would pretend she hadn't seen Elise, then relocate or kill her two captives before Kiara came back with a search warrant.

How long before anyone realises that Elise is gone? None of her old friends will look for her. If they notice she's stopped calling, they'll do so with relief. Her landlord will send a letter when the rent payments stop coming in—but they're automated, so that won't happen until the account is overdrawn. Her unemployment benefits will keep topping up the account until she stops returning the forms. So no one will have any reason to report her missing for at least a couple of months. More than enough time for Stephanie Hartnell to do . . . what, exactly?

'What does she want?' Elise examines the moisturiser and hairbrush. 'Is she going to sell us as sex slaves? Steal our organs?'

Callum takes a deep, shaky breath. 'She wants me to confess to something.'

'What?' Elise looks up sharply. 'What does she think you did?'

He opens his hands. 'If I knew that, why would I still be here? I'd say anything to get out of this place.'

'You must have some idea,' Elise presses.

'I don't know if she's mixed me up with somebody else or if I'm part of some imagined conspiracy, or what. I've told her over and over again that I haven't done anything, but she doesn't believe me.'

Hope flickers in Elise's heart. 'Well, I can vouch for you. Maybe she'll believe me.'

'Oh, you think?' Callum lifts up his shirt.

Elise gasps. She's seen stab wounds before, when she worked as a paramedic. Men in the pub would fight, usually at 2 a.m., defending the honour of some woman who was screaming at them both to stop. But those wounds, examined in the neon glow of the ambulance, were usually fresh. She's never seen anything like this—hundreds of pale, hook-shaped scars, all over Callum's torso. He should be dead. He would be, if all those injuries had happened at once.

'You can't reason with her,' he says. 'If you try, she'll hurt you, too.'

Elise is about to ask what happened, when she hears a sound from above. Stephanie is coming back. Instinctively, Elise backs away. She trips over the low wall across the middle of the septic tank. Her fall is broken by a bag of fertiliser on the other side.

Callum's whole demeanour changes. He lowers his head and hugs his knees. Submitting, defending his tender parts and trying to become invisible, all at once.

The lock rattles. The hatch creaks open, spilling more daylight into the tank. Fresh air flows through the gap.

'Miss Thatcher,' a voice calls.

For a moment, Elise is baffled. Then she remembers her missing wallet. Stephanie must have been fooled by the fake private investigator's licence.

'I'd like to talk to you,' Stephanie continues. 'Come on up.'

Elise looks at Callum, anxious. She's desperate to get out of the tank, but she doesn't want to be any closer to the woman who shot her and has been torturing her brother. Callum doesn't offer any useful advice. He just stares, chewing his scabbed lips.

'If you're still too weak, I can come back later,' Stephanie offers.

'No!' The fear of being trapped down here wins out. Elise approaches the ladder and squints upwards. She can't see Stephanie. She shoots a last look at Callum, who's trembling like a wounded bird.

Still weak from the tranquilliser, Elise climbs the rungs slowly and emerges into the daylight.

Stephanie is wearing a linen blouse with a daisy pattern and some of the jeans Elise saw in her wardrobe. She's holding a rifle. Elise doesn't know much about guns. She can't tell if this is the tranquilliser gun or the one that fires bullets.

'Shut the hatch, please,' Stephanie says.

Elise looks down. Callum is at the bottom of the ladder, eyes wide.

She closes the lid.

'Lock it,' Stephanie says.

The big padlock is on the ground next to the hatch, open. No key—Stephanie must have it in her pocket.

Elise threads the bar of the padlock through the latch and snaps it shut, sealing her brother in.

'Thank you.' Stephanie lowers the gun. 'I'm Stephanie.'

Cockatoos flutter in the distant trees.

'You're Tina, right?'

Elise nods numbly.

'Nice to meet you.' Stephanie holds out a hand.

Elise just looks at it. It's a worn hand, freckled and bony. No jewellery.

'Quiet, aren't you?' Stephanie withdraws the hand. 'Tell me—what's your interest in Mr Glyk?'

It's unnerving to be face-to-face with Stephanie. To be having a conversation, as though she didn't shoot Elise in the back only hours ago.

Elise forces herself to speak. 'Mr Glyk?'

Stephanie jerks her head in the direction of the hatch, as though Callum isn't even worth a pointed finger.

'My interest,' Elise repeats, still catching up.

'You visited his house, and the school that he worked at. You even turned up at the home of one of the police officers on his case. Why?'

Apparently Stephanie has been following her for some time. But she doesn't know Callum has a sister—or she's done an image search and seen hundreds of photos of a fit young blonde in track wear. Not a tattooed redhead, less fit, less young.

'I'm a private investigator,' Elise hears herself say.

'I know. But who hired you?'

Elise says nothing, her mind racing.

Stephanie changes tack. 'What led you to the art studio in Canberra?'

'Mr Glyk, uh, bought a painting.'

Stephanie waits for more information, but Elise can't think of anything else to say.

'I appreciate that you want to protect your client,' Stephanie says. 'But you don't have a lot of options here, Tina.'

Still Elise keeps quiet.

'Okay,' Stephanie says. 'Come with me. I have a proposal for you.'

CHAPTER 11

'Rafa,' Elise said. 'Can I have a word?'

Rafa looked up from his clipboard. He was in his thirties, but already had the hollow eyes of a long-serving paramedic, and the jowls of a man who ate every meal at the King George pub. He put the clipboard on the counter and wiped his hands on his scrubs. 'Can it wait?'

'I'd rather it didn't.' It had taken Elise some time to work up the courage for this.

Rafa sighed and started walking along the squeaky linoleum towards the vending machine, as though he could already tell this conversation would require a Mars bar. Elise followed.

'I saw Mr Stoppard yesterday. He's looking much better.' Rafa seemed to know what was coming, and was trying to change Elise's mind.

'I'm glad.' The resignation letter burned in the back pocket of her jeans.

After high school, she had spent every day studying for her paramedical science diploma, and every night at the track. When she became a qualified paramedic three years later, her schedule had flipped—she ran during the day and drove the ambulance at night. Pulling mangled bodies out of cars. Wrapping blankets around old people with pneumonia. Sitting on the backs of ice addicts, pinning them to the road so they couldn't punch her. All the while winning race after race after race.

Sometimes she'd go without sleep for forty-eight hours. Other times she'd find herself at home, twitchy, knowing she should lie down but instead rearranging the contents of her pantry or watching trashy dramas on TV.

Physically, she was stronger than she'd ever been, her legs like tightly wound springs. But her mind felt like a tightly wound spring, too, and she couldn't take it anymore.

'Stoppard would be dead if not for you,' Rafa said.

'We were lucky.'

'Well, we might not be so lucky with the next one.'

Stoppard was a balding, red-faced man, fired by the local credit union for forging signatures. He'd been found slumped sideways on a park bench outside the library, bug-eyed, making popping sounds with his mouth. A friend said he'd tried some synthetic pot, which was consistent with the e-cigarette clenched in Stoppard's meaty fist. Guessing that the substance was tainted with either arsenic or lead, Elise had injected some dimercaprol into his muscle. A blood test later proved her hunch.

Stoppard's dealer was still out there. Maybe they knew their stock was poison, maybe they didn't. Either way, they were likely to sell it to someone else, who might not have a friend ready to call the ambulance.

'We're doing good work here, Elise,' Rafa said.

'I know.'

'No, you don't.' He didn't look at her as he counted coins for the hospital vending machine. 'You think no matter what we do, the people in this town will keep taking drugs, driving too fast, beating the shit out of one another.'

'It's not—'

'If you weren't thinking that, you wouldn't be leaving me to do this on my own. And for what?' He pushed some buttons on the machine. 'So you can run around in circles for a living.'

It wasn't really a living. Athletes weren't paid. Oddly, that was part of the appeal—it made the effort seem noble. Elise could only afford to quit this job because she'd convinced Mum and Dad to support her. She'd told herself she would pay them back when she had endorsements, speaking fees, a book deal.

Inside the machine a coil rotated, slowly freeing a packet of pork rinds, which fell into the collection tray.

'I have an opportunity.' Elise took the letter out of her pocket. No point hiding it anymore.

Rafa stuck a hand through the flap, rummaging around. 'To get out of this place.'

Elise couldn't pretend that wasn't part of it. 'To do something great.'

'Saving Mr Stoppard wasn't great?'

'That's different.'

'I agree. No one will write about that in the paper. It won't have the whole town talking about how great you are. Even Stoppard himself told me to get fucked when I went to check on him. But it makes a difference.'

At the worst possible moment, a young woman approached. She was pretty, wearing a dress with an autumn leaf pattern over black trousers, rolled up at the ankles. Not a patient, not hospital staff—she must be here visiting someone.

'Excuse me,' she said, 'are you Elise Glyk?'

Rafa snorted.

Elise felt the heat rise to her cheeks. 'Have we met?'

'I saw that article about you.' The woman beamed, brown eyes twinkling. 'Congratulations!'

'Thanks.' Elise didn't tell her there had been a few articles—in *The Warrigal Times* and the *Tablelands Chronicle*, and even a line in *The Sydney Morning Herald*: '*Elise Glyk, the fastest woman in regional New South Wales.*'

The woman waited for Elise to say something else, but she'd never been good at small talk.

'Well, good luck at the nationals,' the woman said eventually. 'I'll be keeping my fingers crossed for you. We all will.'

She walked away without seeming even to notice Rafa, still crouched next to the vending machine. It looked like he couldn't get his wrist at the right angle to grab the pork rinds.

'Who would turn down the opportunity to have more conversations like that?' he said drily.

Elise took a deep breath. 'You've been very generous with time off. I can't ask you for any more.'

'Don't act like you're doing me a favour,' Rafa snapped.

She held out the letter to him. 'I'm sorry.'

He didn't take it, still trying to get a grip on the pork rinds.

'Here.' Elise knelt down to assist him. Her wrists were thinner.

'I don't need your help.' He took the letter and stuffed his hand back into the machine. 'Get out.'

As she was leaving, she was surprised to see the back of Callum's head in the waiting area. It was a handsome head, she knew objectively. Dark hair cut short, symmetrical ears, good posture that made his neck seem longer. Callum had gone straight from cute little boy to handsome man without a pimply, awkward teenage phase in between. Elise's friends always wanted to know if he was single.

Callum was sitting next to a girl, sixteen or seventeen, ash-blonde hair. The girl's head was bowed, her fists crushed between her knees.

'Callum?' Elise said.

He turned. 'Elise? I didn't know you were working today.'

'I wasn't. I . . .' She trailed off, not ready to talk about the resignation yet.

The girl shrank into her chair. She didn't look like she wanted to be introduced. Callum gave her arm a reassuring squeeze. 'Be right back, okay?'

'Who's she?' Elise asked, when they were under the gull-wing-shaped awning outside.

'Ophelia?' Callum glanced back. 'One of my students— or she was, a couple of years ago. I hadn't seen her since she dropped out, but she called me out of the blue and wanted to know if I could come to a medical appointment with her.'

Elise was confused. 'A student asked you to come to the doctor with her?'

He gave her a significant look. 'There are some medical appointments you can't invite your parents to, you know?'

'Oh. Poor kid.' Elise got it now. He taught at a Catholic girls school just over the river. Some of the parents had what Mum called 'strong views'.

'You don't know the half of it. Her father sounds like a piece of work. And she has no one else. I mean, she asked a *teacher* to come with her.' Callum looked haggard, now that Elise could see him up close. She wondered how many students turned to him in times of crisis.

'Are you sleeping okay?' she asked.

'No.' He rubbed his face, then forced a tired smile. 'It turns out teaching is hard.'

It had shocked her when he'd decided he wanted to become a teacher. Privately, she had wondered if he had the patience to watch kids get things wrong over and over.

His grades at uni had been shoddy, but the school had accepted him out of desperation. Educators were abandoning the profession all over the state. And to Elise's surprise, Callum had done well. He had dedicated himself to teaching, in a way she'd never seen him commit to anything. The students found him inspiring, perhaps because he was the only teacher at the school under forty. And the staff were charmed, like everyone always was.

Elise had managed to push down her guilt about resigning, but now it came back with a vengeance. Who was she to follow her dream while Rafa treated drug addicts and Callum comforted crying students?

'I'm not sure this is technically teaching,' she said.

'Well, I hope she's learned something anyway. Shit, that was unkind.' He sighed. 'I'd better get back in there.'

'Yeah.'

'I shouldn't have told you any of that stuff about Ophelia. Shouldn't even have told you her name. You'll keep it to yourself?'

'Of course.'

He went inside to sit with the girl, who now had her feet on the chair and was hugging her knees. Elise headed for the car park, then decided she would run home instead. She could always pick up the car later.

She ran, feeling the wind in her hair, her legs carrying her into the future at a speed no one else could match.

'Are you sure you have everything?' Mum asked, yet again.

'Bit late now, Mum,' Elise said. They'd been driving for almost an hour.

'We could still go back.'

'No, we couldn't. We're halfway there.'

'That doesn't matter. It's never too late to turn around for something important.'

Elise leaned back against the headrest. 'Well, I have everything.'

'Okay.' Mum made a nervous laugh. 'It's just such a small bag.'

She was right. The sports bag on the back seat held a phone charger, two sets of casual clothes and her running gear, and that was it. Elise had been told that the apartment would be fully furnished, and she wouldn't be spending much time there anyway. She'd be at the Australian Institute of Sport all day, every day.

It was just Elise and her mother in the car. Callum had marking to do—he'd seemed horrified to discover that even PE teachers sometimes needed to grade answers on tests—so he had farewelled them in the driveway, tears in his eyes. Dad hadn't been there. He'd gone to the office early, even though it was a Saturday.

'Ugh. Look at that.' Mum pointed at a rise in the distance, where a new town seemed to be under construction. The land had been cleared, but there were no buildings yet. Just a maze of streets, all going nowhere. A playground stood in the centre, shining and empty. A billboard said, GOLDEN-VALE—CLOSE TO EVERYTHING.

'It's not close to *anything*,' Elise observed.

'No, but it will be,' Mum said darkly. 'It'll get bigger and bigger until it merges with Canberra, and Canberra will keep getting bigger until it merges with Sydney, and soon there will be no bush left anywhere. I should write to the paper.'

Mum was always sending letters to the editor. Actual letters, not emails—she scrawled them longhand, like she was eighty. By the time they were delivered and published, the public conversation had usually moved on from whatever she was complaining about. It was odd that someone who kept so quiet at home was so opinionated in public. If *The Warrigal Times* could be called public, since hardly anyone read it.

'I hope Dad's okay,' Elise said, wanting to change the subject.

'How do you mean?'

'He seems pretty busy at work.' What she meant was, he was pretending to be busy. He was just a grouchy old man who couldn't be bothered to see off his own daughter.

'He's had to make sacrifices,' Mum said. 'We both have.'

Elise imagined subtitles under her mother, as though she was an actress on SBS. *Your father and I are so proud of you.*

'This isn't where we pictured ourselves when we got married,' Mum continued.

'What? Driving your daughter to train for the Commonwealth Games?'

'Oh! That's a surprise, but I meant Warrigal in general.'

Elise was confused, and a bit annoyed. 'It's not my fault you had to move to such a crap town, Mum.'

Mum shot her a sharp look. 'The whole universe doesn't revolve around you, Elise.'

'What's that supposed to mean?'

'Just that you could ...' Mum checked the rear-view mirror '... just remember that other people exist, from time to time.'

Stung, Elise fell silent. She could tell that Mum regretted what she'd said but couldn't find her way back to safer ground. Elise wasn't interested in guiding her. She just looked out the window for the rest of the journey, watching paddocks become vineyards, then the city appearing on the horizon.

CHAPTER 12

Elise sits in Stephanie Hartnell's living room, shell-shocked. Even after being followed, being tranquillised, being held prisoner overnight, she can't believe what she just heard. It's too dramatic, like something from a soap opera.

I promise I'll set you free. All you have to do is kill him.

The world spins. Her blood pressure is falling, her hands shaking. She wants a transfusion. Years after she stopped, the craving is still there.

'You want me to kill . . .' Elise almost says *my brother*, but stops herself just in time.

'That's right,' Stephanie says.

The strangeness of the situation is overwhelming. Elise is in a well-presented living room, discussing murder over iced water and biscuits.

She glances at the rifle on the hooks above the back door. What will Stephanie do to her if she refuses?

'I assume your client won't be a problem.' Stephanie notices a spot of grime on the blade of the knife. She scratches the mark off with her fingernail and puts the knife back on the coffee table. 'You can say you never found Callum. That's the outcome in most missing persons cases, isn't it?'

'But—'

'I'll deal with the body,' Stephanie says, as though this must be Elise's main concern. 'I already dug the grave. You'd be free to get on with your life as though this whole thing never happened. And I wouldn't have to worry about you telling the cops.'

Elise swallows. 'I can't do what you're asking.'

'It might not be as hard as you think.'

The question feels dangerous, but it slips through Elise's lips. 'If you want him dead, why have you kept him alive all this time?'

'He was supposed to confess. He never did. I've decided that he's had enough chances.'

'Confess to what?'

Stephanie says nothing.

Elise knows she should pretend to go along with this. If Stephanie thinks she's cooperating, she might let her guard down, and Elise could escape. But she can't stop herself from poking holes in Stephanie's crazy plan. 'If I did talk to the police, they wouldn't charge me for murder. You forcing me to kill Callum is the same thing as you killing Callum.'

'I'm not forcing you,' Stephanie says. 'I'm making you an offer.'

'An offer at knifepoint.'

Stephanie slides the knife across the coffee table and rotates it so the handle faces Elise. Technically, Stephanie is now the one at knifepoint.

'If you went to the cops, what evidence would you have? Those scratches on your arms could be ...' Stephanie trails off, but Elise can guess what she's thinking. The wounds look like self-harm. She wonders if that was how Moon died—slashed wrists.

'Anyway, by the time they got here, Callum would be gone,' Stephanie continues. 'You don't know where the grave is. Your word against mine about what happened. Who would they believe?'

She doesn't know how right she is. With Elise's reputation, no one ever believes her about anything.

'They'd search,' she says.

'You're not a violent person. I respect that. But he—' Stephanie tilts her head towards the backyard '—doesn't deserve your mercy.'

A dark suspicion grows in the pit of Elise's stomach. 'Why not? Just tell me what you think he did.'

'That's private.'

'Private!?' Elise finds herself rocking in the chair, fighting down the frustration.

'Come on. If we spend too long in here, he may start to suspect what we're up to.'

'We're not up to anything.' Elise changes tack: 'You know I'm a PI. It won't be hard for my colleagues to pick up my trail. They'll be here in two days, tops. They could be on their way right now.'

Stephanie looks unmoved.

Elise presses on. 'You have a choice. You can let us go, turn yourself in, plead temporary insanity. No jail time.' This part may be true. Stephanie doesn't seem sane. 'Or you can wait until my friends arrive, and get caught. That's a life sentence. Callum and I get to walk away.'

'You don't understand.' Stephanie's face is like one of the stone heads on Easter Island. 'If anyone knocks on my door, I won't answer. I'll just switch on the pump.' She points to the bathroom. 'The septic tank takes about twelve hours to fill. You'll both drown, slowly, in the dark. Your bodies will never be found.'

Elise stares at her.

'Or I could go out back and roll that boulder onto the hatch. You'd be buried alive. Or how about this? I'll just drop a lit match into the tank. That fertiliser is highly combustible. The whole house could go up. Callum will burn. You'll burn. I'll burn. No one walks away.'

The floor seems to sink under Elise. When she was an ambulance officer, she often dealt with older patients who turned out to be suffering from dementia. She would get this same feeling—the sudden, uneasy sense that the person she was talking to didn't occupy the same reality as her.

'I don't want to hurt you,' Stephanie says. 'But I'm willing to, if that's what it takes to stop Callum going free. Do you see?'

'Yes,' Elise says. 'I see.'

She snatches up the knife and points it at Stephanie's throat.

'Give me the key,' she says.

CHAPTER 13

'Ah, good.' Stephanie is stiff in the chair, keeping her face away from the blade. 'I hoped a spine was under there somewhere.'

Elise stands over her, brandishing the knife with a trembling hand. 'The key,' she repeats. 'To open the septic tank. Now.'

'No.'

Elise can't believe it. She holds the knife even closer to the woman's neck. 'I'm not messing around.'

'Didn't you hear me? I'm willing to die, as long as Callum does, too.'

'I'm going to give you thirty seconds to rethink that answer.' Elise immediately regrets this. Thirty seconds is way too long.

'No,' Stephanie says.

'If you don't give me the key, I'll just take it off your dead body.'

'Makes sense. If you're willing to stab an unarmed, innocent person in cold blood.'

Elise wants to scream. 'That's exactly what you're asking me to do to Callum!'

'Callum isn't innocent,' Stephanie says firmly.

'Ten seconds,' Elise snaps, though she hasn't been counting. 'Nine.'

'You're being ridiculous.'

'Eight. Seven.'

'What will you tell the police?'

'Six. Fi—'

Stephanie kicks Elise's knee inside out.

Elise shrieks. The pain is unbearable, like the joint is full of broken glass. She tries to twist sideways to absorb the impact, but her leg crumples under her. Stephanie makes the most of it, grabbing her wrist and yanking her downwards. The knife misses Stephanie's face and plunges into the stuffing of the sofa. Stephanie punches Elise in the side of the head. Stars burst throughout her skull, the world spins, and she finds herself on the floor.

Stephanie leaps off the sofa and runs across the room. Elise tries to get up, but it feels as though she's in a rocket, the tremendous g-force crushing her against the floor.

By the time she manages to roll over, Stephanie has grabbed the rifle off the hooks near the back door. She whirls around and takes aim at Elise.

Elise feels sick. She's failed. Like always.

Stephanie stares at her for a long time, then lowers the gun. 'When you stab Callum, don't give him thirty seconds' warning. That's bloody stupid. Got it?'

Elise just nods. The movement sends vomit rushing up her throat, but she chokes it down.

'Take off your top,' Stephanie says.

As they walk back through the garden towards the septic tank, Elise's mind is racing. Obviously she's not going to kill Callum. But after a few days, Stephanie will realise no one is coming. She might even discover that Elise isn't a real private investigator. Then what?

Her knee is killing her. It's not broken, as she first thought, but it's badly jarred. After years of running, her knees were already a mess, the cartilage burned away like brake fluid in a revhead's car. Now she can barely put weight on her left foot.

The knife is duct-taped to her back. It's sideways, so it won't stab her if she arches her spine. Stephanie told her the handle is on the right-hand side. Elise didn't tell her she's left-handed. There's no real reason to keep this a secret, but she's desperate to exert power of any kind. She was never in control of this situation, and it feels especially out of control right now.

'Stay back.' Stephanie stoops to unlock the hatch. It only takes her a second, then the key disappears back into her pocket, and the rifle is trained on Elise again. Stephanie steps away from the hatch, then jerks the gun barrel towards it. 'Down.'

Elise stoops to open the hatch. The circle of darkness yawns.

'Get a wriggle on,' Stephanie says.

Elise takes a deep breath, and climbs down into the dark. Slowly, and not just because of her twisted knee. Panic rising.

Callum is in the shadows up the other end of the tank, crouched like Gollum between the stacks of fertiliser bags.

'See you tomorrow.' Stephanie shoots a meaningful glance down at Elise. Clearly she expects Callum to be dead by then. Then she slams the lid shut. The padlock rattles and clicks. Her footsteps fade away towards the garden.

Callum approaches cautiously. 'So? What happened?'

'Shh.' Elise waits until the last of the footsteps fade out. Stephanie isn't hanging around to listen.

'Tell me,' he demands.

Elise turns on him. 'What have you done?'

He looks taken aback. 'What do you mean?'

'That lady is seriously pissed off with you, Cal. This is deeply personal to her. She wants me to kill you.'

His eyes bulge. 'Kill me? How?'

Elise wonders why this is a surprise to him, given everything Stephanie's done so far. She pulls up her top and peels the knife off her back. 'She gave me this. She doesn't know I'm your sister—she thinks I'm some hard-core private investigator who might be willing to murder a stranger. That way, she'll be rid of you, and I won't be able to turn her in without getting arrested. Just tell me: what did you do?'

She waits for Callum to insist, again, that he hasn't done anything. Instead, he hedges his bets. 'What did she say I did?'

'Oh, fuck.' Elise puts her face in her hands.

'Hey,' he snaps, 'get it together. If she gave you some kind of clue, cough it up. I don't even know what I'm accused of.'

'She wouldn't tell me anything about it. Said it was personal.'

'Personal? I never even met her before I got here!'

'What about her daughter?'

Callum looks blank. 'Daughter?'

'Moon Hartnell. Fifteen years old, killed herself in February. Did you know her?'

His mouth falls open. 'She was in my class. This woman is Moon's mum?'

'God, you're slow.' Elise told him Stephanie Hartnell's name last night. She can't believe he's only just making the connection now. 'Could she be blaming you for Moon's suicide?'

He frowns. 'Why?'

'Did you give her a bad grade on a test, or something?'

'Yeah, she failed her nutrition exam. Right before she died. But she got the answers wrong—what could I do? The idea of blaming *me* for her death, is . . . it's just crazy.'

And Stephanie seemed so well balanced until now, Elise thinks. She stabs the blade into one of the bags of fertiliser like it's a knife block, then limps around the septic tank, getting her brain moving as well as her body. The low wall across the middle is like a hurdle—a reminder of where she might be right now, if not for her mistakes. It's as if God is making fun of her.

'She got the answers wrong,' Callum says again.

'Is that really all you know? Moon was your student, she died, you never met the mother?'

He gives a helpless shrug. 'What else am I supposed to know?'

'I don't know, was she being bullied? Maybe you should have noticed, but you didn't?'

'How am I supposed to know what I didn't notice?' Callum's voice cracks. 'After I heard, that was all I thought about. I went over and over every conversation I'd ever had with her. Was there anything I should have seen, anything I could have done? Did I say something that pushed her over the edge? I couldn't sleep. I just kept picturing Moon under a sheet in a morgue drawer somewhere. Later I realised I'd been at Kingo's that night. At that stupid dateless dinner. When Moon was bleeding out, when she needed help from someone, anyone, I was eating a fucking schnitzel with my mates. Laughing at one of Jono's stupid jokes.'

Elise knows the dinner he's talking about—she saw the photos afterwards. It was a Valentine's Day event Callum had organised for singles.

'All the other teachers were the same,' he continues. 'Probably the students, too. No one acted up in class that week. No yelling or laughter in the playground. A quarter of the kids didn't even come to school, and it was like the rest had been replaced by zombies. In case you're wondering, it's bloody hard, losing a student, even one you don't know well. Maybe especially then.'

As he wipes his eyes on his sleeve, Elise blinks away some tears of her own. She never met Moon, but Callum's grief is contagious, and she's just so tired.

She's only been down here for one night. Callum has been trapped for weeks. He must be losing his mind.

'Obviously Moon's mother had it worse than all of us. I get that.' He's starting to sound hysterical. 'But it wasn't my fault. And this?' He gestures wildly at their underground prison. 'This is just nuts!'

'Okay, okay.' Elise hugs him. He smells awful.

He trembles in her arms, like a kitten. 'I just want to go home,' he sobs.

'I know.' She rubs his back. 'Me too.'

Eventually he stops whimpering into her hair, and she releases him. He doesn't say anything else. Just sniffs some snot back into his throat and hobbles over to his pile of fleeces, like the purging process has aged him.

Elise is tired, too. She sits down on a bag of fertiliser to think. Nothing she's learned so far will convince Stephanie to let them go. It's a shame she didn't see Callum's grief just now—it might have helped.

Hours later, Callum is asleep on one of the stacks of fleeces, and Elise is massaging her knee on another. The joint is badly inflamed, but her ACL doesn't feel too bad. She tells herself the pain is mostly from the cold. Their body heat is sucked out through the ventilation tube above, and the concrete walks are chilled by the tightly packed dirt on the other side.

She listens to Callum snoring, every exhalation hissing like bacon in a pan. His face is slack, his lips slightly open. He looks innocent.

I never even met her before I got here. But Callum did meet Stephanie at least once before. In the Woolies car park, where she kidnapped him in broad daylight, like he said.

Elise supposes that doesn't count. They didn't *meet*—he wouldn't even have seen the woman's face. She lies down on the fleeces and tries to sleep.

CHAPTER 14

A voice behind Kiara's shoulder: 'Good, you're here.'

'Yep.' Kiara spins in her chair, trying to act like she's been interrupted doing something important. Like she was actually reading that email, instead of just staring at the words, thinking about Elise.

It's Rohan—her narrow-shouldered sergeant, his sideburns neatly trimmed, his nose hairs plucked. A biro is clenched in his fist like a sword, and he's holding a manila folder close to his chest like a shield. He looks anxious, as usual. Acutely aware that she should have his job by now. But with her screw-up last month, she won't make sergeant for years.

The police station is well lit but stuffy, with windows that are out of reach and never opened. A fern is slowly suffocating in the corner of the room. It's Wednesday, and the blue carpet still has neat lines from the vacuum cleaner on Monday. That's how little has happened this week.

'Got a minute?' Rohan asks.

Kiara gestures to the screen. 'Iris Bandola says her neighbour has stolen her cat for the fourth time. The neighbour, a Mr Clarence Jones, says the cat keeps climbing into his yard by itself.'

'Can we interview the cat?'

Kiara keeps a straight face. 'I've already requisitioned a polygraph, Sarge.'

Rohan chuckles. He brushes some dust off her filing cabinet before perching on it and opening the folder. 'I have something for you.'

The first thing Kiara sees is Zach Locat, smiling for a school photo. He has thin eyebrows, a crooked nose and a vaguely cynical smile. Kiara has seen the picture many times. She keeps it in view whenever she's working the case. Reminding herself there's a human being behind all the evidence tags and file numbers.

Zach disappeared on 2 May. According to the location tracking on his phone, he left school and went up to Fogherty's Lookout. After that, he jumped off the cliff into the river, or was pushed, or fell off accidentally. Or—the best but least likely possibility—he tossed his phone over the edge, then skipped town. In the eleven weeks since, there have been no sightings of him, here or anywhere else, but his family is holding out hope that he's alive ... so they say. Kiara hasn't ruled them out as suspects, since Zach must have travelled to the lookout by car. There's no other way to get up there as fast as he did.

'Don't get excited.' Rohan spreads some papers across the desk, and points to one page. 'It's a bit of hearsay. But I thought you'd find it interesting.'

Kiara peers down at the printed sheet. It's a witness statement.

Rohan doesn't give her time to read it. 'William Yu. Came in yesterday, after you went home.' He pauses just long enough to let Kiara know that he's noticed her leaving early, arriving late, endlessly rearranging her desk. 'He says Zach was bullying a girl in his class—the one who suicided on February 14.'

'Moon?' Kiara can't recall the surname straight away.

'Right. Will didn't want to say anything after the suicide—didn't want to get his friend in trouble. And then, after Zach disappeared, he didn't want to say anything because he was worried about getting in trouble for not saying anything earlier.'

It's a loop plenty of witnesses get stuck in. 'So why is he coming forward now?'

Rohan shrugs. 'Sounded like the guilt just burned him up. You know how it is. Anyone who isn't a total sociopath, eventually they need to tell someone. We're just lucky he's talking to us instead of a therapist, or a priest.'

'What kind of bullying are we talking about?'

'According to Will—' Rohan points his pen at the sheet '—it was mostly text messages. Nothing physical.'

'Threatening messages?'

'More like humiliating. But there may have been more he never saw.'

Kiara is building a timeline in her head. 'So Zach sends some humiliating texts to a girl, who then kills herself, then Zach vanishes three months later.'

'Right. Any thoughts?'

She takes a sip of her coffee and suppresses a grimace. Too much milk—a good excuse to make another one. 'I suppose it could support the theory that Zach jumped.

Maybe he felt guilty, too. But it wouldn't explain how he got up there. Did Will supply any evidence to support his statement? Screenshots of the texts, maybe?'

'No,' Rohan says. 'And Zach used an encrypted messaging app. We can't get the messages from his provider. We'd need his actual phone to confirm, and it's missing.'

'Encrypted messages? Was this kid a spy, or what?'

'All the kids use those apps these days,' Rohan said gloomily. 'I don't know if they're running interference for drug dealers, or if they're just making our jobs harder for no reason.'

'I don't remember hearing about any suspicious messages on Moon's phone,' Kiara says. 'But I guess the lead investigator might not have been looking in the right apps. I can get it back from her family—it'll upset them, though. Did it seem to you like Will was telling the truth?'

'Hard to say.' Rohan is never too confident in his own judgement. It's one of many things Kiara likes about him. She's worked with cops before who were happy to arrest someone on a hunch, and leave her to deal with the resulting paperwork.

Kiara herself has sometimes been guilty of putting too much faith in her own instincts. She thought Elise was trustworthy, despite what everyone said. And look where that got her.

'I'll go to the school,' she says. 'Chat with some of Zach's other friends again, see if anybody other than Will has become more talkative.'

Rohan nods and stands up. 'Want me to come with you?'

'No,' Kiara says quickly.

'You sure?'

It's a four-person station. They can't afford to dispatch two police officers to anything less dramatic than a terrorist attack. But apparently Rohan doesn't think she can handle this alone. Why would he? Anyone can see she's distracted. These days, victims give up hope before she's even finished taking their statements.

'It's fine,' she says. 'I'll let you know what I turn up.'

'Okay. I've got your back if there's anything you need, all right?' He's not just talking about the interview.

'I know. Thanks, Sarge.'

Rohan smooths down his buttoned shirt, picks up his pen and marches away, leaving the folder behind.

Kiara starts digging through the names and contact details for all Zach's friends. She should focus on the ones who also knew Moon. The school principal will help her identify them.

She smiles at the thought of the principal, a cheery, big-haired lady who wears bright dresses like the Queen and uses strange expressions like, 'There's a donkey's chance of that happening, my girl.' Kiara hasn't seen her since . . .

Since just after Callum Glyk disappeared.

Kiara hesitates, her hand on her leather jacket. Callum fled because he was about to get busted for possession with intent to distribute. Everyone accepts that, except for his sister, who betrayed Kiara and got her thrown in disciplinary counselling. Was Zach in Callum's class? Could Callum have been selling drugs to his students?

This should have occurred to her earlier. She hasn't had her head in the game.

Kiara picks up her phone. Elise isn't going to like these questions. And talking to her still hurts. *Be a professional*, she tells herself, and hits the call button.

The phone rings and rings.

Kiara closes her eyes. Tries not to think of Elise's laugh, beautiful because it was so rare. Her strong core, pressed against Kiara's belly. And that awful moment, reaching across the bed and finding her gone.

She still loves Elise. But she can't be with someone she can't trust.

'This is Elise.'

Kiara's heart skips a beat, but it's a recording.

'I don't listen to messages,' Elise continues, 'so send me a text. Unless you want to give me a hard time, in which case you can piss off.'

Beep.

Kiara leaves a message anyway. She can imagine Elise listening to all the hateful voicemails, even after she's promised herself she won't, like picking at a scab.

'Ms Glyk, this is Senior Constable Kiara Lui. I haven't found your brother,' she adds quickly, 'but I do have some questions. Call me, please. It's important.'

She pushes the red button. Then she taps out a text message. It's almost the same as the voicemail, word for word. When she's done, she puts on her jacket and braces herself for a visit to Warrigal Public School.

CHAPTER 15

Kiara gets some stares on the way into the school. She tells herself it's just the uniform. A conversation between a group of boys falls silent. One girl turns to look and gets hit in the shoulder with a basketball. The ball bounces away, ignored.

Her father is a Wiradjuri man, and her mother was a Vietnamese refugee. They met at a protest against a planned nuclear waste dump north-east of town. 'Star-crossed love,' Dad told Kiara, which was a romantic way of acknowledging that her two extended families were often at loggerheads over how the children should be raised, schooled and fed, and also acknowledging that the nuclear dump was built anyway.

Warrigal has what Kiara thinks of as a high level of low-level prejudice. There's nothing obvious. She doesn't get refused service or shouted at in the street. But there's a bubble of awkwardness that seems to follow her around. Some people avoid her gaze, while others are painfully friendly. She suspects that everyone relaxes whenever she leaves the room. Some well-meaning prick once told her, 'You can get away with being Black, or Asian, or gay, or a woman, or a cop in this town—but you're trying to do them all at once, which is very ambitious.' That night, Kiara wondered which part of that sentence had pissed her off the most. She was torn between *get away with* and *trying*.

She signs in at the front desk. Under REASON FOR VISIT she scrawls: *police*.

'I'll take you down to the principal's office,' the receptionist says, getting out of her chair.

'I know where it is.' Kiara doesn't wait for her.

Mrs Fripp's office is decorated with pictures of the principal, all drawn by children in smudged texta. Hundreds of warped versions of her, hair like matted straw, eyes too high on her crooked face, looming like a giant over smiling children. It's terrifying.

Kiara clears her throat. 'You have some, uh, talented students.'

'I have some *hard-working* students,' Mrs Fripp corrects her cheerfully. 'We're all about the growth mindset here.' She settles into a squeaking chair and takes a sip from a chipped mug printed with a slogan: *Reading! It's how you install software in your brain.* 'It is a shame, though. The kids stop making pictures of their teachers at exactly the time when their drawings become good. I never get anything from my Year Twelves.' Fripp notices a blob of Blu-Tack on her desk and starts scratching it off with a fingernail. 'So, what can I do for you today, Constable?'

Kiara takes the seat opposite the principal and immediately feels like she's in trouble. 'I came to talk to you about Zach Locat.'

Fripp stops scraping. She looks hopeful. 'Any sign of him?'

'I'm afraid not. I'm trying to get some more information about his social life. Was he in a relationship?'

It's a warm-up question. There's a delicate rhythm to interviewing witnesses. Whatever the crucial question is, Kiara has to ask it at the right moment. Too early, and the subject is still guarded. Too late, and she'll get an abridged answer, because they're sick of her.

'I'm sorry,' Fripp says. 'As I told you last time, these kids swap partners so fast. And for a fifteen-year-old, there seems to be little agreement about what the word "relationship" even means.'

'Was he close to William Yu?'

Fripp frowns. 'Close romantically?'

'In any way.'

'They spent a lot of time together, sure. You don't think Will had something to do with Zach's disappearance?'

'Nothing like that.' Kiara has considered this, but decided that if Will were trying to mislead the police, his statement would have had more detail.

'Will's a good kid. A bit of a boofhead, but honest.'

'He said Zach had been bullying another student.'

'That's awful.' But Fripp doesn't sound entirely shocked. 'Who?'

'Moon. The girl who took her own life.'

Fripp says nothing for a moment. Then, 'Close the door, will you?'

Kiara does, gently, and sits back down. 'Did you know about the bullying?'

'No. I remember thinking Zach might have had a crush on Moon. He followed her around like a puppy. She either didn't notice or pretended not to. Actually, she probably wasn't pretending—there was a bit of fairy dust sprinkled over our Moon. Off in her own world a lot of the time.'

'But it never came to anything?'

'No. Zach seemed to lose interest. Her death hit him hard, though. All of us, but him especially.'

'Like he felt guilty?'

'Maybe.'

Kiara waits. She can tell there's more.

'I want you to know that I almost called you about this,' Fripp says. 'But you hear so much gossip in this school, and almost all of it turns out to be distorted, exaggerated or utter fiction. If I contacted the police every time a teacher said a parent had told them that a student's best friend's boyfriend had done whatever, you'd stop taking my calls altogether. And with the girl dead already, I thought it might do more harm than good to rake up old ground.'

'What gossip did you hear?'

'The rumour was that Moon Hartnell was pregnant.'

Kiara's eyebrows shoot up. 'She was fifteen, correct?'

'That's right. A few weeks ago, a member of the cleaning staff overheard something in the girls' toilets. But she only heard half of it, and English isn't her first language. Honestly, those kids could have been saying anything.'

Kiara hides her annoyance, remembering how often people assumed her mother had missed or misunderstood something, just because she talked with a Vietnamese accent. How often she was disbelieved. How people who had never bothered to learn a second language spoke louder and slower to her, as if she was stupid. And Mum had to keep smiling and nodding, behind the counter at the bakery.

'I investigated, of course,' Fripp goes on. 'I logged into my son's social media—with his blessing—and had a look around. I asked some of the good kids if they'd heard anything. No one had.'

'You thought Zach might have been the father?'

'It occurred to me. But as I said, Moon never seemed interested in him. And if she had really been pregnant, the autopsy would have uncovered that, right?'

Kiara says nothing, making a mental note to read the medical examiner's report again and check that all the usual tests were done.

'So I eventually concluded that it was nothing,' Fripp continues. 'But if Moon was being bullied, that rumour could have been what the bullying was about.'

Kiara chews her lip. Sometimes police work is like taking a metal detector to the beach. Other times it's more like peering through a keyhole. Trying to guess at the shape of something, having seen only a tiny piece of it.

'Can you think of anyone who was close to both Zach and Moon?'

Fripp looks up at the ceiling, like she's visualising a constellation of friendships. 'Indica Aigner,' she says at last. 'Social butterfly, in several different groups. I can give you contact details for her parents.'

'Thank you.' Something clicks. 'Was Moon Hartnell's mother Stephanie Hartnell?'

'That's right. You have a good memory.'

Not as good as she thinks. Kiara heard that name only yesterday, when Elise said Stephanie's car had been following her.

So, Moon Hartnell is cyberbullied. She commits suicide. Her bully goes missing. Then a PE teacher at her school goes missing. Then her mother is accused of following the teacher's sister.

A sister who still hasn't called Kiara back.

'Constable?'

Kiara snaps out of it. 'Sorry, what?'

'I asked if you'd like Stephanie's contact details.' Fripp frowns. 'Are you feeling okay?'

'Fine. And, no, thank you. I have her number and address.'

'Righto. Be gentle with her, will you?'

'With Stephanie?'

Fripp nods. 'She acts like a tough old bird, but under the surface I think she's still very fragile. What happened to her . . . Well, you'd never get over it, would you?'

CHAPTER 16

Elise uses her good leg to kick every section of every wall. She stomps on the floor, pushes on the ceiling. It's all solid concrete.

'Tried that,' Callum says, cross-legged on the floor.

There are two horizontal flow pipes at either end, so the tank can be filled and drained. One presumably leads to the house, the other to an absorption trench. Elise attempts to climb into the one at the back of the tank, but her shoulders are too wide, and even having her head inside is a claustrophobic nightmare.

'Tried that, too,' Callum says.

By dragging a pile of fertiliser bags across and standing on them, she can push her hand up the narrow ventilation tube in the ceiling. But she can't reach the other end, and she's not sure what she'd do if she could.

'Tried that.'

'Not helping, Cal.'

Elise spends an hour bashing the little square window with the handle of the knife. If she can get an arm through, she might be able to pick the padlock with the tip of the blade. She's never picked a lock before, but how hard could it be?

She doesn't get the chance to find out. The window is perspex, or something. She can't break it. She stabs the thick, hard plastic around it, and can't break that, either. All this does is blunt the knife.

The hinge plate is held in place by eight big screws. Elise tries twisting them out with the knife. But they're too tight, and the blade is the wrong shape. None of them budges.

She reaches for her keys so she can use them instead, then remembers that Stephanie took them. The spares are in her car. Her phone, too. And *no one knows she's here.*

When she presses her face against the perspex, she can't see the surrounding landscape—only a sliver of the boulder. The sun is crawling across the middle of the sky. She's running out of time. Stephanie will be back soon, expecting Callum to be dead.

Or worse, Stephanie *won't* come back. She'll slip in the shower and break her neck, or trip on the porch stairs, or have a heart attack in front of the TV, leaving Elise and Callum to die of thirst down here in the dark.

In one corner of the tank, a PVC pipe is mounted flat against the ceiling. Maybe once it was used to pour treatment chemicals into the tank, but now both ends have been cut off—it goes nowhere. The pipe is held up by a metal bracket, fixed to the concrete with two rusted bolts. Wondering if the bracket might be strong enough to break the little window, Elise tries to pry it off the ceiling. But her fingernails aren't strong enough, and the knife isn't either— the blade starts to bend.

She can't stop thinking about Guppy. Running out of food and water. Waiting for her to come home. No one else will rescue him—her neighbours hate her, and if anybody other than her comes to the door, he'll just hide.

She could ask Stephanie to go to her house and feed him. But someone who's willing to kidnap and torture people probably wouldn't care about a starving dog. And if Stephanie did go, she might notice the photo of Callum in the hallway, and realise that Elise is his sister.

Would she trade Callum's life for her dog's? She shakes off the thought. It won't come to that. She has another idea.

She just wishes she hadn't blunted the knife.

'You want to cut me?' Callum sounds appalled when she explains her plan.

'Both of us.'

'I've been cut enough. It's amazing I have any blood left.'

'There's no other way,' Elise says. 'It's not like Stephanie left us with any red food colouring, or a great big bottle of tomato sauce.'

'I can just play dead.' There's an edge of panic in Callum's voice. 'I'll be very convincing.'

'No, you won't. She'll assume it's a trick unless there's a puddle of blood under you. I can lose a litre without getting sick, but a litre won't be enough to make it look real. We'll need at least two.'

'Of course *you* would think of this.'

Elise flinches. It's been two years since the ban. Callum is the one person who's never mentioned it. He's always spoken kindly to her, until now. She tells herself he's just scared. 'It's the only way—'

The septic tank darkens. A shadow has fallen across the window.

Elise looks up. Stephanie's face appears behind the perspex. She peers at Callum, alive and well. Then she looks at Elise, eyes narrow.

The padlock rattles. The hatch creaks open.

Stephanie doesn't give her the chance to climb the ladder. A box of cornflakes falls through and thuds to the floor. It's followed by an empty bucket with a wire handle and a lid, then a ten-litre bottle of water.

The hatch shuts. The lock clicks. Stephanie's footsteps crunch away.

Callum crawls over to the supplies. He twists the spout of the water bottle and slurps greedily. Then he tears open the cornflakes and starts packing them into his mouth, like a toddler.

'How do you know that's not poisoned?' Elise asks.

'Never has been before,' he mumbles, his mouth full. 'And I'd rather be poisoned than starve.'

She supposes that the sealed plastic bag inside the sealed box is a good sign. And as Stephanie has already pointed out, there are easier ways she could kill her captives.

Elise says, 'Does she always look through the window before opening the hatch?'

Callum grunts, still eating.

'To check that you're far enough away from the ladder?'

'That's the point of the window, I think.'

'In that case, you'll need to lie somewhere she can see you. Otherwise she might not even open the lid.'

Elise presses the knife against the stone floor and bends

it until the cheap steel snaps. She slides the handle across to Callum and keeps the severed blade for herself.

He looks uneasy. 'Whoa, hang on. No point doing it now.' He gestures at the supplies. 'She won't come back for two or three days.'

'Yes, she will.' Elise saw the way Stephanie looked at her and Callum—not just annoyed, but impatient. 'She'll be back soon to see if I've killed you. If I haven't, she'll start to suspect that we're planning something together. Then the trick won't work.'

'At least let me eat first.'

Elise eyes the food and water. 'Yeah, okay. Good idea. We need to keep our iron levels up.' She knows that an injection of red blood cells can make someone feel like a superhero, but a lack of them can make the person feel like the walking dead.

They eat in grim silence. The light from the window glints off the broken blade. Elise tries to get into that calm space she always entered before an event, breathing in through her nose and out through her mouth, flexing her joints one by one, counting them as she goes. Letting the anxious thoughts drain out.

Callum breaks into her trance. 'You remember that time I pretended to be sick, to get out of science?'

She does. He hadn't finished his model of a carbon atom by the due date, so he stayed in bed, moaning and writhing. Mum didn't seem convinced until Elise played along, putting her hand on his forehead and insisting it felt hot, and saying she'd heard him vomit during the night.

Their plan worked too well. Mum took Callum to Dad's practice, and Dad correctly guessed there was nothing wrong with him. Furious at being made to look foolish in front of Dad, Mum built a bonfire in the backyard, and threw both Callum's and Elise's phones into the flames. Mum didn't often get angry, but when she did, it was terrifying.

Despite everything, Elise finds herself smiling at the memory. Given enough time, tragedy becomes comedy. 'Let's hope your acting is as good now as it was then.'

'I just have to stay still, right? I think I can manage that.' He guzzles some more water. 'The week after that, I really *was* sick. Mum made me go to school anyway. Half my class ended up catching it.'

'Hmm, if only there had been some kind of childhood fable to warn you. Something about a boy who tells a lie, and later discovers that people don't trust him when he's telling the truth.'

Callum snorts.

It wasn't only him who lost his credibility. Every time Elise got sick after that, Mum and Dad accused her of faking. She doesn't mention this now.

They finish eating and push the empty cereal box aside. Callum takes the bucket into the corner. Sees Elise looking. 'A little privacy?'

'You should wait,' she says. 'Piss your pants.'

He looks disgusted. 'For real?'

'Yeah. Dead people do that.'

'Shit.'

'No need for that. Some urine will do.'

'Not funny.' He leaves the lid of the bucket on, comes back and stretches out at the bottom of the ladder.

She sees pretty quickly that there's a problem with the plan. When she holds the knife handle flush against his chest, it looks like the blade is stuck in between his ribs—but she has no way of making it stay upright. Even when she cuts a small hole in his shirt to hold it in place, the handle just falls sideways.

She sits back, thinking. 'Maybe you can hold the handle under your chin. Like I stabbed you in the throat.'

He lies on his back and lowers his chin. He can hold the handle in place, but now he doesn't look dead. A dead man wouldn't hold his head up like that.

'Roll onto your side,' she suggests.

He obeys. 'Does it look real?' The angle of his neck makes his voice choked, like that of Kermit the Frog, or Yoda. It would be funny if their lives weren't depending on this.

'Not exactly.' Elise rubs her brow.

'Forget this plan. You can pretend to be sick, like you need a doctor.'

'Great idea. That'll work, as long as Stephanie has never seen any prison movie, ever.'

'Like you said, she doesn't want you to die. She'll let you out, and then—'

'Put the handle in your mouth,' Elise says.

He looks repulsed. 'In my mouth?'

'Yeah. Between your teeth, like I stabbed you in the face.'

'Jesus.' He wipes the knife handle on his grimy shirt, probably making it dirtier rather than cleaner, and puts it in his mouth.

The illusion is surprisingly convincing. The protruding handle makes it look like the blade is wedged deep in the back of his throat. No one could survive an injury like that.

Elise studies the tableau. *Yes*, she thinks. *This will work.*

'How do I look?' His voice is muffled by the handle.

'You look extremely dead.' She feels a flicker of excitement. 'Now we just need the blood.'

He spits out the handle and sits up, slowly. They look at each other for a moment.

'How do we do this?' he asks finally.

She prods the sharp edge of the blade with a fingertip, looking at the veins in his forearms. He's lost so much weight that they're easy to see. But while she's used to having her blood taken, she's never been the one doing the taking. And the implement was always a sterilised needle, never a broken kitchen knife.

This sounded easy in the abstract. Much harder, now that the cold steel is actually in her hand. *At the pointy end*, her coach would have said.

The wind moans, distorted by the ventilation tube.

Stalling, Elise says, 'Will we be able to overpower her once she's down here?'

'I figured you'd just stab her in the back while she's checking my pulse.' His casual tone is jarring.

'I'm not sure I can do that.'

'Are you kidding? She tortured me for weeks. She's a monster.'

'This isn't much of a weapon without the handle.' Elise holds up the broken blade. 'I'm more likely to stab myself. We'll have to try to get the gun off her.'

'And then shoot her, right?'

'She'll do what we say once we have the gun.' Elise hopes this is the truth. But she remembers how easily Stephanie shrugged off her threats. Her flat voice: *No one walks away*.

Elise saws through part of her tank top, tears off the midriff and slices it in half, for makeshift bandages.

'We'll have to put pressure on the wounds,' she says. 'As soon as there's a decent-size puddle. Otherwise we'll both go into shock.'

'I get it,' Callum says.

She touches the tip to the inside of her elbow. There's a scar already, from all the needles.

'You want to go first?' she asks.

He shakes his head.

She wills herself to push down. Her skin stings. But she can't apply enough force to draw blood.

She thinks of Moon Hartnell. What caused her to make that final push? She must have felt so lonely, so unloved. Elise knows what that's like—and yet she can't do what Moon did. Elise wants to live, but apparently not as much as Moon wanted to die. The poor kid.

'Let me.' Callum holds out a hand for the blade.

She gives it to him gratefully. But then he points it back at her. He wasn't offering to go first—he was volunteering to cut her.

'Not too much.' Her voice wavers.

'I promise.' He squeezes her wrist, then brings down the blade.

CHAPTER 17

Stephanie switches off the vacuum cleaner, and hears screaming.

It's so faint that it might be mistaken for a bird's call. She listens for a moment longer, then drops the vacuum and runs. It's starting to get dark, so she snatches up a torch from the kitchen bench and bursts out the back door into the cold, trying not to get her hopes up again.

These past few hours have been driving her insane. She's been pairing socks, ironing clothes, sponging mould off the ceiling of the shower recess. At four o'clock she started preheating the oven for dinner, as if she was an old lady. Her father spent the last ten years of his life in a home, complaining that the bloody dinner was served in the middle of the goddamn afternoon so all the idiot staff could go home.

The housework doesn't need doing. But anything is better than just pacing around the house, wondering if Callum Glyk is dead yet.

She couldn't sleep last night. The more tired she became, the more her thoughts got trapped in a loop, orbiting

Callum as though they didn't have enough momentum to escape his terrible gravity. Would the private investigator do the job? Stephanie wasn't sure. Callum was like Schrödinger's cat, both dead and alive until she opened the hatch to check.

When she saw him still breathing that morning, the disappointment nearly flattened her, before the rage swept it away. She listened for a while, then stormed back to the house, grabbed some matches from above the stove, and lit one. She watched it burn all the way down until it singed her fingertips, while she imagined throwing it down the hole to ignite all that fertiliser. The flames consuming Tina Thatcher, and Callum, and her, and probably the farmhouse. Maybe burning half the country before anyone put it out.

One more day, she told herself. *I'll give her one more day.*

Now, as she races through the garden in the twilight, she wonders what she'll find. Someone is definitely screaming. Who, though? It sounds like a woman, but she knows that Callum makes a high-pitched squeal when punctured, like a tractor tyre.

What if Thatcher made the right choice but messed it up? What if Callum managed to fight her off?

This worry is dispelled as she gets closer. It's not a scream of pain. It's desperation. She can hear Thatcher shouting, 'Let me out of here! I did it, okay? It's done! Let me out!'

Stephanie's heart rate spikes. She leans over the hatch. Can't see anything in the fading daylight. She clicks on the torch and points it down through the window.

There's Callum Glyk, sprawled in a halo of blood. One of his arms is twisted behind his back. There are dark stains all over his shirt, probably stab wounds. The knife is sticking out of his face.

Stephanie flinches, before she remembers who she's looking at. The relief is huge. It's like she's just taken off a heavy hiking backpack. He's gone. At last.

She fumbles with the key, about to unlock the hatch. Then her brain catches up with her body. She hears her father's voice: *Look before you leap, Steph.*

She hurries back to the house and grabs the rifle off the hooks above the door. Callum looked dead, but he may need one more shot. And she may need to threaten Thatcher again. Make sure she understands that she can't go to the police, not now that she's a murderer.

Still, Stephanie is elated, practically floating through the garden towards the hatch. She can't believe the plan worked.

She looks through the little window again. Callum's body wasn't a mirage—it's still there, in all its bloody glory. Her hands tremble as she unlocks the padlock and slips it into her pocket.

She lifts up the hatch.

Did Callum's eyelids just flutter? She might have imagined it—or there might be a trace of life left in him. She watches for a moment. His chest isn't rising or falling. If he's not dead, he's very close.

The private investigator is huddled in a corner, hugging her arms. She's pale, exhausted. The bloodstains on her hands extend all the way up to her wrists. She must have stabbed Callum over and over.

'I did what you wanted.' Thatcher's voice is hoarse from the screaming. 'Can I come out now? Please just let me out.'

Stephanie feels a flash of pity for the wretched woman. 'I need to make sure. Stay back.'

She clambers down the ladder, landing next to Callum's corpse. She nudges it with her foot. It's like pushing a sack of grain. She bends down to check the pulse, then notices Thatcher approaching.

Stephanie points the gun at her. 'Hey. Get back.'

Thatcher stops. 'There's a knife in his brain, all right?' Her voice wobbles. 'He's dead.'

She sounds scared. Guilty.

'You don't need to feel bad,' Stephanie says. 'The world is safer without him.'

'What do you mean?'

Thatcher is hiding one arm behind her back.

'What's in your hand?' Stephanie keeps the gun trained on her.

'Nothing.' Thatcher exposes her hand. Empty. But there's a scrap of fabric tied around her elbow. A makeshift bandage.

Tension grows at the base of Stephanie's skull, though she's not sure why. 'You're hurt.'

Thatcher touches the bandage. 'He fought back.'

'I'm sorry,' Stephanie says, truthfully. She risked the PI's life, putting her down here with him, without even thinking about it. She's become obsessed.

'We're in this together, now.' Thatcher's eyes are haunted. 'Just tell me—what did he do?'

It seems cruel to let her carry the guilt. Stephanie owes her the truth, or at least part of it. But it's hard to find the words. She swallows. 'My daughter. He—'

A hand squeezes her ankle.

She looks down in time to see Callum spit out the knife, his bloodied lips parting to expose yellow teeth. Back from the dead. His arm whips out from behind his body to claw at her. She sees another bandage, like the one around Thatcher's elbow, and realises how she's been tricked.

Panicked, she tries to rip her leg out of Callum's grip, at the same time lowering the barrel of the gun so she can shoot him—

But Thatcher crashes into her, grabbing for the rifle and knocking her off her feet. They both slam into the wall, Stephanie's vision blurring as the side of her skull crashes against the concrete. The gun clangs against the ladder, and she loses her grip on it.

'No!' She swipes, trying to snatch the gun back. But Callum kicks her ankle out from under her, and she hits the floor, jarring her shoulder.

'Stay down,' Thatcher says.

Stephanie doesn't. She scrambles to her feet, the world still swimming, her ears ringing.

Callum is already halfway up the ladder. 'Shoot her!' he shouts over his shoulder.

Thatcher jabs the gun at Stephanie. 'Back off!'

Stephanie can't let Callum escape. She would die to make sure he never leaves this place. 'No.'

'I'm warning you—'

Stephanie lunges. Thatcher doesn't shoot. Instead she swings the rifle upward, slamming the butt into Stephanie's nose. *Crunch*. Pain flares across her face. She staggers backwards with a choked squawk, and trips over the low wall in the middle of the room. She thuds to the floor on the other side.

Winded, she claws her way back up the wall, into a kneeling position. She doesn't have the torch anymore, and she's still seeing stars. They clear just in time for her to see Thatcher's feet at the top of the ladder. Then they're gone, and the hatch slams shut, trapping Stephanie inside.

'No!' she screams.

CHAPTER 18

'What are you waiting for?' Callum demands. 'Come on!'

Elise looks around, panic rising. 'Where's the padlock?' It's not hanging from the bolt, or lying in the dirt, or hidden behind the hatch. It must be in Stephanie's pocket. Without it, they can't seal the septic tank.

'Just run!' Callum is already sprinting towards the farmhouse.

Elise tries to roll the boulder onto the hatch, but it won't budge. She gives up and dashes through the garden after Callum, wincing at every twinge from her sore knee. The howling wind snatches away her ragged breaths.

Will Stephanie be able to chase them? She has a head injury, and maybe a broken nose. But she's also furious, and Elise has seen anger keep people upright long after they should have collapsed.

Elise herself is weak and dizzy. Callum cut her too deep, draining her like he was a medieval doctor. And Stephanie took too long to check on them, leaving Elise screaming and bleeding for ages. Her bandage is tight enough to make her arm numb, yet too loose to stop the bleeding.

It's getting cold. She didn't put her jacket back on, not wanting to dislodge the bandage. The twilight is becoming night. Or is she losing consciousness?

Just get to the car, she tells herself. *Black out later.*

She and Callum sprint around the house rather than going through it, in case the front door is locked. Soon they're racing down Stephanie's driveway towards the road. The rifle bounces on her hip, the strap cutting into her shoulder.

As she runs, she keeps an eye out for good-sized rocks. The plan is to smash a window when they get to the car. Then one of them can start the engine with the spare key while the other—probably Elise, since she's too dizzy to drive—calls the police.

Callum's breaths are ragged. 'Which way?'

'I parked over there.' Elise jabs a floppy arm forward and to the left, about eleven o'clock.

'I don't see it.'

'It's there.' Her heart is pounding, a motor low on fuel. Her extremities are cold. 'Just keep running.'

They reach the road and turn left. No headlights in either direction. Elise can't hear anything over the wailing wind.

'I don't see it,' he says again.

'It's right . . .' She trails off as they reach the spot where she parked, just off the road, between the trees.

Callum grabs her shoulder. 'Where's the car?'

'She must have taken it somewhere. Fuck!' The Suzuki could be anywhere. Crushed in a ravine or burned out in a paddock. They're stranded.

His eyes are wild. 'What do we do?'

'Uh ...' She turns around and around. The chances of someone driving past are minuscule, and she doesn't know how much time they have. She presses her palms to her forehead. *Think, Elise.* 'Maybe she moved the car to her garage. Or maybe we can find her keys, take *her* car. Maybe—'

A light clicks on at the farmhouse. Stephanie is loose.

A vice of panic squeezes Elise's lungs. She grabs Callum and drags him off the road, back onto Stephanie's property, into the trees.

'What are you doing?!'

'Shut up!' she hisses. 'She's out.'

He looks like he's going to be sick. 'Oh, Jesus. Why didn't you just shoot her?'

They duck, using the shrubbery for cover. Elise watches the house. There's movement behind the curtains. Then nothing.

She keeps her voice low. 'She'll think we're running down the road. Probably west, since that's where I parked. She'll drive after us. Then we can search her garage.'

'But what if the—what if your car's not there?' His words trip over each other. 'Or maybe it's there but she's taken the keys, or—'

'Then we call the police on her phone ... No, wait.' Elise remembers the slashed phone line. It's as though Stephanie anticipated Callum might get free at some point and wanted to stop him from calling for help. What other preparations has she made?

'What?' he asks.

'If the car's not there, we'll head back to the road on foot and go the opposite way to her. Got it?'

He nods vigorously. 'Got it, yeah. Okay, good plan.'

'Come on.' Elise starts creeping away from the road, deeper into the bush—and further onto Stephanie's land.

'Where are you going?'

'We can't stay here. She'll see us when she drives off.' It's surprising that Stephanie hasn't come out the front door yet. Maybe she's concussed and can't find her way through the house.

Or maybe she's not in the house anymore. Elise peeks between the trees. The lights inside are still on, but there's no more movement. Stephanie could have entered the house then left via the back door. She might already be in this patch of bush, looking for them.

Elise puts her finger to her lips. Callum's eyes widen.

She raises the rifle and turns in a slow circle, her finger inside the trigger guard. It's heavier than she thought it would be, or maybe she's just weak from her injuries. One end is a wooden wedge, the other a long, narrow barrel. There's a leather shoulder strap from the back to about the halfway point. No scope, just two small metal divots to peer through. She's never fired a gun before. Hopefully it's as simple as pulling the trigger.

No sign of Stephanie. But she hasn't left—the Barina is here, parked in front of the house.

'Give me the gun,' Callum whispers.

'Shush.'

They're still too close to the driveway. They'll be visible as soon as the headlights come on. Elise motions to Callum, and they edge deeper into the forest, painfully slowly. Every crunching twig sounds like the crack of a whip. Waves of nausea wash over Elise—from fear, from blood loss, from cold—

Blood loss. She turns, squats. They're leaving traces—red drips on leaves and on the ground. Dad used to hunt feral goats on the weekends. His aim wasn't always good enough to hit the animal in the head, but if he got the shoulder or the rump, he could always follow the blood to the wounded creature's hiding place.

The trail is hardly visible in the moonlight. But if they're still out here at sunrise, or if the Barina's headlights turn this way . . .

'Keep moving,' she whispers to Callum, one hand clamped over her wounded arm, trying to stop the flow.

Their path is blocked by a pit, two metres long and a metre wide, mostly concealed by fallen branches. Elise spots it almost too late. One of her feet skids over the edge, but she manages to keep the other on solid ground. She stumbles back, dirt cascading over the edge into the darkness.

Callum bumps into her. 'What?' He hasn't noticed the pit.

Elise is disoriented. She's sure this is the route she took through the trees when she first arrived at the farm. But there was no pit then. Just a flat patch of dirt—she remembers thinking it might have been an abandoned vegetable patch.

Now Callum sees the pit. 'Shit, I nearly fell in that.' The way around is blocked on both sides by stunted bushes—he turns slowly, uncertain which way to go.

But Elise is leaning down, peering into the pit. There's a curious shape under the dirt, like an enormously fat tree root.

Stephanie said, *I already dug the grave.* Why would she do that before Callum was dead, before even asking Elise to kill him?

Elise lies down and reaches in, extending every joint in her arm so her fingertips brush the dirt. There is something under it. She leans further over, scratching away the earth, uncovering the mass beneath.

Callum looms over her. 'Come on, what are you—yeargh!'

His cry of alarm is loud enough to make Elise's heart skip a beat. She shushes him, even as she sees what he saw in the pit.

A face.

It looks like that of a child, or maybe a teenager. A boy. Elise sweeps the dirt off his thin eyebrows, his crooked nose, his inky hair. His eyeballs are missing, devoured by grubs. His mouth hangs open, the jaw twisted sideways, his teeth gleaming in the moonlight.

'Oh God.' Callum has realised why Stephanie reopened the grave. He sounds hysterical. 'Don't let her put me in there!'

Elise finds herself lifting one of the branches and using it to scrape off more dirt. More of the boy's body is revealed—he's wearing a shredded T-shirt and skinny jeans, the creases black with sediment. She is more familiar with the recently dead, but she guesses the body has only been buried for a few months, or there would be more decay.

Callum is gulping like a fish, on his hands and knees a few metres back from the pit. Elise is glued to the spot, her mind racing.

This has to be that kid Kiara was looking for. She can't remember his name. If the Warrigal police ever raid this farm, they'll solve all three of their missing persons cases—assuming Elise is reported missing by then. Stephanie is a one-woman crime wave. But why?

Something moves in the corner of Elise's eye.

She whirls around, but too slow. Something punctures the side of her abdomen. A hum fills her head, like a swarm of bees. Her arm lashes out against her will. She screams and tries to leap away from the source of the agony. One of the fallen branches catches her foot, and she crashes to the forest floor.

The dark figure between the trees doesn't look human at first. Its head is angular, and a strange bulge protrudes from its neck. One of its arms is too long. But as it swings again, the shapes suddenly make sense to Elise's brain. It's Stephanie. Wearing night vision goggles, with the tranquilliser gun slung over her back—and brandishing a cattle prod.

Elise scrambles away through the dirt. 'Runun, Callul!' Her tongue is stiff.

Stephanie lunges after her. The cattle prod looks deceptively harmless—a short rod with a rubber handle, the electrified needles invisible at night. But when it smashes against her shin, her whole body goes rigid. Her skin tingles and fizzes all over, like a prawn cracker dissolving on the tongue.

Run! But this time the word doesn't leave her lips, just bounces around and around the inside of her head.

'I gave you a way out,' Stephanie snarls.

Elise tries to kick her, but she's paralysed.

She can hear Callum fleeing but can't turn her head to look. Helpless, she watches as Stephanie squints down the sights of the tranquilliser rifle and pulls the trigger. There's a sharp pop, and a second later, the distant thud of Callum hitting the ground.

Stephanie lowers the gun and turns back to Elise. 'I'm *very* disappointed in you.' She swings the cattle prod again. Elise can't even scream as the blackness comes crashing down.

CHAPTER 19

When Stephanie reaches Callum, he's facedown in a puddle of leaf litter. She can't see the tranquilliser dart sticking out of him anywhere. Maybe he's faking. She stabs him in the armpit with the cattle prod. His body goes stiff, then limp. Now it doesn't matter.

She used to enjoy hurting him, with a boot, a fist, a fireplace poker. Not anymore. The anger is still there, but hitting him no longer releases the pressure. Now it just grows and grows, leaving her pacing her house, grinding her teeth, glaring at the carpet without seeing it.

He tried to run. To save himself, leaving Thatcher to face the music. Bloody typical. Every time she thinks she has him figured out, he finds a new level to sink to. As Moon would have said, *he's just the worst.*

Stephanie puts her hands on her hips, trying to figure out how to get her captives back into the septic tank. They'll be incapacitated for somewhere between five and sixty minutes. She can't carry both of them at the same time without her wheelbarrow. If she carries one, the other might escape. And if she goes to get the wheelbarrow, they both might. It's like that old riddle with the wolf, the goat and the cabbage.

Luckily, she has her handcuffs. She bought them online—they were the number-one-ranked brand for 'reliability and sexiness'. They're covered in fuzzy red fabric, but they have a steel core, and she's superglued the quick-release mechanism in place. She drags Callum back to the private investigator and cuffs his wrist to her ankle. Now neither of them is going anywhere in a hurry, conscious or not.

The septic tank is a long way away, but the pit is close. Stephanie could just cave both their heads in with a rock, then push them in on top of Zach's corpse.

But the private investigator, Thatcher, hasn't done anything wrong. Stephanie can't kill a woman who's just doing her job. Therefore she can't kill Callum, either, because Thatcher needs to do it. Otherwise Stephanie can't let her go. Jesus, what a mess. She jogs up the driveway to the garage, where the wheelbarrow is.

She heaves the door open with a rattle and a screech. The night vision goggles illuminate Thatcher's Suzuki and the rest of the garage in grainy grey. There are plenty of tools, mostly gathering dust. When she first moved here, she struggled to predict which things she would need to take with her—and, she now realises, what she would need them for. The wheelbarrow, the shovel and the pitchfork have all been unexpectedly useful lately.

The barrow has a ball at the front instead of a wheel. Better for rolling across the soft dirt with a heavy load. She bought it just after Vic left. With his broad shoulders and thick arms, it hadn't mattered what kind of wheelbarrow they owned. Once he was gone, everything seemed harder.

There's just enough room to manoeuvre the barrow past Thatcher's Suzuki. Stephanie lifts the rubber handles, does a three-point turn and is suddenly blinded.

She rips off the goggles and finds herself staring into a pair of headlights. A spike of fear impales her heart. She hadn't even heard the car coming up the driveway behind her.

There have been no visitors in months. It can only be the police. She reaches for the tranquilliser gun on her back—

But then hesitates. It's a tan ute, not a police car. An old man steps out of the driver's seat, wearing a red raincoat and a matching beanie, rubbing his hands against the cold.

'Stephanie?' he says. 'Herbert Conway from next door.'

It takes her a moment to find her voice. 'We've met.'

Next door is almost a kilometre away, and she'd thought the occupants were long gone. Why is Herbert here—and how much did he see on his way up the drive?

As he approaches, he takes in the wheelbarrow, the night vision goggles, the rifle. 'What are you up to?' he asks cautiously.

'Shot a feral goat,' Stephanie says. 'Not before it ate half my garden, mind. Now I have to get rid of it.'

She's talking too fast, too loud. She's not sure if Herbert can tell.

'Ah,' he says. 'Would you like a hand?'

'No. Thank you. I thought you moved to Wagga?'

'We did. But the estate agent is having trouble selling the property. She thought it might help if we cleaned the house up a bit. I'd have thought that was her job, but apparently not.' He harrumphs, the way old men do when the world doesn't bend over backwards for them.

'Real estate agents,' Stephanie says. 'Don't get me started. Anyway, thanks for stopping by.'

Thatcher or Callum could wake up and start screaming at any moment. Stephanie has to get Herbert out of here.

'I spent all day scrubbing windows,' Herbert continues, as if he hasn't heard. Maybe he hasn't—there's a flesh-coloured hearing aid in his ear. 'All done now, though. I'm driving home in the morning. But I wanted to ask, do you know anything about a car parked in front of my fence?'

'Car?' Stephanie says, as though she's only familiar with horses. She resists the urge to glance at Thatcher's Suzuki, which is right next to her.

'The agent spotted it. Said it looked like someone had abandoned it there, maybe.'

'Sounds about right. You want me to help you get rid of it?'

'It's gone now.'

'Oh, good! Problem solved. Now if you'll excuse me, Herb, I have a goat to bury.'

'Just seems strange.' He coughs into his fist. 'To dump a car way out here. And where did it go? Did the owners come back for it, or did someone steal it, or what?'

'I guess we'll never know.' Stephanie starts rolling the wheelbarrow towards Herbert, slowly herding him out of her garage.

He takes the hint. He glances at his wrist and realises he's not wearing a watch. 'Well, I'd better get going.'

'No worries. Have a nice evening.'

He opens his car door, goes to get in, then stops. 'I wanted to say I'm sorry. For your loss.'

Stephanie just looks at him.

'Vic showed me some pictures,' he continues. 'She was a beautiful girl.'

And there's the anger, burning hotter and hotter in her chest. Tectonic plates shifting, ready to release the lava. She has the sudden urge to shoot Herb and throw him into the septic tank, even though he has nothing to do with anything.

'It's a terrible thing,' he says.

She keeps staring at him until, clearly embarrassed, he gets in the car and starts the engine. He reverses down the driveway, fast enough that the wheels slide on the gravel when he reaches the open gate.

Stephanie watches the headlights swing to the right, not the left. He must be staying at the motel in town rather than the cold, empty house. She's alone again. She rolls the barrow out of the garage and down the hill into the trees.

By the time she gets back to the two prisoners, Thatcher is stirring slowly, like a spider sprayed with Mortein. Stephanie doesn't want to use a tranquilliser dart—the dosage is calibrated for Callum's weight. Thatcher is lucky the last one didn't kill her. Reluctantly, Stephanie blasts her with the cattle prod again. Both prisoners shudder, the current apparently reaching Callum through the metal in the cuffs.

Why didn't Thatcher just kill him? She has no other way out—can't she see that?

It's possible that Stephanie will have to tell her what Callum did. What he is.

But she really doesn't want to dig all that up again.

When her captives stop twitching, she unlocks the handcuffs. She pushes one arm under Callum's knees and the other under his neck. She hates touching him, but there's no way around it. Gritting her teeth, she hauls him up. Even thin from hunger, he's heavy. She's relieved to drop him into the barrow. His head thunks against the steel.

She carries Thatcher more carefully, trying to avoid touching her injured elbow. But when she lowers her onto Callum, the barrow is too heavy. Stephanie will have to take the prisoners one at a time.

Annoyed, she pulls Thatcher back out and handcuffs her to a tree root, then starts pushing the barrow back through the forest towards the septic tank, Callum's body bouncing around inside. The ball gets stuck on a rock, and she has to push harder to get over it.

'You fucker,' she mutters. She only ever swears when she's alone. 'You piece of shit. Look what you've done to me.'

She can't wait to be rid of him.

CHAPTER 20

The sun beat down on the running track, reflecting the heat back up into Elise's face as she doubled over, clutching her abdomen. Everything hurt, from her toes to her scalp. Each thump of her heart sent ripples through her vision. She could barely see her shoes, or her bare legs.

It felt like that flu she'd caught when she was nine—trembling agony all over, her brain throbbing like it wanted to explode inside her skull. She had begged to go to hospital, but Dad had prodded her glands with a rough hand and said, 'You'll be right.' The fear that he was wrong was almost worse than the fever. But after Dad went to bed, Callum snuck upstairs and brought her water and Panadol. She was pathetically grateful. Without him, she might have died—or so she had believed, at the time.

Now, dry-heaving beside the finish line, she wished her brother had come with her to Canberra. He would put a hand on her forehead and tell her not to worry, that she was going to be okay. Essentially the same thing that Dad had said, but somehow more comforting.

Mr Panagoulis had been right. It was different, racing the best of the best. She'd barely placed at the nationals, and it had taken everything she had. Now she and twenty other young women were training at the Australian Institute of Sport, and Elise's times were never in the top ten, no matter how hard she pushed. This was killing her.

The other athletes were stretching and laughing. A few were circling the stadium again, slower, to cool down. Some of them wore full makeup, apparently immune to sweat. The coaches—mostly men, with sagging bellies and thinning hair—were muttering, making emphatic gestures or massaging calf muscles. A couple of mysterious strangers in suits watched from the otherwise empty stands. Sponsorship brokers, maybe.

Elise peered through the blur of exhaustion at one of the runners, who was doing sumo squats. She didn't even look sweaty.

Maybe she's a robot, Elise thought dizzily. *Maybe they all are. It's some crazy reality show, where the producers surrounded me with machines to see if—*

'Hey.'

Elise spun around, too fast. The world spun with her, and she nearly collapsed.

'Whoa!' Someone caught her. Strong arms. White teeth. That was all she could make out.

'Easy, tiger,' a voice said. 'You okay? You barely made that last hurdle.'

The woman sounded friendly, and a bit rough. Someone from the country, like her. Not like all these posh girls from private schools in Brisbane and Melbourne.

Elise found the ground beneath her feet and slipped out of the woman's grip. 'Sorry.'

'Don't be.' A sly smile at the corner of the woman's mouth. Sweat beaded her angled brows and upturned nose. Her cheeks were pink from the run. A long brown ponytail dangled over the straps of her sports bra. A thin gold chain hung just under her throat.

Her name came to Elise. 'Narelle, right? I've seen you.'

'I've seen you, too.' Narelle's smile grew wider. 'That was quite a run—near miss aside.'

Elise looked away. 'I was pretty slow.'

'Faster than last time, though. And that time was faster than the time before that.'

'I suppose.' Elise was surprised that Narelle had been paying such close attention.

'You might be a bit behind right now, but you're improving faster than any of us. Three months, and you'll be leading the pack. Maybe—' Narelle broke off. 'Sorry. I'm not your coach. You probably don't want a pep talk from me.'

'It's okay.' Elise did feel a bit better.

Narelle looked around. 'Where *is* your coach?'

'Smoko.'

Narelle laughed. Elise would have joined her if she could breathe.

Elise's coach, Jim McConnell, was a thirty-year-old man with a soul patch and a sports science degree. He'd cornered her after a race in Sydney, and promised to be the wind beneath her wings—he'd literally said those words. Elise had laughed, but had also been disarmed by his earnestness. He'd turned out to be a decent coach, when he bothered to show up.

'Mine told me he needed to organise some logistics,' Narelle said. 'I took that to mean he was going to stuff his face at Macca's. Why do they do that?'

'Eat fast food?'

'No—hide their bad habits. I'm not expecting *him* to run a race. He can eat whatever he wants.'

'Maybe he's ashamed. Seeing you, being all—' Elise almost said *beautiful* '—fit. He can't bear to eat rubbish in front of you.'

'Maybe. Pretty inconvenient time for him to go AWOL, though. Help me stretch?'

'Sure.'

Narelle put her ankle on Elise's shoulder. The extra weight nearly flattened her. But she kept her footing and pushed up Narelle's leg, gently.

The angle left her looking past Narelle at the other athletes, still running around in circles like soldiers training for an invasion. None of them had said more than a few words to Elise since she arrived. It was high school all over again—she was insignificant, and found herself on the outside of every conversation, peering in.

'They don't even look tired,' she said, marvelling.

'Yeah, well.' Narelle sounded like she knew something Elise didn't.

'What?'

'Don't worry.' Narelle switched legs, leaning her other ankle on Elise's shoulder. 'You'll get there, okay?'

Elise doubted this. She was already eating exact portions at precise times. Running the right distances on the right days.

Tracking her weight, how long she slept, how much she urinated. What more could she do?

'Trust me.' Narelle lowered her leg. 'You have more potential than you think.'

Elise didn't want potential. She wanted to go home. But she couldn't. She was the pride and joy of Warrigal. No one else from that little town had ever done anything of note.

She pictured herself begging Rafa for her old job. Telling her parents she'd failed, after they'd *made sacrifices*.

'Hey. You okay?' Narelle squeezed Elise's arm.

She didn't usually like being touched. She liked running because you got your own lane, that no one else could enter. But this time it felt nice.

She just nodded.

'I'm sneaking out tonight,' Narelle said. 'For a proper meal, not this protein shake bullshit. Come with me?'

———

Canberra was an inland city, but Narelle had somehow found a waterfront restaurant. Lights sparkled across the lake, and a tea candle burned on the table. A handsome waiter set down pre-warmed plates, and soon came back with a small metal bucket of lentil curry.

'I'm not sure I've ever eaten out of a bucket,' Elise said.

Narelle was already scooping it onto her plate. 'Welcome to the big smoke.'

Elise spooned some curry onto her garlic naan, and nibbled. 'Wow.'

'Right? I think it's ninety-nine per cent cream.'

'Coach would kill me if he knew I was eating this.'

'I can keep a secret.' The candlelight sparkled in Narelle's eyes, her lipstick gleaming.

Sitting opposite her, Elise felt an excited fluttering in the pit of her stomach, one she'd felt before—with a girl in her maths class, and with a couple of her brother's girlfriends. Elise had never felt it when talking to a boy. She'd always tried to ignore it.

'Tell me about yourself,' she heard herself say.

'Well, I'm from Melbourne.' Narelle sipped a mango lassi. 'Grew up in a flat in Elsternwick. Mum and Dad are accountants, and they both really loved sport, so they got me on to little athletics when I was basically a foetus. Lucky they did, too. I can't throw a ball through a hoop, or hit one over a net, or kick one between two goalposts. But running in a straight line? I can do the hell out of that.'

She didn't sound like a city girl. 'You can jump, too,' Elise said.

Narelle laughed, sparking a warm glow all over Elise's body. 'So can you.'

Her smile was beautiful. Elise watched it for a while, then realised she should probably say something. At least make an encouraging noise to keep the conversation going. But *which* noise? Her brain was frozen.

Narelle rescued her. 'Anyway, I placed at the regionals, and now I'm here on a state scholarship. How about you?'

'No scholarship for me.' Elise tried to make it sound like this was no big deal. 'But Mum and Dad are supporting me.'

Narelle seemed to detect the tension. 'For how long?'

It was a blunt question, so Elise gave it a blunt answer. 'Until I win a gold medal, or until their money runs out.'

'That's a lot of pressure.'

'No pressure, no diamonds.'

Narelle cracked a poppadom in half. 'Ooh, I like that.'

Elise didn't want to admit she was quoting her coach. 'Thanks.'

A boat glided past, people leaning against the railing on the top deck, champagne flutes in hand. Narelle gave them a cheery wave. Someone waved back.

'Do you know them?' Elise asked.

Narelle laughed again. 'No! There's just something about boats. I wouldn't wave at a stranger in a car, or on a bike, but if they're on a boat? Sure. Or if they're in a hot air balloon—that's worth a wave.' She shrugged. 'Doesn't make much sense, when I say it out loud.'

'Maybe it's because they can't come over and talk to you. You're willing to wave because you know that'll be the end of it. You're not going to get stuck making small talk with them.'

'They're the ones who'd be stuck. I love talking to people.' Narelle pulled some lipstick out of her handbag and scribbled a phone number on a napkin. Elise took it, feeling tingly.

'It's for a doctor,' Narelle said. 'All the other girls go to him. He can make sure you're getting the best out of your body.'

Disappointed, Elise looked down at the napkin, and the blood-red digits on it.

Narelle reached across the table and squeezed her hand. 'Don't worry. We're going to win you that gold.'

CHAPTER 21

'Where are you?' The Scottish accent made McConnell sound more annoyed than he probably was.

Elise was standing in front of a narrow, two-storey stucco building, preparing to meet Narelle's doctor. But if she told her coach that, he'd want to know why she hadn't told him earlier.

'I went for a run,' she said instead.

'It's your rest day. And there are plenty of available tracks here, Glyk.'

'I wanted some variety.'

McConnell huffed. 'Well, come back. I want to talk about our strategy for next week's event.'

Elise already had a strategy: run as fast as she could, jump over all the hurdles. She doubted that McConnell could improve on that. But she said, 'Got it. See you soon, coach,' and ended the call.

The sign at the front of the building had clearly once featured two names, but the second one was scratched out.

Only DR E. MICKLEHAM remained. The glass door was liver-spotted with Blu-Tack residue.

When Elise had made the appointment, she'd pictured something more like a day spa, with bamboo and incense. She had also hoped that Narelle would come with her. But they both trained six days per week, and their rest days didn't line up. Neither was willing to lose a day of preparation for this, not when races were won or lost in a tenth of a second. Now it was the following Wednesday, and Elise was no longer sure what she was doing here.

Her hand hovered over the buzzer. She felt as though touching it would commit her to something, though she wasn't sure what. A short cut that wasn't on the map.

She suddenly remembered Lacey, a hardcore Christian at one of her schools who had primly referred to masturbation as 'ringing the devil's doorbell'. The memory made her laugh, made the whole thing seem less ominous. She pushed the button. *Buzz.*

A voice crackled from a speaker: 'Come up.' The door unlocked.

Elise made her way up a dim set of stairs to a small, shabby office. It was nothing like her father's practice. Medical instruments were strewn across a desk. A computer monitor stood on a thick textbook.

The doctor had pale blue eyes, deep set in a gaunt face, and thick brown hair that hung to the top of his glasses. There was no 'How are you?' or 'What brings you in today?' He didn't even look up from his clipboard. Instead, he just said, 'Name?'

She cleared her throat. 'Uh, I'm Elise. Elise Glyk. Are you Dr Mickleham?'

'Time?'

'What?'

'What is your fastest time?' He enunciated the words with exaggerated care, like she was stupid or didn't speak English. 'You are an athlete, yes? You are not, perhaps, a different Elise Glyk?'

Ringing the dickhead's doorbell, more like, she thought. She would have walked out right then, except that Narelle liked this doctor, and Elise liked Narelle.

'My best time for the 400-metre hurdles was fifty-four seconds,' she said.

'Fifty-four exactly?'

'Fifty-four point oh four.'

'It's important to be precise.' Mickleham paused to have a coughing fit, then took a gulp from the coffee mug on his desk. 'My specialty is endurance athletes, but I can probably help you shave off a quarter of a second. In hurdles, that can sometimes be the difference between a loss and a world record. Stand on the scales, please.'

After checking her weight, height and blood pressure, the doctor took her hand gently—then pinched her finger and touched it with a red-and-white stick that looked a bit like a pregnancy test. The stick made a *ka-chunk* sound, like a stapler. Elise inhaled sharply. Her fingertip stung.

The doctor examined the readout on the stick. 'Hmm. Your haemoglobin's not bad.'

Tension was building in her neck and shoulders. She wanted to get out of there. To tell her coach she was going to the hotel gym—and then to sneak off to the movies instead, with a big bag of Maltesers and a Coke.

But the doctor wasn't done yet. He produced a syringe and a vial from a drawer.

Elise flinched. She had never liked needles but had learned not to say so. She could still hear her father's voice: *No one likes needles. Get over it.*

'Is that necessary?' she asked.

He lifted his chin so he could look down his nose at her. 'How did you think this would work?'

Elise imagined herself telling Narelle that she had chickened out. Then failing to place in yet another race and being sent home. Just another reject from Warrigal.

She held out her arm.

The sting caught her by surprise, but she managed not to flinch. The doctor was good, at least at this—he didn't need a second try. The blood trickled into the vial, filling it slowly, brighter than she had expected. She knew from her work as a paramedic that bright blood was likely to be arterial. Oxygenated.

As soon as the vial was full, the doctor unscrewed it and attached a second one to the syringe.

She watched the second vial filling up, as the doctor prepared a third. 'What is this test for?'

'Test?' he asked.

She suddenly felt ill. Her vision tunnelled.

'Ah.' The doctor was filling up a third vial now. '*Test.* Yes.'

She should have guessed much earlier—but no one had said any of the keywords. Cheating. Doping. Did Narelle know about this? Had she done it herself?

All the other girls go to him. No wonder Elise could never beat them.

She took a deep breath. 'I have to go.'

The doctor kept his eyes on her arm. 'We're nearly finished.'

'I don't want to do this.' She would have pushed him away, but she was worried the needle would tear her artery as it came out.

'It's already done.' He detached the third vial, screwed on the cap and sat down on a squeaking swivel chair.

That wasn't true, she knew. It wouldn't be done until he centrifuged the blood and injected the red cells back into her, giving her more oxygen than she was supposed to have. Up until that point, she hadn't broken any rules.

'Just a small sample to begin with,' he was saying. 'We have to see how your body will react. Has someone told you how the cash deposit system works?'

'There's been a misunderstanding.'

'Has there?' He reclined in his chair, looking thoughtfully at her.

'I'll pay you for today. But I won't be coming back.' Elise resisted the urge to apologise. This man was a cheat. A criminal.

'You really should. You've lost a lot of blood. If you don't replace it, you'll be at a substantial disadvantage.' His voice became gentle. 'It's okay. Everyone is nervous, their first time. You're the girl from the country, yes? Your parents looked very proud, on the television.'

This wasn't true. Mum and Dad had sweated under the lights, forcing rictus grins as they sat shoulder to shoulder on the couch. They had looked less like proud parents and more like politicians getting grilled.

'And not just them,' the doctor continued. 'Your teacher was interviewed, and the town mayor. It must be hard, living with all those expectations.' He tilted the vial to watch the blood slosh back and forth. 'It will be harder still, if you fall short of them.'

Elise stood up too quickly. Her legs buckled, but she caught the doorhandle and stayed upright.

'You should stay for at least ten minutes,' the doctor said.

She ignored him, opening the door and walking out, so woozy she nearly fell down the stairs. She didn't feel like she could breathe until she was out through that dirty glass door, standing in the sunshine. The doctor didn't follow.

She staggered along the cracked footpath to her car, then realised she was in no condition to drive it. The doctor was right—she'd lost a lot of blood. What had she been thinking? She'd be too weak to train tomorrow. Maybe the day after that, too.

Leaning against the bonnet, she squeezed her eyes shut. She wanted to call Narelle, but wasn't sure what to say. She should ring her coach instead, but he'd give her an earful. After a minute, she dialled Callum's number.

'Hey, Sis. What's up?' He was chewing something. Toast, maybe. A little late for breakfast, but that was always him. Eat whatever and whenever he felt like, stay fit somehow. Was he doping, too?

'Nothing much.' She closed her eyes and turned her face up to the sun. 'Just wanted to hear your voice. How's the new job?'

Callum had recently left the Catholic school, taking a position at the public school he and Elise had attended. She found it hard to picture him there, standing exactly where Mr Panagoulis had, yelling at kids on the track.

'Ugh,' Callum said. 'All the other teachers are nice in the staffroom, but they keep saying nasty things behind one another's backs.'

'Well, it *is* a high school, right?'

'Oh yeah. Good point.'

'It's just the other teachers who are like that?'

'Well, obviously. I would never complain about my co-workers, especially not when talking to my famous sister over the phone. How's life in the big city?'

Elise glanced back towards the doctor's office. 'Pretty much like everyone says. Loud, busy. No one has any time for anyone else.'

'So, what you're saying is, you're not the centre of attention anymore.'

'Ha, ha.'

'Made any friends?'

Elise thought of Narelle. 'There's this one girl. But I'm not sure it's going to work out.'

'How do you mean?'

Callum had always been too invested in Elise's friendships, constantly giving her advice and encouraging her to invite people over. She wasn't sure how he'd react if she told him about the butterflies she felt when Narelle looked at her. Now wasn't the time for that conversation.

She changed the subject. 'How are Mum and Dad?'

'Excited. They're already sending out save-the-dates for your next race.'

She was surprised to hear this. She wondered if Callum was just trying to buoy her spirits. 'They're not coming here, are they?'

'God, no. Mum's heart wouldn't take it. But they've invited all their friends over to watch it. They bought a bigger telly. And signed up for Foxtel, finally. I've been enjoying it.'

As Callum rambled on about some pseudo-pornographic HBO show he'd been watching, Elise imagined her parents and all their friends huddled around their new TV—their expensive new TV, which they probably expected her sponsorships to pay for. She imagined their faces falling as they watched her come last. *Well, that's a shame*, her mother would say, with too much cheer, trying not to cry in front of the guests.

Elise interrupted Callum's monologue. 'I'm not sure I can do this.'

He was instantly on high alert. 'What? Why not?'

'I'm not like these other women.' She crouched next to the car and leaned against the door, as though taking cover from gunfire.

'No, you're not,' he said firmly. 'They're stuck-up, privileged city kids—'

'They're adults. And you don't even know them.'

'I know *you*. And I know you always do whatever it takes to win.'

Elise looked at the doctor's office again.

'You got this.' Kind words from Callum, as usual. He sounded like the instructor in a workout video. 'Don't give up. We all believe in you.'

Elise checked her watch. Ten minutes had passed. Had she recovered enough from the blood loss to drive?

'I have to go,' she said.

'Okay. Call me later, all right?'

'Thanks, Cal,' she said. 'For always having my back. No matter what.'

She could hear the smile in his voice. 'What are brothers for?'

CHAPTER 22

Elise wakes up under a heat lamp, wet towels beneath her body. The walls are tiled with rectangles of alternating pink and mint. An extractor fan whirs.

Someone is massaging her calf muscle. 'Coach?' she mumbles.

'Shh,' says a voice. 'It's okay. You're safe.'

She lifts her throbbing head. She's back in the farmhouse, in the bathroom. Stephanie is rubbing a salve into an electrical burn on her shin. A large, clean bandage is wrapped around Elise's elbow. Her ankles are bound together with duct tape.

'I accidentally shocked myself with a cattle prod once,' Stephanie is saying. 'It was like getting bitten by a bull ant. I was reluctant to use it on the sheep after that. But my foot recovered pretty quickly.'

It all comes rushing back. The escape attempt. The missing car. The boy in the grave.

'Where's Callum?' Elise croaks.

Stephanie doesn't look up. 'Back where he belongs.'

'Is anybody else here?' Elise has an indistinct memory of bright lights and engine noise from the driveway. She thinks she tried to call out, but couldn't speak, like in a nightmare.

'No,' Stephanie says. 'It's just us.'

Dizziness swirls around Elise. She slumps to the floor.

'Take it easy.' Stephanie picks up a cup of water. 'You've lost a lot of blood. Here.'

She holds up Elise's head and presses the cup to her lips. Elise sips the cold water carefully, but her throat spasms, and she chokes. Stephanie rolls her sideways and thumps her back as she coughs the water out. Tears trickle into Elise's ear. Stephanie strokes her hair. Eventually Elise stops retching and lies still. Exhausted and hungry, she has a delirious thought: *Stephanie would have been a good mother.*

Elise can't recall her own mother ever taking care of her like this, but that could be because she never asked her to. Mum seemed to resent her children, for reasons she kept to herself. Elise was always too proud to turn to her for comfort.

Then again, Mum never locked Elise up, or shot her, or hit her with a cattle prod.

'Are you okay?' Stephanie asks.

Elise manages a shaky nod. Stephanie helps her roll onto her back.

'You nearly died for him,' Stephanie says. 'How did he convince you to do that?'

'It was my idea,' Elise rasps. Callum always gets the credit for her work. When they were children, Aunt Tania often visited, and Elise would announce that she'd learned to tie her own shoelaces, or count to ten in Japanese, or spell 'accommodate'. Tania would respond, 'Wow! Did your big brother teach you that?' As adults, people assumed Callum was a good PE teacher because Elise was an elite athlete. But he never got the blame for her failures. The scandal at the Games didn't seem to make a dent in his social life.

'You might *think* it was your idea.' Stephanie is bandaging Elise's leg, too tight. 'But that's what he does. He convinces people that they care about him.'

Elise swallows. 'Who's the boy in the grave?'

'His name was Zach Locat.'

'You killed him?'

'I did.'

'Why?'

Stephanie opens a small plastic container. Elise shrinks back, but what comes out of the container is just a cracker with some tinned salmon spread across it.

'You're not a vegetarian, are you?' Stephanie asks. 'I have some beans and some spinach—but I hear the iron in those is harder to absorb.'

Her kindness makes Elise uneasy. She doesn't know when the psychopath with the cattle prod will reappear.

Elise can't put much weight on her left elbow, where Callum cut her. She props herself up on her right and nibbles on the cracker. Her guts churn.

'I've had some time to think.' Stephanie spreads more fish on a second cracker. 'I misjudged you, and I put you in an impossible position. The sort of woman who would risk her life to save a stranger—that sort of woman wouldn't kill one.'

Elise realises she's holding her breath.

'Not,' Stephanie continues, 'without a good reason.' She holds out the cracker and waits for Elise to take it.

'What are you saying?' Elise asks.

'I'll tell you the whole story,' Stephanie says. 'When I'm finished, you can go.'

'Go?' Elise's pulse quickens.

'Leave. Your car is in the garage. I'm hoping that if you know all the facts, you won't talk to the police—but I can't stop you.'

It sounds too good to be true. She could drive home, feed her dog, and cry. 'What about Callum?'

'Don't worry about him. I'll finish the job as soon as you're gone.'

Elise flashes back to the grave between the trees. Nothing has changed. She can live—but only if her brother dies.

Stephanie's intense expression heightens her unease. Elise thought she understood the situation. Callum gave Moon a poor grade on a test, and Moon killed herself. But if that's the story, then how is Zach involved? Clearly there's more to it—or at least, Stephanie thinks there is.

'What happened?' Elise asks.

Stephanie clears her throat. 'I have to warn you—parts of this will be hard to hear.'

'I'm ready.'

CHAPTER 23

Stephanie had never been fazed by blood. She had rinsed it off her arms after the sheep gave birth, hosed it off the concrete floor after killing a lamb with a broken leg, felt it squirt out of a fox in a trap. Now she hardly noticed it. One of those protesters from the city had once tried to splash her with pig's blood, but only got her shoes. She had laughed, because the protester spilled much more on himself, and he looked to be on the verge of vomiting.

Everything changed on Valentine's Day. As Stephanie fell to her knees beside the tub and cradled Moon's head in her arms, screaming and sobbing, feeling how cold the girl's flesh was already, some part of her brain took note of the horrifying inversion—the water in the white bathtub had turned pink, while Moon's formerly pink skin had turned white. The wounds on her wrists had yellowed like an old photograph. The knife on the floor was the only red thing in the room. Stephanie didn't realise that she'd stepped on it, slicing open her foot, until much later.

There had been warning signs. Little cuts on Moon's thighs and her belly, like she had been scratched by a cat. The doctor had reassured Stephanie that twenty-two per cent of girls self-harmed at some point, and it rarely became anything serious. He'd given Moon a rubber band to wear around her wrist and told her to snap it against her skin whenever she felt the urge. Stephanie had tensed up whenever she saw Moon doing it. It worked, though. Soon Moon didn't need the band anymore. There were no more incidents.

Until now. Her little girl. Her baby.

Gone.

The paramedic, a tattooed guy named Rafa, asked Stephanie some questions. So did a jittery police officer named Rohan. Later, she couldn't recall what either of them had wanted to know, or what her answers had been. Her call logs showed that old friends had left voicemails for her, and that she'd called them back, but she had no memory of doing it. When ironing clothes for the funeral, she burned a triangular patch of her dress. She was oblivious to the smell of smoke as she stood there, picturing her daughter, all grown up, in some parallel universe where Stephanie and Vic had come home from the restaurant early enough to stop her.

People said they were sorry. They said they understood how she must feel. Then they went back to their lives.

They understood *nothing*.

To spend nine months growing someone in your belly, to sweat and groan your way through fourteen hours of labour, to change thousands of nappies and play with toys and read storybooks and watch your beautiful little girl take those first few wobbly steps, laugh at silly faces, mispronounce words, cry, eat birthday cake, hold your hand when Grandpa died, and then just . . . disappear.

Stephanie couldn't believe it. She *wouldn't* believe it. Moon rode horses, painted birds, argued with her friends about which boy in which fantasy novel was the cutest. She wrote poetry, and not that emo stuff, either—nice poems. She played the ukulele. Whoever heard of a suicidal ukulele player?

Even after the police located the note on Moon's laptop—*I'm sorry*. Even after they tested the knife and found no one else's prints. Even after they found the web searches on Moon's phone—*painless deaths, important arteries*. Even after all that, Stephanie knew in her bones that they were wrong.

She and Victor had been talking about buying a nicer home on a bigger plot of land. In their grief, they rushed the process, as though their problem was a cramped house rather than a dead daughter. The real estate agent cheerfully commented that he'd never seen such a quick settlement.

It helped, briefly. The process of selling their old farm, reading the contracts, and moving the sheep and their possessions to the new place was all-consuming. It was hard to fall apart when they were so busy. But it was over too soon, and the sadness came rushing back in.

Stephanie clung to increasingly convoluted theories. Someone must have held Moon down and slashed her wrists. Or poisoned her, made her delusional. Or they must have threatened her. *Kill yourself or we'll kill your family*, that kind of thing. Every night Stephanie shared her newest idea with Vic, and every night he clenched his jaw and told her to 'drop it'.

Then to 'Just drop it, all right?'

Then to 'Shut up, for fuck's sake!'

Soon she was telling her theories to his empty side of the bed, while he slept on the couch. Not long after that he was gone.

Vic had always acted like his relationship with Moon was somehow more special than hers. When Stephanie hadn't wanted to put her body through the trauma of a second baby, Vic had taken that to mean she was indifferent to their first. He was an involved father. He had named Moon, he had been the one at every parent–teacher interview, and she'd looked up to him as though he were a god. Whenever Stephanie asked her to do anything—feed the sheep, take out the bins—Moon rolled her eyes or sulked. Stephanie wouldn't let her use her phone at the dinner table, and dinners often turned into shouting matches or icy silences. Sometimes Moon stormed off to her room to cry, leaving Stephanie pleading with a closed door.

But none of this meant Moon hadn't loved her mother, or that Stephanie hadn't loved her daughter. That was what Vic didn't understand. He was always in bed by the time Stephanie and Moon made up, put a movie on and snuggled on the couch with mugs of Milo. If the movie was long, sometimes Moon fell asleep with her head on Stephanie's shoulder. Stephanie would get pillows and blankets from Moon's bedroom, tuck her in on the couch and give her pink hair a gentle kiss.

After he left, Vic completely rewrote history. When he spoke to their friends, he made it sound as though Moon and Stephanie had been bitter enemies. That the suicide was all Stephanie's fault.

Soon people stopped calling her. She was glad.

When one of the sheep got shipping fever, Stephanie couldn't kill it. She just stood there with the bolt gun, weeping as she stared into the sheep's sad eyes, stroking the rough wool on its neck. She ended up letting it rejoin the flock. They all caught the disease, and died. She didn't buy more.

Every time she tried to unpack Moon's possessions, she found the task impossible. She ended up smelling hairbrushes, staring at sketches she couldn't see through the tears, hugging clothes as if her daughter's warmth might still be on them.

Then she found the phone, tucked into the back pocket of some jeans.

The police had taken Moon's phone away. Whose was this?

Moon's smiling face was the lock screen. When Stephanie unlocked it—Moon's birthday was the passcode—she found more photos, mostly selfies. This was Moon's phone. Moon's *secret* phone. Who had bought this for her? Why?

There was a social media app linked to an anonymous profile with a gibberish name and no followers. Moon had been posting about an unnamed boy.

One post read: *Everything he says has two meanings. One for everyone else, and another that only I can hear.*

Another: *Afterwards, my mouth was dry, my heart raced, my whole body tingling—is that what love is?*

And another: *He says it's over.*

The phone trembled in Stephanie's hands. This was her daughter's diary. Public, but anonymous.

He says we can't tell anyone. They wouldn't understand. But how can I heal if I don't? Wounds fester in the dark.

I don't want him back, but I don't want to be tossed aside like a tissue after a nosebleed, either. Forgotten.

I want him to suffer.

The thought that Moon had killed herself to punish some boy was horrifying. Stephanie tapped the default messaging app, hoping to search for the boy's name, but the inbox was empty. There was a second app, apparently designed for encrypted messages. She opened it—and recoiled.

You slut.

You fucking bitch.

You disgusting pig.

The messages all came from the same number. Each one was a knife through Stephanie's heart. Her daughter had endured all of this in secret. Why?

And then she saw it—the text that filled her with white-hot rage:

You're a whore. Why don't you kill yourself?

CHAPTER 24

For the next few days, Stephanie seldom slept and barely ate. But rage was an efficient fuel source, keeping her awake and focused.

Identifying her daughter's bully was easier than she had expected. The sender had used an encryption app, but the phone number was still attached. She called it from her own mobile. 'Hi, you've called Zach Locat,' a voice said. 'Leave a message.'

She didn't leave a message.

Was cyberbullying illegal? If so, it wasn't illegal enough. Stephanie knew what would happen if she went to the cops. The kid would get some stern words from a police officer, or, at worst, a magistrate. He would say he was sorry, and that would be the end of it.

A quick social media search showed her what Zach looked like. Dark hair, dark eyes, and what she thought was a slimy sort of smile. In some pictures his parents were hugging him, and in one he was brandishing a debate team trophy like a club.

Stephanie wanted to know why he'd sent those messages, and whether he had also been Moon's secret boyfriend. She didn't want to confront him at home, or near his school. She wouldn't get the truth if he had a friend or a parent or a teacher to hide behind.

She didn't go to bed that night. She made cup after cup of tea and let them go cold, undrunk, as a dark plan formed.

At about 4 a.m. she printed out some religious pamphlets on her computer. She made the language as forgettable as possible—*Jesus saves, avoid hell, call for more information.* She put the phone number of St Barnabas' Church down the bottom.

Then she checked out some crazy survivalist websites, the kind that recommended buying potassium iodide pills, canned non-hybrid seeds and gold bullion. On her back porch, she mixed bleach with nail-polish remover and ice in a glass jar. The result, according to one of the websites she'd checked out, was chloroform. She didn't have any sheep left to test it on, but the fumes gave her a hell of a headache. She took that as a good sign.

At 2.55 that afternoon, she parked across the road from her daughter's school and waited for the students to emerge. She hadn't slept at all. Her eyes ached, and there was a fuzzy heat in her head. A man watching the school like this would have looked shady. But as a woman, she figured that anyone who didn't know her would assume she was waiting for her kid. And anyone who *did* know her, well, they'd keep their distance.

She was wrong about that. The principal, a big-haired lady in a bright dress, spotted her and walked over. 'Steph!' she said. 'It's good to see you.'

'You too.' Stephanie couldn't remember the principal's name. She didn't take her eyes off the front entrance. The kids had just started to flow out. Laughing, screaming, shoving each other in the sunshine. Stephanie was reminded of chickens, jostling for food and pecking at one another's necks.

'What brings you here?' the principal asked.

'I wanted to talk to Kelli-Anne. I've lost her number, but I figured she'd be here to pick up Sara.' The lie came easily. Her voice didn't waver, and there was no urge to fidget. Why should she be nervous, when the worst had already happened?

The principal's face fell. 'Oh, you just missed her.'

Stephanie knew that—she had watched Kelli-Anne drive away a minute earlier. 'That's a shame.'

'I can't technically give you her number. But if you'd like me to give her *your* number, I can . . .'

Stephanie wasn't listening. She'd spotted Zach Locat, walking out the front of the school, his bag slung over one shoulder. He said goodbye to a blonde girl with glasses— Indica Aigner, one of Moon's old friends. He slapped her on the backside, and she squealed. As Indica lined up for the bus, Zach started walking down the street. He must live nearby.

The principal was still talking. '. . . sure she'd like to hear from you.'

'That'd be great.' Stephanie watched Zach get further and further away. 'I have to go.'

'Sure.' The principal reached through the open window and squeezed Stephanie's shoulder. The contact was electrifying. No one had touched her since Vic left. Even before then, come to think of it.

'How are you coping?' the principal asked.

Zach disappeared around a corner.

'Everything's under control.' Stephanie started the engine. 'But I do have to go.'

Zach wasn't difficult to follow. He never once glanced back, wireless headphones jammed deep in his ears. When he reached a long, quiet street—no traffic, no parked cars, curtains drawn in all the houses—Stephanie overtook him. She parked fifty metres further along, got out and started walking towards him, but slowly. She didn't want to be too far from the car when she grabbed him.

She took the religious pamphlets out of a saddlebag and pushed one into each letterbox. The wind was against her, tugging at her hoodie, as though trying to make her turn back. Zach didn't seem to have noticed her, his head down.

There was a tightness in Stephanie's chest. What if someone saw her? What if Zach turned out to be a black belt in karate, and he fought her off? What would the police do, once she let him go?

I don't care. The thought was like a plughole opening up, sucking the pink bathwater down into the darkness, leaving Stephanie entirely empty.

She and Zach were about forty metres apart. Then thirty. Twenty.

He had seen her, but didn't look concerned. He kept up the same pace, moving to the left side of the footpath, preparing to pass her. Fifteen metres to go.

With shaking hands, Stephanie tried to push a pamphlet into a mailbox, but because she was watching Zach, she missed the slot. The pamphlet fell. She quickly snatched it up, crumpling it a bit. Now it didn't fit, and as she shifted her weight to push it through, some other pamphlets spilled from her saddlebag onto the muddy footpath.

'Oh no!' Zach ran up to her. 'Here.' He crouched down and started picking up the pamphlets. The perfect picture of a helpful young man.

Stephanie stared down at the back of Zach's head with disbelief that quickly became fury. Who did he think he was? The monster that had told her daughter to kill herself, acting *nice*?

She crouched next to him and reached into a side pocket of the saddlebag. The chloroform-soaked dishcloth was wrapped in plastic. She pulled it out, holding her breath.

Zach had time to look at it and recoil from the strange, sweet smell. 'Wha—?' he began.

Then Stephanie pushed the cloth into his face.

He spluttered. Tried to stand up but didn't make it. He toppled onto his back and lay there like a turtle, legs moving slower and slower. Some of the chloroform splashed Stephanie's wrist, a cool burn on her exposed skin. She held the cloth over the boy's face until his limbs stopped moving. The whole attack took less than ten seconds, and was almost silent.

She looked around. Still no sign that anybody was watching from the surrounding houses, but that could change at any moment. Woozy from the smell, she dragged Zach back to her car and heaved him up into the boot. There wasn't time to gag him or restrain him. Hopefully he'd stay unconscious throughout the journey. She slammed the lid.

She'd done it. She'd kidnapped her daughter's killer. Her plan was to drive him to Fogherty's Lookout. She could march him right up to the edge of a cliff overlooking the Murrumbidgee River. There she would finally get the truth.

She drove slowly out of town, compulsively checking her mirrors. At the base of the hill, she stalled the engine—a mistake she hadn't made since her driving test, twenty-five years ago. She took each bend with care on her way up the slope, seeing no one, and pulled up in the empty car park with its view of the distant mountain range. It wasn't until she opened the boot that she realised how strong the chloroform had been. Zach was dead.

CHAPTER 25

Stephanie sat on the edge of the cliff, thinking. The brown water swirled far below, carrying dead leaves downstream. The clouds were pink and gold in one direction, bruised and stormy in the other.

She had picked this spot because it was isolated, and threatening. A good place to scare a confession out of somebody. But it turned out to be a good spot to reflect on death, too.

When she'd checked Zach's pulse, she had been shocked, then scared. She had crossed a line. In fact, she had crossed it the moment she typed 'how to make chloroform' into a search engine, and now it was way too late to go back. The police would soon be after her. And she hadn't found out why Zach had sent those messages. The whole exercise had been pointless.

There was another regret, from a darker place in her psyche. Zach had never known *why* she had killed him. He hadn't had any time to feel fear, or to regret what he had done to Moon. She had snuffed him out in a few chaotic seconds.

A search of his schoolbag turned up nothing of interest. There was a tablet. A change of clothes for PE. A lunchbox containing mandarin peel and a mustard-stained scrap of a tortilla. She could bury or burn all that stuff when she got home.

But the phone in his pocket could be traced. She couldn't take it anywhere near her house. Maybe she should chuck it into the river. If anyone followed the trail later, they might think Zach had gone to this clifftop and jumped.

Stephanie licked her teeth, mulling it over. Then she went back to her Barina and popped the boot. She used Zach's soft, limp thumb to unlock the phone, then swiped through his messages.

She saw nothing interesting. Nothing coherent, even. Teen lingo had certainly changed since her day. Half the time Zach didn't even use words—he expressed his emotions using pictures of celebrities or cartoon characters, none of whom Stephanie recognised.

She had the idea that she could message one of his friends about Moon. It was too late to make Zach regret what he'd done. But she could make others *think* he regretted it, enough to throw himself off a cliff. There was a certain symmetry in that.

Before she tried it, though, she searched for 'Moon' in his messages.

She found what she expected to. The messages he'd sent to Moon, the ones she'd seen already. But there were also messages he had sent to others *about* Moon.

Stephanie stared at the screen. It felt like she was falling— she had to steady herself on the side of the car.

Did you hear Moon Hartnell fucked a teacher?!

Under the message, there was a gif of a clown looking shocked.

Later, Stephanie would have no memory of throwing the phone into the river or driving home. She wouldn't remember digging the grave and dumping Zach's corpse inside. Her body did these things while her mind was elsewhere. The two weren't reunited until she was in her daughter's room, going through the secret phone again.

Some of Zach's other messages made more sense now. *I bet you're getting As in PE* had seemed innocuous before— even complimentary. Not anymore. *Hey, meet ME behind the bike cage after school.* Stephanie had interpreted that as a threat when she first read it, but this time it seemed like a sexual request.

The messages had fresh potency, like they'd found a new angle to lance her from. It wasn't until she tasted blood that she realised how hard she was biting her lip.

There weren't many male teachers at Warrigal Public School. The only one who had taught Moon's year group was Callum Glyk, and he was indeed a PE teacher. Stephanie found him online, photographed alongside other school staff, smiling like a politician. He had social media profiles on various platforms, with posts she couldn't see because of the privacy settings.

She thought of how often she and her daughter had fought, because Moon wanted to go out. Out where? 'Just out, okay? Jeez, Mum.'

Stephanie hadn't thought Moon was the type to have a secret relationship with a teacher. But Stephanie hadn't thought she was the type to kill herself, either. Every day she peeled back another painful layer, exposing the raw wound of how little she'd known about her daughter's life.

Moon had been under the age of consent, but Stephanie couldn't go to the police. Firstly, she would be arrested if she revealed how she had found out what she knew. And secondly, she didn't really know anything, not for sure. All she had were messages from a teenage dickhead. Without proof, she would go to prison, and Callum would go free.

She needed to be sure. Not just whether or not Callum was guilty—she wanted to know what had pushed Moon over the edge. Was it vicious cyberbullying from a classmate, or exploitation by a predatory teacher? Or both?

This time there would be no chloroform, no pamphlets, and no mistakes. Stephanie would need to lay a more sophisticated trap.

She spent hours making a fake social media profile and populating it with stolen photos. She wasn't sure how suggestive to be in the captions. She settled for lukewarm statements like *Girls just want to have fun!* and *Check out this super-cute top I found!*

Soon her profile looked authentic, other than the lack of 'friends'. After a bit of searching, she found a few users with thousands of connections. Assuming they said yes to everyone, she sent requests, which were granted within minutes.

It was almost scary, how easy all this was. But it was kind of a thrill, too. Stephanie was discovering something about herself. Deep down, she had never been a farmer. She was a hunter.

Soon she was ready to send Callum a message. She agonised over it, like it was a cover letter for a resumé.

Hey Mr Glyk!

I hope it's not weird, me messaging you out of the blue like this. I'm struggling with my Year Nine physical education class, especially the sexual health component.

Too obvious. Stephanie changed it.

. . . especially the anatomy component. My sister's friend, Alex, went to your school last year or maybe the year before? Anyway, Alex said you were a really great teacher.

I was wondering if maybe I could ask you some questions sometime? I promise it won't take long. I don't know if there's rules about hanging out with people from the Catholic school, but I won't tell anyone if that's an issue.

Sincerely,

Neve XX

Stephanie hit send and immediately started second-guessing herself. Were the two Xs too much? And why had she put salutations at the start and the end? Teenagers didn't do that.

Callum would smell a trap. She had failed.

She threw her phone across the room. She made fists of her hair and pulled, as though the thoughts could be torn out through her scalp.

Then the phone dinged.

She found it behind the armchair, the screen chipped in one corner, a notification light blinking.

Hi Neve! Of course, I'd be happy to have a chat. What's your number?—Callum.

Every time Stephanie went to the hardware store, she wore a different disguise.

She bleached her hair, then hid it with hats. Sometimes she wore glasses. Once she added fake freckles and a mole to her face.

None of it mattered. No one took any notice of her. She was a woman over forty—invisible. Just some lady, buying bolts. Glue. Padlocks. Duct tape. For each useful item, she added two useless ones, like light bulbs and peach paint. She had prepared a cover story about building a granny flat, but no one asked. It was as though she had died alongside her daughter and was now a poltergeist, just moving objects around, hoping to take revenge upon the living.

She kept waiting for the police to knock on her door with a search warrant and questions about Zach. They never did.

Preparing the septic tank was backbreaking work. She had to install a new lid, one that could withstand pressure from the other side. The lid needed a window, so she would be able to tell if Callum was waiting underneath before she opened it, but the window had to be tough. She mounted a pulley next to the hatch so she could lower in Callum's unconscious body.

The tank had been used for storage, and she had to take out anything he might use to attack her or to break out. Some days she never even saw the sun—she was down there sorting things before it rose and long after it set. The tank started to feel like her own prison, rather than Callum's.

She ignored her landline whenever it rang, but paid close attention to the dings from her mobile. They were always messages from Callum. At first, he had only discussed teaching. But he had allowed her to lead him to more personal topics. She had asked him for advice about a fictional best friend, then about a fictional crush. All of her stories made her sound isolated and vulnerable.

Stephanie felt ill, sending these messages. But his responses convinced her she was doing the right thing. An adult shouldn't talk to a child the way he was. He'd called her beautiful at one point, and the word chilled Stephanie to the bone.

Now, finally, she was sitting in her front room, watching the driveway through the window. She had told him she was lonely with her mother interstate, and had begged him to visit her.

He'd said he would.

She wondered, squinting into the sunshine, if she should confront him on camera, like on *To Catch a Predator*. Expose him to the whole world as the monster he was.

But then what? He would be fired. Possibly arrested, maybe jailed. Then after five or ten years, he would be released, free to live the rest of his life in peace. Moon, who should by then have been a grown woman, with a career, perhaps a husband, maybe even children of her own, would still be dead.

Also, the police might link Stephanie to Zach's disappearance. If they searched the property and unearthed his body, she would be locked up for even longer than Callum. No one would visit. She had no friends or family left. He had taken everything from her.

While she waited, she cooked a pasta sauce, but was too nervous to eat more than a spoonful. She tipped the rest into the rubbish. As she washed the dishes, unease swirled around her gut. Callum should have arrived by now. Had he realised this was a trap?

Or was he innocent after all? Sitting by the window, Stephanie re-read the messages. All the flirty ones had been written by her. Callum hadn't said anything overtly sexual. He might just be friendly and a bit oblivious. Maybe Zach had been full of shit. There were no messages from Callum on Moon's secret phone. Moon had never mentioned him by name.

And yet. In the last few weeks of Moon's life, it had seemed like she wanted to tell Stephanie something but couldn't find the words.

If only Stephanie had been the kind of mother that Moon felt she could talk to.

The damaged screen blurred. Stephanie hadn't thought she had any tears left. If Callum was innocent, then the past few weeks of work had been for nothing. What was she supposed to do now? What was the rest of her life supposed to look like?

Then she heard a vehicle approaching.

She had so thoroughly convinced herself Callum wasn't coming that for a second she wondered who could possibly be visiting at this time of night. It was only when she heard footsteps crunching up the gravel towards the door that everything snapped together in her head.

She leapt to her feet and grabbed the tranquilliser rifle. This time there would be no messing around with chloroform. Each dart contained precisely the right amount of midanol to knock out, but not kill, an adult human male of average weight.

She raced to the door, clutched the handle and took a deep breath. Then, just as the footsteps thumped up onto the porch, she pulled the door open and raised the gun.

CHAPTER 26

Elise feels feverish, her whole body trembling. She's on the living room floor in front of the fireplace, wrapped in a towel. The flames are popping and crackling, but she can't get warm.

The story she's hearing can't be true. Callum is a decent man. A bit too slick sometimes, sure. Easily convinced by others, and by himself. But fundamentally good. He would never do anything inappropriate with a student.

Would he?

Stephanie confessed to murdering a teenage boy as matter-of-factly as she might discuss the cricket scores. Why would she tell the truth about that, then lie about the rest? It doesn't make sense.

As Stephanie tells her about Facebook-stalking Callum, Elise wonders if the woman is delusional. Mad with grief. She might have misinterpreted Callum's messages. Seen sleaze when there was only kindness.

Then Stephanie gets to the part about Callum arriving here, after sunset, expecting to find a girl whose parents weren't home.

Elise remembers what he said in the septic tank: *I never even met her before I got here.*

Why would he have come? Elise racks her brain for an innocent reason. He thought the girl might be in danger, perhaps. Or he didn't understand the parents wouldn't be home.

But then why would he tell Elise he'd been abducted from a Woolworths car park?

Someone is lying. She wants to think it's Stephanie. But a shadow lurks in the corner of her mind. A bad feeling that predates what she's being told. Something she's been trying to ignore for years.

She thinks about the new clothes, the shaving, the work-outs. Signs that Callum was dating someone, even though he denied it. He's had plenty of girlfriends and never kept them a secret before. And as he got older, they seemed to be getting younger.

Elise shakes her head to dislodge the thought. Whatever Callum has done—and it's nothing, she's sure of it—she can't let Stephanie kill him.

'So.' Stephanie dries her hands on a towel. 'Now you see why I can't let him go.'

'Do I?' Elise heaves herself up into a sitting position, fighting off vertigo. 'You still don't know he's guilty.'

Stephanie's nose twitches. 'Why else would he turn up here?'

'If you were sure, you wouldn't have spent the past month and a half trying to make him confess.'

Stephanie snatches away Elise's towel, balls it up and tosses it into a basket. She keeps staring at the basket, as though she expects the towel to crawl back out.

'You took Callum's phone, right?' Elise says. 'Did you find any messages between him and your daughter?'

'If he was smart enough to buy Moon a secret phone, then he was smart enough to delete her messages off his.'

'So that's a no. Did you put the drugs in his house?'

After Elise discovered that Callum hadn't showed up at work, then called him and got no answer, she let herself into his home with her spare key. She immediately spotted the little bag on his bedside table, stuffed with pills. Callum didn't do drugs, so she left them there, thinking the police could use the fingerprints to solve the crime. Later, she wondered if she should have removed the bag. The police would have taken Callum's abduction more seriously if they hadn't thought he was a user.

'I bought some GHB.' Stephanie's voice is flat. 'Pretty easy, these days, with the dark web and all. I used Callum's key to enter his house, left the pills in his bedroom. I wanted the police to think he'd just skipped town.'

'Right,' Elise says, feeling vindicated.

'But I needn't have bothered. When the police searched the house, they *also* found some ecstasy.'

'That wasn't yours?'

Stephanie's eyes are hard. 'No. That was his.'

Elise is thrown, but only for a moment. 'Lots of people use ecstasy. I think it's even been decriminalised. And the cops didn't find any—' she tries to remember the police terminology '—child exploitation materials, did they?'

Stephanie throws up her hands. 'For God's sake. You're free to go. Have some more water, then get out.'

'But then you'll kill Callum, right?'

'Why do you care what happens to him? He's a bloody paedophile.'

'He's not,' Elise snaps.

'How do you know?'

Elise clamps her mouth shut. If Stephanie finds out Callum is her brother, she'll realise that Elise *can't* walk away—and she'll kill them both.

Stephanie doesn't wait for a response. 'Your car's in the garage. I'll have to hang on to your phone, I'm afraid— I can't risk the police arriving before I've finished the job.'

An idea surfaces. 'Don't you see? I can help you.'

Stephanie blinks. 'Help me?'

'I'm a private investigator. I can help you find out if he's guilty.'

'He's guilty. I'm a hundred per cent sure.'

'Listen to me. He was never going to confess to you, his kidnapper, the mother of the victim. He might confess to me—he thinks I'm on his side.'

'He won't. He's a sociopath.' But Stephanie sounds thoughtful, like she's considering this.

Elise keeps pushing. 'At least I can trick him into giving me some clues. Something I can pass on to you, so you can find the proof for yourself.'

'Then what?'

'Then you can take him to the police.'

Stephanie's mouth is a hard line. 'I'm not doing that.'

'Or kill him.' Elise tries to sound nonchalant. 'Whatever. But you won't have to live with the doubt about whether you got the right guy.'

Stephanie doesn't seem troubled by these doubts. 'And you'll leave?'

'If we can prove he's guilty, I'll leave.'

Actually, Elise is hoping to find something that proves Callum's innocence, so Stephanie might let them both go. But Elise doesn't say this out loud. Stephanie won't consider that possibility yet.

'You won't tell the police what you found here?' Stephanie asks.

Elise holds her gaze. 'Why would I?'

This might be too much, but Stephanie seems to buy it. 'All right,' she says, and holds out her hand to shake. When Elise reaches for it, Stephanie pulls back. 'Forty-eight hours,' she says.

Elise doesn't ask what happens if she takes longer than that. Maybe Stephanie will tranquillise her and dump her somewhere, then kill Callum. Or maybe she's still considering dropping the match into the tank. Igniting the fertiliser, and burning them both to death.

'Deal,' Elise says.

CHAPTER 27

They go out the back door, into the moonlit garden. The air is wet with fog.

Stephanie keeps the torch pointed at Elise with one hand as they walk, and the gun aimed at her with the other. They're theoretically on the same side now, but Elise acts like she hasn't noticed. Despite her stiff knee and wobbly arms, she trudges across the dirt with purpose. She has a plan now. She just hopes it will work.

The scraps of duct tape, now sliced through, flap against her ankles as she walks. When she glances back, she sees bags under Stephanie's eyes. The woman has had a draining night, recapturing Elise and Callum, carrying them back up the hill, bandaging Elise's wounds and then telling her about Moon, and Zach, and Callum. Hopefully Stephanie will go to bed once Elise is back in the tank. Give Elise some time to update Callum and quiz him.

'Stay back.' Stephanie unlocks the hatch and lifts it up. Elise can't hear any sound from below.

The circle of blackness still causes a spike of fear. Elise might not be able to prove Callum's innocence. Stephanie could change her mind once Elise is down there. Or Stephanie could get arrested for Zach's murder, or simply die of a stroke. In any of these scenarios, Elise and Callum would be left underground, slowly dying of thirst.

'Down you go,' Stephanie says, with a jerk of the gun.

Elise stuffs the fear deep inside herself, playing the role of a hardened PI. She steps onto the ladder and descends. The rungs toll like a grandfather clock striking midnight.

Stephanie doesn't say anything, knowing Callum can hear. She just closes the lid and locks it. Her muffled footsteps fade away.

Callum is lying on a fleece, one foot elevated against the wall, using a fertiliser bag like a pillow. He's pale. Stephanie hasn't treated his wounds with as much care as she has Elise's. There's a puddle of vomit in the corner. Maybe he had a bad reaction to the tranquilliser.

He rolls his head sideways to look at Elise as she clambers over the low wall.

'Hey,' she says.

'Oh my God.' He looks relieved. 'I thought maybe she killed you.'

'Not yet. You okay?'

He wiggles his mouth around, as though his lips are a bit numb. 'Been better. You?'

'Yeah.' Elise sits next to him and goes into paramedic mode, checking his injuries. There's some swelling where the tranquilliser dart hit him, in his lower back. Some bruising on his face, probably from when Stephanie dumped him down here. A rough bandage is stuck to his inner elbow, where he bled, but Elise can't smell any antiseptic. At this point, Stephanie doesn't care if he dies from an infection. He might not even last the forty-eight hours they've been given.

'I'm sorry about the vomit,' he says.

'It's okay.' Elise isn't sure how to help him. She's never heard of midanol. It must be used mostly on animals.

'I didn't have anything to mop it up with. We could cover it with a fleece, but the smell will probably—'

'Here. Drink this.' She helps him into a sitting position, and holds up a jug of water. Callum sips from it cautiously.

'I might have a way out of here,' Elise says.

Callum chokes, coughs. 'You do?'

'Yeah. But it's important you tell me the truth, okay?'

Callum wipes droplets off his chin. 'About what?'

She gives him the whole story. Moon's suicide, Zach's murder, Stephanie's conclusion that Callum is responsible for her daughter's death. Elise watches him closely as she talks but keeps her voice level, trying not to sound accusatory. She expects him to interrupt, to object, but he listens in silence, looking more and more perplexed and alarmed.

'Well, that's ridiculous,' he says, when she's finished.

'Which part?'

'All of it. I barely knew Moon, like I told you.'

'You never saw her outside of school?'

'No. I barely even saw her *inside* school. She skipped a lot—I was told she had mental health issues.'

Elise takes time choosing her words. 'You didn't tell me about driving out here.'

'I *didn't* drive out here. The last thing I remember, I'd been shopping, I was in the car park, and she must have grabbed me.'

'Must have?'

Callum frowns. 'That's what I assumed. I think I remember that happening, but my head was pretty scrambled when I woke up. I did intend to visit Neve, but—'

'What?' Elise swallows. 'You were going to meet a teenage girl on her own at night?'

Callum waves his hands frantically. 'No, no! I thought she was a teacher. She said she was struggling to teach anatomy to her Year Nine class. She didn't talk like a teenager—she sounded like a middle-aged lady. Which makes sense, now I know who was writing the messages.'

'What about her picture?'

'Jesus, her picture was a tiny little circle next to the message. I was too busy to click through to her profile—I had no idea what she looked like.'

'You went to visit a stranger at her home without even looking at her profile?'

Callum gestures at the septic tank around them. 'What, you're saying I should have *expected* this?'

Elise would never go to a stranger's home without researching them thoroughly. But she supposes that men aren't taught to be wary like that, and Callum's always lived casually, assuming everything will work out fine. Until now, he's been right.

'Why didn't you tell me you drove to Neve's house?'

'Because I never made it there! I—'

'Yes, you did.' Elise is thinking it through as she speaks. 'When you arrived, she shot you immediately, and when you woke up, you didn't remember driving here. So you assumed she'd grabbed you in the car park.' She wonders how Stephanie disposed of Callum's car—it wasn't in the garage.

'Oh.' He nods slowly. 'Right. That makes sense.'

It does. And Elise is desperate to believe her brother's version of events. But she keeps pushing. 'Why would Moon's classmates think she was in a relationship with you?'

'I have no idea.' He looks sickened. 'There was a boy named Callum in the year group above hers. Maybe she was seeing him? If she told someone that her boyfriend's name was Callum, and that he was older than her, that person may have jumped to the wrong conclusion.'

'What about your girlfriend?'

'Heidi? What about her?'

It's the first time Callum has admitted he was dating someone. 'Why did you keep her a secret from me?'

His mouth falls open. 'You thought my girlfriend might have been Moon?'

Elise hesitates. 'No.'

'Jesus, Leesy.' He pulls his hand away from hers. 'You know me better than that.'

'I do. It's just—'

'Heidi's married, okay?' he snaps. 'She and her husband are going through a trial separation. She didn't want me to tell anyone we were dating. She thought it might get back to Jamie—her son. He knows me, but he doesn't know I'm seeing his mum.'

'I'm sorry.'

Callum shrugs. He still looks annoyed.

'We need a way to prove that Moon's boyfriend wasn't you,' Elise says. 'Hopefully then Stephanie will let us both out of here.'

'That was the deal you made with her?'

'Not exactly, but I think it's our best chance.'

Callum is watching her carefully. It doesn't look like he believes her.

'What?' she asks.

His gaze slides down to the bandage around her arm. 'She's not going to let me go.'

'She will. She's not a total monster.'

He laughs darkly.

'I mean it,' Elise insists. 'She's gone out of her way to avoid killing me, because I'm a bystander. If she knows you're innocent, she'll let you go, too.'

'Didn't you just tell me she murdered a teenage boy?'

'That was an accident.' Elise can't believe she's defending their captor.

'Well . . .' Callum rests his head against the wall, thinking. 'I guess we can tell her about the other Callum. Maybe she'll find some evidence that it was him, not me.'

'Maybe. But then . . .'

'What?'

Elise is thinking. She narrowly missed out on the Rio Olympics, but once found herself researching the history of the event. This led her to the myths about the Olympians. Now she thinks of Atlas, the Titan cursed to hold up the sky forever, unless he could trick someone into taking his place.

'What?' Callum says again.

'If she finds out about the other Callum,' Elise says, 'she might blame *him* for Moon's death. Then he'll end up down here instead of us.'

CHAPTER 28

The morgue is a separate structure behind the hospital, at the end of a covered walkway. The building is made of three repurposed shipping containers, stacked side by side, holes cut in the walls to link them together. Kiara can still see an old stencil-painted logo from an abattoir on one side, and a power point where a container would have been plugged in for refrigeration.

She finds several people inside, none alive. Circling around the building, she comes across the medical examiner on a folding chair on the grass, apparently enjoying the winter sunshine.

'Hi, Gregor,' she says.

'Impeccable timing as ever, Constable Lui,' the ME says drily. 'I've just started my lunchbreak.'

She doesn't apologise for interrupting. 'I'm here to talk about Moon Hartnell.'

'So you said, on the phone.' He removes his sunglasses and squints at her. 'The girl's dead—surely she can wait?'

'According to that logic, you'd never have to do anything.'

'Hmm.' He looks grudgingly impressed by her point.

Gregor is rake-thin, with black hair swept over a bald spot, and as pale as the bodies he presides over. Kiara has met him several times, and still can't figure out if spending nine-to-five with the dead has given him Zen insights that have put him completely at peace with the universe ... or if he's a sociopath, caring nothing about the people he carves up.

His lunch appears to be a jam doughnut. There's no sign of a sandwich or anything else.

Kiara opens her leather notebook. 'First up, are you sure it was a suicide?'

'Not my department,' Gregor says. 'I can tell you if a victim was shot, stabbed or poisoned, but I can't determine who was holding the gun, knife or arsenic. I leave that to intelligent police officers, such as yourself.' Pleased with that little speech, he takes a bite of his doughnut.

Kiara reframes the question. 'But there's no doubt about the cause of death?'

'Moon Hartnell drowned,' Gregor says. 'I'm ninety-nine per cent sure.'

Kiara's pen pauses over her notebook. 'Drowned? She didn't bleed to death?'

'She lost a lot of blood before her heart stopped, for sure. But there was also water in her lungs. Your clever colleagues concluded that after she punctured the radial artery, the blood loss caused her to lose consciousness, then she slipped under the bathwater.'

Kiara takes a moment to imagine those last few horrible seconds of Moon's life, getting dizzier and dizzier and then ... nothing. Or perhaps she woke again when she started to drown but was too weak to sit back up. In the crime scene photos there was water all around the tub, like Moon began convulsing once she was under.

The sun vanishes behind a cloud, and Kiara shivers.

Gregor waits, apparently comfortable with the silence. The powdered sugar in his beard makes him look older, wiser.

Kiara takes a breath. 'And you'd agree with that assessment?'

'As I said, that's not my job. But it's exactly what I'd expect to see—what I've seen many times before.' He's smiling again, jam between his teeth and gums. 'Suicides often show signs of previous self-harm, and there were also some old cuts on the girl's inner thighs. None newer than a month.'

'You mentioned that you were only ninety-nine per cent sure about the cause of death.'

He scoffs. 'Only ninety-nine, you say? That's as much certainty as you get, in my line of work. In any line of work, probably.'

Kiara isn't surprised. She knows that prosecutors always try to avoid calling on Gregor as a witness. He's never willing to say that anything proves anything else for sure. Defence lawyers love him.

She moves on. 'Were there surprises when you examined the body?'

'Like what?'

She didn't want to prompt him, but he's not giving her a choice. 'Any signs of sexual activity?'

'Not immediately prior to her death—or after,' Gregor says matter-of-factly. 'Before that, it's impossible to know.

There was no trauma to the hymen, but contrary to popular belief, that doesn't prove anything one way or the other.'

Kiara knows what this man does for a living, and she knows why it's necessary. But it's a nasty shock to find herself picturing it—to imagine those sugar-encrusted fingers probing around inside a teenage girl.

She has to ask him directly. 'Moon wasn't pregnant, then?'

The ME gives her a withering look. 'I would have mentioned that, Constable. It's standard procedure to check. The betaHCG test came back negative, and there was no fluid-filled sac in the uterus. She wasn't pregnant.'

'You're a hundred per cent sure?'

He waggles a finger at her. 'Ah, very good.'

She closes her notebook as a way to draw a line under the conversation. 'Thanks for your time.'

'Surely we could have discussed that over the phone,' he complains. 'Or email. After lunch.'

They could have, but Kiara always interviews people in person. Not just so she can observe their faces, but also so she can see how closely they watch hers. In her experience, that's the clearest indication that someone is hiding something.

'That poor girl,' Gregor says unexpectedly. It's the first time he looks like you'd expect an ME to look—serious but gentle, like a movie oncologist delivering bad news.

'Yeah.' Kiara straightens her cap and turns to leave. Still two hours before she's scheduled to meet Indica Aigner—the girl who was friends with both Moon and Zach. Kiara might visit Elise's house first, see why she hasn't returned Kiara's call.

'You met the mother?' Gregor asks.

'Moon's mother?'

He nods.

'Not yet,' Kiara says. 'Why?'

'She came to the morgue to visit the body. I don't know why—it was my understanding that the girl had been identified at the scene, by her and her husband.'

'What happened?'

'You see all sorts of reactions in this job. Tears, obviously. Screaming, sometimes. Even laughter, once—a psychologist later told me that's a natural response to fear.'

'How did Stephanie Hartnell react?'

'She just stood there.' Gregor looks down at his doughnut, reading the crumbs like entrails. 'Didn't respond to anything I said for a minute, maybe two. That's not uncommon, either—but her expression was . . .' He frowns.

'Was what?'

'It's hard to describe.'

'Try.'

'There are two kinds of people,' he says. 'Those who are capable of murder, and those who are not. Doesn't matter if the weapon is a chainsaw or a phone call. It's a psychological thing. Of course, not everyone who is capable actually follows through. And not every killer is capable—the guilt crushes some of them.' He lifts his gaze to meet Kiara's. 'That girl's mother looked ready to kill somebody.'

CHAPTER 29

A sheet of cardboard covers the front window. It's one of Elise's old boxes—there's a picture of her TV.

Kiara jams her hands deep in her pockets so she won't touch anything. When arriving at a location, a police officer's first job is always to ask themselves: *Is this a crime scene or not?* In this case, it clearly is. The glass has been smashed from the outside. But it's equally clear that Kiara is too late to help.

She thinks back to Monday, when Elise called about the Barina following her. It felt like she was holding something else back. This must be it. Elise's window had been smashed, and she was too proud to report it. Or, more likely, she heard the hostility in Kiara's voice and didn't expect any sympathy. So Elise fixed it, badly, silent and alone.

'Fuck,' Kiara mutters. This is why she likes to talk in person. She should have pushed harder. Yes, she's still mad at Elise. But she cares about her, too. And more than that, Kiara is a cop. She should offer sympathy to any victim of a crime, no matter who they are.

She knocks on Elise's door. A cop knock: four quick, loud thumps.

She can hear Elise's stupid little dog skittering away to hide somewhere. Other than that, there's no sound from inside the house.

She knocks again. 'Elise? It's Kiara. You home?'

Still nothing. Elise must be out. Or . . . Kiara looks back at the smashed window.

The 'abuse' Elise claims to have endured is low-level. Harsh language and petty vandalism are predictable, if not acceptable, responses from the town she humiliated. Kiara knows all too well that if Elise wasn't white, or if more people knew she was a lesbian, the anger directed at her would have been a thousand times worse. Just the same, Kiara sometimes worries that one of Elise's detractors will someday go too far and hurt her for real.

What if Elise's body is rotting in that house right now?

Kiara rolls her patrol car further up the driveway so she can climb onto the boot and jump the fence. She circles the whole house, dodging dog shit and peering in all the other windows. Most of the curtains are closed, but there are no blowflies bouncing against the glass, which usually means no corpses.

After using a lawn chair to climb over the gate, she walks back to the broken window. She tells herself that a killer would hardly have repaired the window with Elise's cardboard before fleeing the scene. Still, she might talk to her sergeant about getting a warrant to search the premises, in case—

She senses a presence behind her, and turns. Her instincts are right. There's a man on the other side of the street.

White, heavy-set, forties, lots of ink. Without his uniform, it takes her a second to recognise him.

'Ahoy there,' she says, then wonders when she became a pirate. 'Rafa, right?'

The paramedic just nods. He doesn't cross the street.

Kiara walks towards him instead. 'You know anything about this?'

'About what?'

She points. 'The window.'

'No. Can't say I disapprove, though.'

The hair on the back of Kiara's neck rises. 'Why's that?'

Rafa just shrugs. She waits for a few seconds, but he gives nothing else away.

'Seen Elise lately?' she asks.

'Not in months.'

'Seen anybody else hanging around this street?'

'Why would I have?' He adjusts his stance, kicking a tuft of grass. 'I don't live near here.'

'What brings you here now, then?'

'I was just in the neighbourhood.'

'For work?' No ambulance, no uniform. She's hoping to catch him in an obvious lie.

'Visiting my sister.'

'Can your sister confirm that?'

'I haven't been there yet,' he says.

'Well. Piss off, then.'

Rafa smirks, then turns to walk away. He doesn't seem to have a car with him.

'Oi,' Kiara says.

He looks back.

She feels the need to defend Elise, having let her down during the phone call on Monday. 'Leave Ms Glyk alone, all right? Leave the judgement to actual judges.'

'You don't know what she did,' Rafa says.

'I do, actually.'

'No. You don't.'

He walks away without explaining what he means.

'I have to tell you that you're allowed to have a parent present,' Kiara says.

'No thanks.' Indica Aigner stirs her latte. Imagine a fifteen-year-old girl who drinks coffee, Kiara thinks. It wasn't until she joined the police force that she even tried it.

'You sure?'

Indica nods.

'Okay.' Kiara is relieved. Parents think they bring out good behaviour in their children, but in Kiara's experience, kids are more honest and mature without Mum or Dad looming over their shoulder.

The owner of the café is wiping the specials off the chalk-board. At a table in the corner, a balding man who might have Down syndrome is chatting to a woman who looks like his mother. Other than that, the café is empty. It's a private, neutral place to meet witnesses.

Kiara is trying to concentrate on the interview, but it's hard when she's worried about Elise. 'Tell me about you and Zach,' she says to Indica.

'It was just a casual thing.' The girl takes off her glasses and polishes them with the sleeve of her jumper, then puts them back on. She blinks and squints, eyes adjusting.

'How long had this casual thing been going on?'

'We hooked up at Maxie's birthday party. It was Halloween themed, even though this was, like, February. That's Maxie Elphick,' she adds. 'E-L-P-H-I-C-K.'

She waits for Kiara to write this down. Kiara doesn't. She's learned not to take unimportant notes that might obscure the truth later. When you're looking for a needle in a haystack, the last thing you want is more hay.

'I was dressed as a zombie nurse,' Indica continues. 'Zach was Iron Man, but it was a knock-off costume from the two-dollar shop, so technically he was called Metal Hero, or something. I kissed him on his mask and left a lipstick mark—there are photos.'

Kiara doesn't write any of this down, either. 'Was Moon Hartnell at this party?'

Indica pauses with the coffee halfway to her mouth. 'Dunno. Why?'

'She was a friend of yours, right?'

'I thought you were investigating Zach's disappearance.'

'Well, he and Moon knew each other, didn't they?'

'Yeah. Kinda awkward.'

'Why was that awkward?'

The girl bunches up a serviette and then slowly unfolds it. 'Well, Zach had a thing for Moon for a while. He'd written this letter, like, on paper, and written her name on it with a little heart. He wanted me to give it to her, but I told him she had a boyfriend.'

'This was before the party?'

'Ages before. December, maybe.'

Kiara notes that for Indica, two months equals ages.

'What's it like, being a cop?' Indica asks.

Kiara raises an eyebrow. 'Thinking of joining the force?'

'No. I'm going to be a singer.' Indica says this as though a fortune teller read it in her palm. Kiara wonders if she's any good.

'How did Zach react when you told him Moon was seeing somebody?'

'Oh, he was pissed off. He snatched the letter back and tore it up. He wanted me to give him the guy's name, but I said I didn't know.'

'Was that true?'

'Yeah. She told me how far she'd gone with him, all the bases, you know. But she wouldn't tell me his name. I don't think Zach believed me about that, though. He started sort of following Moon around the school, trying to work out who she was seeing.'

'That must have upset Moon,' Kiara says.

'I don't think she noticed. She was always kind of in her own head. Anyway, then her boyfriend dumped her, so it didn't matter anymore.'

'But Zach never asked her out?'

'No. He asked *me*.' Indica shoots Kiara a challenging stare. She's obviously expecting to be accused of being the runner-up. The silver medallist. She looks like she has her defence ready to go. But Kiara doesn't care for high school drama.

'How do you know Moon's boyfriend dumped her?'

'She said so.'

Indica falls silent. Kiara waits. She's learned to ride out these silences, waiting for the witness to get uncomfortable enough to add something extra.

It didn't work on Rafa, but it works on Indica. 'She had this dumb idea,' she says.

'What idea?'

'She said—I told her not to do this—she said she was going to pretend to be pregnant.'

Kiara hadn't guessed that Moon herself was the source of the rumour. 'Why would she do that?'

'*Thank* you. That's what *I* said. But Moon reckoned he'd feel guilty about dumping her if he thought she was making a baby for him.'

The phrasing chills Kiara down to her core.

'Actually, that's not quite right,' Indica says. 'She didn't just want him to feel guilty, she wanted him to be scared.'

'But the boy would catch on eventually.'

'About nine months later, yeah.' A nervous giggle. 'But Moon thought she could pretend she'd had a miscarriage, then he would never find out she'd lied.'

'Do you know if the boyfriend believed her?'

'I guess so. She called me, crying. Said he'd told her to just kill it. Even though the baby wasn't real, I think she was upset by how it didn't mean anything to him.' Indica's voice starts to wobble. 'And then she . . .'

'Was this conversation right before she died?'

'No. Ages before. Two weeks, maybe.' Indica's mascara starts to run. She doesn't seem to remember the napkin scrunched in her hand. Kiara passes her another one, and she dabs her eyes. 'Thank you.'

Kiara remembers life as a teenager, when everything seemed like a huge deal. Homework, parties, what to wear to the school formal. Actual huge deals, life or death things—pregnancies, suicides—got lost in the noise.

'When you started dating Zach,' she says, 'did you tell him what you knew about Moon's boyfriend?'

Indica hesitates. The answer is clearly yes.

'Including the pregnancy?'

'I didn't tell him it was fake,' she says defensively. 'I thought Moon's boyfriend might hear about it if I did. Her plan was dumb, but I didn't want to screw it up.' Indica sniffs, clears her throat. 'I think Moon thought, *I'll show him*. The boyfriend, I mean. Like it was less about wanting to die and more about ruining his life.' She wipes her eyes again. 'I hope it worked, the piece of shit. Whoever he was.'

Kiara can't phrase the question gently, so she softens her voice instead. 'How did Zach react to the suicide?'

'Oh my God. He didn't talk for, like, three days. I told him it wasn't his fault. How could it have been? Moon barely knew he existed—I didn't put it like that, obviously.'

Apparently Indica doesn't know about the messages Zach supposedly sent, which may have pushed Moon over the edge. 'Did he seem like he felt guilty?'

'Yeah. *He* wasn't Moon's boyfriend, though,' Indica adds quickly. 'Like I said, she was already seeing someone when Zach tried to ask her out.'

When investigating a death, the victim is like a black hole. Invisible, and unknowable. You can guess at their nature by looking at the other things in their orbit, but it's only ever a guess. This time, Kiara has two black holes, circling each other. Moon and Zach. Neither one available to speak for themselves. Their secrets trapped forever beyond the event horizon.

Indica finishes her drink and gets up to leave. Apparently she was only willing to talk for as long as the free coffee lasted. 'You'll tell me if you find Zach?' she says.

Kiara nods. 'You're sure Moon never mentioned her boyfriend's name?' she asks. 'Never told you anything about him?'

'No.' Indica shrugs. Then, with a casualness that astonishes and horrifies Kiara, she says, 'All I know is that it was one of the teachers.'

CHAPTER 30

'Fooled you,' Callum says.

Elise looks at the grid scratched into the floor. 'No, you haven't.'

'All right.' He shrugs, as if he couldn't care less. He's trying to distract her from her next move, and it's working.

At first Elise rejected the idea of passing the time with a game. They should focus on escaping. But after hours and hours of pacing the septic tank and getting nowhere, she needed the distraction to keep her from thinking about how suffocating it is down here, and how hungry Guppy must be.

Stephanie will be back sometime tomorrow. If she doesn't believe Elise about Callum's girlfriend, or about the other boy who might have been seeing Moon, then she's likely to kill them both.

Callum suggested I-spy, and Elise told him to go screw himself. She proposed the alphabet game, but he wanted something competitive. Eventually they agreed to Connect Four, because they could play it without a board or pieces, and it was slightly more interesting than noughts-and-crosses. Elise removed a wire handle from one of the toilet buckets. She uses it now to scrape a circle onto the grid on the floor.

'It's hard to draw with that,' Callum says. 'Do you have anything else sharp?'

'No.' She gives him the wire.

'Fine.' He scratches out a triangle next to her circle. 'Checkmate.'

'That's the wrong game.'

He ignores this, pointing at the grid. 'See? I can't lose. If you block me here, I'll go there and win, but if you block me there, I'll go here and win.'

Elise glares at the grid. Callum won the last two games, as well.

'Fine.' She makes a circle in one of the two spots.

He takes the other and draws a line through the four triangles to illustrate his victory. Then he starts making a new grid next to this one. 'If I win four games of Connect Four in a row, do I win some kind of meta-game?'

'I don't want to play anymore,' she says.

'Oh, come on.'

'It's getting too dark.'

He drops the wire. 'Whatever. You've always been a sore loser.'

It's true. She spent much of her childhood sulking after losing games to Callum. She always lost, because he only agreed to play games he knew he would win. There's no pithy way to say this, though, so she stays silent.

He kneels in front of the low wall that divides the tank and starts tapping his fingers atop it, like he's playing the piano. She reminds herself that it's not just her—he's also going mad down here. But it feels too intimate to watch him fantasise about being a concert pianist, or whatever he's doing. She looks down at the Connect Four grid instead.

Suddenly she sees there was another option—she didn't need to block Callum in either of the spaces he pointed to. She already had three circles in a row somewhere else, and could have made four. Would have, if he hadn't distracted her.

'You cheated,' she says.

Callum doesn't turn around. 'Huh?'

'I could have gone in this space here.' She points, but he's not looking. 'You made me think I had two options when I actually had three.'

'No, you didn't. You would have lost either way.'

'Will you just look?'

He glances at the grid, face blank. 'The game's over, Elise.'

She's seething. Does he really not see what she's talking about? Or did he know the third option was there all along?

'It's just a game, Leese,' he says.

'I could have won,' she insists.

'We can play again, if you want.'

She hates how he can sound so reasonable while still refusing to admit he did anything wrong. 'No,' she says.

He folds his arms. 'Okay.'

She retreats to her sleeping fleece and lies down. Tries to let it go. Because he's right. It *is* just a game.

Elise wakes up to the sensation of hands crawling across her body.

For a second, still with one foot in the dream, she thinks it's Kiara. They're lying together on the cold, hard floor, having not even made it to the bed, or to the shower after. Sometimes it's like that. They're too in love even to clean up the mess.

She hums and rolls over—then smells the fertiliser and the stale air. Opening her eyes, she sees Callum crouched over her.

She pushes his hands away and scrambles back. 'What the fuck?'

He says nothing, staring at her. She wonders just how crazy he's become, down here in the dark.

'I'm your sister,' she says, covering her chest with her arms. 'Jesus.'

'Where's the knife?'

She rubs her eyes with the back of her hand. 'What knife?'

His voice is menacing. 'The one she gave you.'

'We broke it, remember?'

'She didn't give you a replacement?'

'No! Why would she do that?'

He nods slowly. 'Okay. Sorry.'

'You're sorry? What's wrong with you?'

'Nothing. I guess I just had a bad dream. This place . . .' He gestures around at the concrete walls. 'It's messing with my head.'

Now Elise understands. 'You think I'm lying to you.'

'I don't think that.' It's hard to read his expression in the gloom.

'You think Stephanie gave me the same deal as before.' The dread is like quicksand, sucking her down. 'You think she told me to kill you and said she'd let me go afterwards.'

'No, I—'

'And you think this time I was actually considering it.'

'I know you wouldn't do that,' he says. 'Go back to sleep.'

She doesn't believe him, and she can tell he doesn't believe her. They glare at each other for a long moment.

'Tell me about Heidi,' Elise says finally.

'What do you want to know?' he says, after a pause.

'How long have you been seeing her?'

'Ten months. Why?'

'How old is Jason? Her son?'

'He's about to turn eight. He told me he wants a Batman Lego set for his birthday. Look, what do he and Heidi have to do with this?'

'What about her ex? What's his name?'

'Derek. I never met him. What are you getting at?'

There's a lump in Elise's throat. 'I was wondering if Heidi might help us get rescued,' she lies. 'Did you tell her you were coming here? To visit Neve, the Year Nine teacher?'

'I didn't,' Callum admits. 'I didn't want her to get jealous, hearing that I was going to visit another woman, even just to talk.'

Sounds plausible. Like everything Callum has said.

'Okay.' Elise unclenches her fists. 'It was just a thought.' She lifts up her shirt and shuffles around so he can see her back. 'No knife. Satisfied?'

'Yeah. I'm sorry.' He drags his palms down his face. 'It was one of those middle-of-the-night thoughts. You know, those worries that don't make sense, but you can't get them out of your head.'

She nods. Her heart is pounding. 'I know the ones. It's okay.'

He shuffles back over to his pile of fleeces. 'Good night, I guess.'

'Good night.' Elise lies back down. She closes her eyes but doesn't sleep.

Her own brother thought she was planning to kill him. She can't believe it.

But that's not the thought that keeps her awake. The dread isn't like quicksand anymore—it's like a chasm, and she's falling faster and faster, deeper and deeper.

Callum hesitated when she mentioned Heidi's name. Like he was about to ask, 'Who?'

And yesterday, her son's name was Jamie, not Jason.

CHAPTER 31

Elise couldn't see the crowd, but she could hear it. A roar as big as the ocean. She stood in the dark concrete tunnel under the stands, head tilted, marvelling at the sound. Dad and Callum were up there somewhere, screaming her name. Mum hadn't come—she still seemed nervous about all this, like she didn't think Elise could do it—but she would be watching on TV.

'Listen to that,' Elise whispered.

Two of the other athletes ignored her. They were staring at nothing, getting into the zone.

Narelle was leaning against the wall like a supermodel, perfect arms folded. She said, 'I try to tune it out.'

She and Elise hadn't talked much since that dinner on the lake. Elise had been trying to get her alone, but Narelle always left straight after training, surrounded by friends. She was slow to reply to texts, even on her rest days. Eventually Elise had been forced to accept that Narelle was avoiding her. She'd guessed about the butterflies in Elise's stomach—and she wanted nothing to do with them.

Heartbroken and ashamed, Elise had thrown herself into her training. Aching muscles were the kind of pain she knew how to deal with. And it was working. She'd won dozens of races now, and this was the last heat. If she placed, she was going to the Commonwealth Games.

'Why?' she asked.

'What we do takes concentration,' Narelle said. 'If you're focused on the crowd, you're not running your best race.'

'I disagree,' Elise said, for perhaps the first time in her life. 'The sound gives me energy.' It had set her vibrating, like a tuning fork. She always ran better with an audience. What was the point of all this, if not to impress people, to perform for them, to be idolised by them?

It wasn't just the crowd giving her strength. Dr Mickleham had given her an injection of red cells two days earlier. She didn't mention that. None of the women on the team ever talked about the doping, perhaps so they could convince themselves it wasn't happening.

Elise felt unstoppable. The transfusions didn't just help her run faster—they reduced her recovery time. She didn't need rest days anymore. She could train longer and harder than ever without getting tired.

This latest injection had lifted her mood, too. It made her forget all about Narelle's rejection. Gave her the confidence to say things like, *I disagree*. She had no anxiety about this race. She was going to win.

The others didn't look as confident. Their faces were drawn, eyes hollow. Elise wondered if the doses became less effective over time—then she pushed the thought away.

'Good luck,' she said.

The others didn't respond. Narelle forced a tight little smile.

A man in a windbreaker appeared at the far end of the tunnel. 'It's time,' he said.

Elise strode out of the tunnel and into the daylight, letting herself drown in the applause.

The doorbell rang, and there was a sharp knocking at the same time. The downlights clicked on automatically—a feature for hard-of-hearing guests who might sleep through the bell. Elise rolled over, getting tangled in the silk sheets. She looked through bleary eyes at the bedside clock. It was two in the morning. Who the hell could be at her door?

More ringing, more knocking. 'Just a minute,' she croaked.

She climbed out of bed and padded through the serviced apartment to the door. When she checked the peephole, her blood ran cold.

A man and a woman in white polo shirts stood outside. The man had a clipboard. The woman had a ziplock bag and was looking at a stopwatch.

Anti-doping agents.

Elise hesitated. If she didn't open the door less than two minutes after they rang the bell, there would be a mark against her record. Three strikes, and she'd be kicked off the team.

But if she let them in, and failed the test, she'd be sent home right away. Instant ban.

The man's backpack didn't look big enough to contain a rebreathing machine. The agents were probably only after a urine sample. She'd be okay.

Wide awake now, she tugged the sleeves of her pyjamas down, covering the tiny injection scab from yesterday. Then she opened the door.

The woman spoke first. She was in her forties and short, with spiky hair and an engagement ring. 'Hi, Elise. Can we come in?'

'Are you serious?' Elise's voice shook, but she tried to make it sound like anger rather than fear. 'The Games start on Saturday. I need a full night's sleep, to prepare.'

'Sorry for the inconvenience. Can we come in?'

If Elise said no, that was a fail. 'Make it quick,' she said.

The agents entered the apartment. The man flicked on some more lights, looking around at the sparse furnishings. 'You're alone?'

'Yes. Can we just do this?' She faked a yawn. Neither of the agents yawned in response. It was like they were aliens.

'This is a random test,' the woman said. 'You know how it works?'

'Yeah.' Elise had done these before. But not lately. Not since she'd started visiting Dr Mickleham.

The woman opened the ziplock bag and pulled out a sample cup. 'Are you ready?'

Elise had gone to the toilet just two hours earlier. But if she said no, the agents would just sit there on her couch for however long it took.

'Can I drink some water?' she asked.

'Sure.'

The agents followed her into the kitchenette, unwilling to let her out of their sight. Neither of them said anything as she filled a tumbler with water and gulped it down.

'You guys don't do small talk, huh?'

The woman didn't smile. 'Are you ready?'

'Yep.' Elise thought she could force it.

The man sat right on the edge of the couch, as though he'd never seen one before and wasn't quite sure how it worked. The woman went with Elise into the bathroom, closed the door and held out the sample cup.

Elise took it. She told herself there was nothing to worry about. Her blood would have suspiciously high levels of oxygen, but her urine should be fine.

She waited for the woman to turn away, then remembered she wasn't going to. Grimacing, Elise pulled down her pyjama pants and undies and sat on the toilet, holding the cup in the porcelain bowl. The woman stared right at her, making sure she wasn't squeezing someone else's piss out of a hidden pouch somewhere.

Not that there was anything to see. An expectant silence filled the bathroom.

For the first time, Elise saw a glimmer of sympathy in the woman's expression. 'Not ready yet?'

It was hard enough, peeing with someone watching. Harder still with a mostly empty bladder, and with the fear that she was wrong, that the urine would somehow show what she'd done. 'Just give me a sec.'

'It needs to be a testable amount. Might be better off waiting.'

'Hang on.' Finally Elise got a trickle going. She clenched and managed to fill the whole cup. Her hands shook as she screwed the cap on, nearly spilling it all.

'You right?' The sympathy was gone from the woman's expression now. She looked suspicious. Elise guessed she had met plenty of cheats in her career—that she knew guilt when she saw it.

'I'm fine.' Elise held out the cup with both hands, as though it was a bribe. *Please accept this.*

The woman took it with latex-gloved fingers and put it in the ziplock bag. 'Do you have anything to tell me?'

Elise held her gaze. Told herself that a urine sample wouldn't—couldn't—give her away.

'I just want to go back to bed,' she said. 'Are we done here?'

It wasn't until she closed the front door, locking the agents out, that she collapsed to the floor, shivering. Her stomach churned. She held down the vomit with pure will-power. If she let her digestive system shift into reverse gear, it would take almost a full day to get back to her peak. And she had to be at training in four hours.

She wanted a transfusion, to smooth out her jitters and clear her head. But it was way too soon. The doctor had said she couldn't take them too close together. Her heart wouldn't be able to handle it, especially since she had a family history of heart disease.

Elise wondered if this whole thing scared the other girls as much as it did her. She crawled to the bed, lay facedown and screamed into the pillow.

CHAPTER 32

The hatch opens, and the light blinds Elise. She snorts awake. 'Fnyah?'

'Up you get,' says a stern voice from above. Stephanie.

Elise can't believe she got any sleep at all. She remembers lying awake for hours, her dark thoughts trapped in a loop.

If Heidi and Jason aren't real, then what else has Callum lied about? He told her he was abducted from a car park, then changed his story and said he came here to help a fellow teacher, without even looking up her profile first. He seemed devastated by Moon's death, but claimed he'd hardly known her. It all sounded true at the time, but now none of it does.

What if Stephanie is right? What if Callum raped a fifteen-year-old girl?

Stephanie calls down, 'Just you, Tina.'

Callum is crouched behind the low wall, like a soldier afraid of going over the top. Elise makes a calming gesture at him, then says, 'I'm coming.'

Still waking up, she mentally walks through the routine of going out—*need my keys, my wallet, my phone, my glasses, gotta brush my teeth, make a cup of coffee for the road.* Then she realises she doesn't have any of those things. The fact she reached for them means that, subconsciously, this place is becoming her home.

She goes to splash some water on her eyes, then remembers that water is precious down here. Instead she slaps herself in the face, like a man applying aftershave, and climbs the ladder.

Stephanie looks as clean and well rested as Elise is exhausted. Her clothes are pressed, her hair has been washed, and her eyes are bright. It's as if she's Dorian Grey, and Elise is the portrait in the attic.

Stephanie closes the hatch. 'Come,' she says, like she's speaking to a dog.

Elise feels a fresh stab of fear for Guppy, trapped in her house, and surely out of food and water by now. 'Can you feed my dog?' she says suddenly.

Stephanie looks confused and annoyed. 'What?'

'My dog. He has no food or water. I'm worried about him.' Going to the house might lead Stephanie to Elise's real name. But it's worth the risk, especially now that Elise's plan has imploded. She can't prove Callum's innocence if he's not innocent.

'You're trying to trick me,' Stephanie says. 'You have a security camera, or—'

'There's nothing like that, I swear.'

The woman turns away. 'The sooner you do your job, the sooner you can go back to your dog. Do you have any proof yet?'

Elise follows her through the garden. 'Please. He must be so thirsty.'

'So that's a no?'

Elise grits her teeth. It makes sense that a sheep farmer would have learned not to be sentimental about animals, but most people care about dogs.

'No proof?' Stephanie prompts.

'It hasn't been forty-eight hours yet.'

'True, but I thought you would have made *some* progress.'

When they reach the back veranda, Elise sees a steaming teapot and two cups in saucers set up on the little glass-topped table. Apparently they're meeting outside today.

Stephanie eases herself down into a rocking chair and pours the tea. 'Tell me where you're up to.'

Elise sits on the edge of a nearby bench seat and picks up a teacup, grateful for the warmth. 'I've questioned him,' she says, trying to sound like a PI.

'And?'

'So far, I've found out that Callum had a girlfriend named Heidi, with an eight-year-old son. She was going through a trial separation from a man named Derek. Not sure if he's the boy's father. No last names yet.' Elise says all this as though it's established fact. As though she hasn't spent all night counting the holes in this story.

'So what?'

'Callum and Heidi were trying to keep the affair on the down low, because of Derek and the kid. The secrecy around the relationship could have led to the rumour about Moon.'

Stephanie's expression darkens. 'It wasn't just a rumour.'

'Moon was definitely seeing someone,' Elise says quickly. 'But it may not have been Callum. It seems more likely to have been one of the boys in the year above hers.' She stops herself from mentioning the other Callum by name. It's unfair to put him in danger, now that she knows her brother is the guilty one.

Then she wonders if the other Callum exists at all. Her brother could have made him up, too.

There's a long pause. Then Stephanie hurls her teacup at the wall of the house. The fine china bursts apart against the bricks. 'You were supposed to prove he's guilty,' she snaps. 'It sounds like you're trying to exonerate him.'

'I'm trying to find the truth.' Elise stalls with a sip from her own cup. 'If all you want is a coerced confession from an innocent man, then you can get that without my help.'

Stephanie licks her bared teeth, like a nervous dingo.

'Except you can't, can you?' Elise holds Stephanie's gaze. 'You've imprisoned him, starved him and tortured him, and still he's sticking to his story. In my experience, guilty men don't do that. In fact, the opposite is true—people often admit to things they haven't done.'

She has no experience. But the statement sounds true, and it catches in her mind. Why hasn't Callum tried begging for mercy?

'He drove here thinking he'd find a helpless teenage girl,' Stephanie growls.

'Did you specify the girl's age?' Elise prays that Callum thought through this part of his story, even if it's a lie. 'He claims he was coming to visit the teacher of a Year Nine class, who was struggling to explain anatomy to her students.'

'I filled the fake profile with pictures of—'

'Pictures Callum may not have seen. We don't know if he looked at the profile, and he may only have skimmed the messages.' She stresses the *we*, still trying to pretend to be on the same side as the dangerous woman.

Stephanie clenches her jaw. 'If this is the best you can do, I don't know how you make a living as an investigator.'

'I'm trapped here.' Elise finds herself oddly defensive about her fictitious career. 'But you're not. You can track down this girlfriend, see if that part of his story holds up.'

'It's bullshit.'

'I'm not saying he's innocent. I'm saying we have no strong evidence either way. If you want proof, you're not going to get it by torturing him. You have to actually get out there and look.'

Elise holds her breath. It will take Stephanie at least a few days to track down every Heidi in Warrigal and work out that none of them has an ex called Derek or a son named Jamie. But then what?

'Fine,' Stephanie says at last. 'I'll do some digging. But keep pushing him. I'm ninety-nine per cent sure Callum is guilty. I'm sure you can trick him into confessing, if you try.'

'You have my word,' Elise lies.

As they walk back towards the septic tank, the words keep echoing through her mind.

Ninety-nine per cent.

Not a hundred anymore. She's making progress. But can she really convince Stephanie that Callum is innocent, when she's no longer sure of it herself?

Stephanie unlocks the hatch and heaves it open. 'I'll be back tomorrow,' she says darkly.

Elise climbs down into the hole.

CHAPTER 33

Callum has dragged the fleeces and buckets to the edges of the room, and swept away some of the empty cereal boxes and bottles. He's shivering, pale and gaunt. Hollow around the eyes. It reminds Elise of that time he got food poisoning at a party and vomited all night. He promised Mum and Dad that he hadn't been drinking—he'd just eaten a pizza that got left out in the sun. They believed him. Elise did too. Even after she smelled the vodka on his clothes, she assumed someone must have spilled something on him. Because he didn't drink, and he wouldn't lie to her, would he?

Throughout Elise's life, whenever she saw evidence that Callum had done anything wrong, she always ran from it. But down here, there's nowhere to go.

Elise steps off the bottom rung to the concrete floor, and sinks to her knees. Stephanie slams the hatch shut. Her footsteps crunch away.

'Where's she going?' Callum asks.

'Huh?'

'She said she's coming back tomorrow. Where's she going?'

Elise can't even look at him. 'To get some more clues about what you did.'

'I didn't do it.'

'You told me that already.'

Her brother is silent for a long moment. Almost long enough for her to forget he's there.

Maybe he's not. Maybe the brother she thought she knew never existed.

She braces one foot against the low wall, stretching. 'I've put some doubt in Stephanie's mind. She's looking for Heidi. But when she finds out there's no such person, I don't know what she'll do.'

Callum opens his mouth, then closes it.

'What?' Elise stands up. 'You have something to say? Another excuse? Some plausible reason that she'll find nothing? Here, let me help you. Maybe Heidi told you she was about to move to another town with her son, Jason. Or was it Jamie?'

'Leesy—' Callum begins.

Elise lunges at him. The movement catches them both by surprise. Callum doesn't get his arms up in time, and suddenly Elise's hands are around his throat, squeezing. His eyes bug out. He makes a choked gurgling sound as he squirms.

'How could you?' she screams. 'How could you?'

Mum shouted the same thing at Elise after she was sent home from the Games. Saying the words brings the moment back—the heat of the front porch, the sick hollow in her belly, her inability to look up from her scuffed runners.

The shame of what she'd done, the fear of what might come next.

Callum probably shares those feelings now. Elise releases his neck and shoves him away. Then she scrambles backwards to the ladder, as far from him as she can get.

She's never felt so horribly alone. Everyone else has given up on her. Her friends, her co-workers, her girlfriend, her father. The only person who stuck by her was her brother. And he's . . . he's a . . .

'I'm sorry,' Callum says.

An admission, at last. Elise hadn't realised that part of her still believed him until she felt her heart break.

'You're sorry.' She slowly rolls onto her side, the cold cement against her ribs, and closes her eyes. The air in her lungs dries up. She can't find a reason to take another breath. What if she chooses not to? Can you die by choosing not to breathe?

Apparently not. The air seeps back in, somehow.

'Stephanie's going to kill us,' Elise whispers. 'Why the fuck didn't you tell me the truth?'

'I . . . I couldn't.' His voice wobbles. 'I'd been down here alone for so long. I thought that if you knew, you'd hate me. I couldn't take it.'

He's right. She does hate him. 'That girl was fifteen, Cal.'

'I know.'

'And she died.'

'I know.'

The silence is suffocating.

'I loved her.' His voice is thick with tears. 'But I told her I didn't, because I knew we couldn't be together. It was wrong, for so many reasons. I thought, she's young.

221

She'll get over it. And then she . . .' He swallows. 'I couldn't even grieve for her. Not properly. I couldn't tell anyone how much she meant to me.'

Elise squeezes her eyes shut and plugs her ears with her fingers. She doesn't want to hear anything that might tempt her to forgive him. What he's done is unforgivable.

The silence inside her head is deafening. She stares at the back of her closed eyelids for God knows how long.

She wishes Kiara were here—or rather, wishes she were wherever Kiara is. Elise would give anything. She would cling to Kiara and never let her go. *You're the best person I ever knew*, she thinks. *Please, take me back.*

When she eventually removes her fingers from her ears, Callum has stopped talking. She turns to look at him. He's sitting on the low wall, watching her.

'What?' she says.

'Are you going to kill me?'

She lets out a laugh that's more like a cough. 'That's still your theory? That I made a deal?'

'You strangled me a minute ago,' he points out.

'Yeah.' She refuses to apologise.

'That's why she said she'd be back tomorrow, right? To check that I was dead.'

'Not this time. I told you: she wants me to prove your guilt, so *she* can kill you.'

'Oh. Yay.' He still doesn't look like he believes her. He's a dirtbag, like the bundle of fertiliser next to his feet. She finds herself glaring at it, surprised the rage in her eyes doesn't set it alight. She'd welcome that. The blaze would consume them both, along with anything else not made of concrete or wool—

'Leesy,' Callum begins.

'Shut up.' She chews her lip.

'I don't—'

'Shut up! I'm thinking.' She picks up one of the empty cereal boxes and takes it over to the ladder. Puts it on a rung and leans it against the wall.

'What are you doing?'

Ignoring him, she looks from the box to the hatch to the fertiliser, then back to the box. She drums her fingertips on the sides of the ladder, considering her plan from every angle. There are weaknesses, but she's sure she can overcome them.

'I have an idea,' she says finally.

'What kind of idea?'

'A way to get us out of here.'

Callum's mouth falls open. 'Really?'

'Yeah. But after that, I don't have a brother, and you don't have a sister. Got that? We're done.'

He swallows. 'I said I was sorry.'

'I don't care.'

Apologies have always come easily to him. When they were kids, he discovered that 'sorry' was the magic word, the one that always got him out of trouble. Whereas Elise would always rather take the punishment than admit she was wrong.

'Deal,' he says, after only a second of hesitation.

She's almost offended. 'I wasn't offering,' she says, and starts searching the septic tank for something made of metal.

CHAPTER 34

They turn the septic tank upside down. They still have the wire from the game of Connect Four, but it won't work—they scraped it against the concrete plenty of times without creating a spark.

'What's the plan, exactly?' Callum asks.

She's still pissed off at him. 'Zip it.'

There are no surprises. She finds only the things she knew were there—the bike helmet, cereal boxes, basket of toiletries, water bottles, fleeces, buckets, bags of fertiliser. Nothing metal.

Eventually she needs to pee and drags one of the buckets back into the corner. As she squats over it, she finds herself looking up at the ceiling—at the bracket, the one holding up the PVC pipe that goes nowhere. There's a rusted bolt at each end.

She pulls up her pants and approaches the bracket. She can't prise it off the ceiling with her nails, so she picks up the wire from before, wedges one end between the bracket and the ceiling, and pushes until the tip emerges on the other side.

'Grab that,' she tells Callum.

He doesn't ask why. He takes one end of the wire, and Elise holds the other.

'Pull on three,' she says.

'*On* three? Or one, two, three, pull?'

'I meant what I said,' she snaps. 'One, two, *three*.'

They yank the wire downwards. The rusty bolts creak but don't break.

Elise twists her end of the wire around her fist for a better grip. 'Try again.'

The second time, one of the bolts comes free, bouncing off Callum's skull and jingling away into the corner. She hopes the impact was painful.

With one side of the bracket detached, she has enough leverage to pop out the other bolt. The pipe falls and cracks, but she ignores it. All she needs is the bracket in her hands. It's about thirty centimetres long, three wide, half a centimetre thick. Straight at both ends, with a semicircular bend in the middle to make room for the pipe. Lighter than she expected.

Callum is keeping very still. Elise realises that the bracket might make an effective club against an unarmed man, although it's no match for Stephanie's rifles.

Ignoring his discomfort—maybe even enjoying it a little bit—Elise goes over to the wall. She scrapes one end of the bracket against the concrete. No spark. She tries again, faster. Nothing.

As she keeps scratching, he says, 'Careful. You might set fire to the fertiliser.'

'Not at this rate,' she grumbles.

'You *want* to do that? Are you crazy?'

She's still scraping. The corner of the bracket starts to wear away, leaving pale marks on the wall, like chalk.

'Stephanie said the fertiliser is very flammable,' Elise mutters. 'If we put some into one of those cereal boxes, we could make a small bomb.'

He looks even more alarmed. 'Your plan is to blow us up?!'

'Not us. The hatch. It's just plastic.' *Scrape, scrape.* The end of the bracket is slowly sharpening to a point. 'We can prop the box against the top rung of the ladder, set fire to the cardboard and stand back. Hopefully the heat will melt a hole right through it.'

'If it's hot enough to melt plastic, it's hot enough to kill us both.'

'Like I said, we'll stand back. And those wool fleeces won't burn. We can use them like fire blankets. But we need—' *Scrape.*

'A—' *Scrape.*

'Fucking—' *Scrape.*

'Spark!'

She throws the bracket down. It clatters to the floor.

Callum keeps an eye on it, like it's a hibernating snake.

'Must be the wrong kind of metal.' She's breathing hard. 'We need copper or something else that conducts.'

'The opposite, I think,' he says. 'Sparks are molten metal. If the metal conducts the heat, it *won't* melt. You want a metal with low thermal conductivity.'

Elise stares at him. 'I thought you were a PE teacher.'

'I'm a PE teacher who watched *Breaking Bad*.'

She notices his belt buckle. 'What kind of metal is that?'

He looks down. 'Dunno.'

'Give it.'

Uneasily, he starts taking off the belt. She gets a horrid mental image of him undressing for Moon. She can't shake it off.

'Why were the drugs in your house?' she asks.

'Stephanie planted them, remember?'

'She planted the GHB. What about the ecstasy?'

'Oh.' He looks uncomfortable. 'Moon got that from a friend—or, she said she did. She wanted us to try it together. I said no.'

'Why was it still there?'

'I wouldn't let her take it back home. But I wasn't sure how to get rid of it safely.'

'How responsible of you.'

He hands over his belt without replying.

Elise hefts the buckle. It's light. 'Maybe aluminium or titanium. Are they conductive?'

'There weren't any episodes about that.'

She scrapes it against the wall. Nothing. She tries again, faster. Still nothing—but the buckle is getting warm. If sparks are molten metal, then heat must be a good sign.

On her third try, she sees a flicker. Like a glint of phosphorescence. Perhaps a proto-spark.

'I think we might be in business,' she says.

CHAPTER 35

The house is low and wide, the roof cutting a razor line across the horizon. Big windows, probably double-glazed to handle the weather. Summer gets up to forty-five out here. Winters can be fifty degrees colder. Double-brick walls, a whopper of an air conditioner tucked around one side. Someone paid good money for this place.

Most cases have a financial angle, and Kiara wishes she could find one here. But this is shaping up to be something far yuckier. The sort of case that nudges cops towards therapists, alcohol and early retirement.

She parks her patrol car next to the white Holden Barina that Elise told her about. Elise still hasn't called back. Kiara is telling herself it's just because she's too proud, too defiant. Kiara remembers that night six weeks ago, waking up, rolling over to put her arm around Elise, feeling vaguely like they might have sex. But her arm fell flat on the mattress. Elise was gone.

If Kiara had just stayed in bed, she and Elise would probably still be together. But her cop brain wouldn't let her. She knew that Elise always got up at midnight—you could set your watch by her bladder—but it was now after two. She noticed that the mattress was cool, so Elise had been gone for a while, too long for a quick trip to the toilet.

So Kiara got out of bed and crept around the corner to see Elise on the couch, her face illuminated by Kiara's laptop. The one Kiara wasn't supposed to take home, but often did. The one she shouldn't have written down the password for, but had.

They'd made eye contact. That long moment of silence, the sound of Elise not apologising—Kiara can still hear it.

Despite all this, she's spent the drive to Stephanie Hartnell's property muttering, *Please, Elise, please be okay.*

Kiara prods the doorbell, listens to the echoes. The curtains twitch. But there's a long pause before a figure appears behind the frosted glass door.

It opens part way. 'Officer,' Stephanie says, peering through the gap.

'Mrs Hartnell?' Kiara says, but it's not really a question. She recognises the woman from a photo in the newspaper. Stephanie looks thinner now, her grey hair tangled. A purple bruise stains the bridge of her nose.

'That's right.' Stephanie doesn't invite her in.

'I'm Senior Constable Kiara Lui. I'm sorry to intrude— I was hoping I could ask you some questions about your daughter.'

Still Stephanie hesitates.

'Are you alone? I can come back later, if—'

'It's okay. Come in.' Stephanie opens the door all the way, and Kiara enters the house.

The living room has a large, faded rug and floor-length curtains with patterned pelmets, the cords hanging loose, the edges frayed. Stephanie is looking around anxiously, as though the old furniture might somehow make Kiara suspicious.

They both see the roll of duct tape on the table at the same moment.

'I had a fall and landed on one of my solar lights.' Stephanie gestures at her injured nose. 'I was about to fix it.'

'This happened just now?' The bruise looks a couple of days old.

'Yesterday. Can I get you a cup of tea? Coffee?'

'No, thank you.' Kiara takes off her hat, then realises this makes it seem like she's here to inform Stephanie of a death, so she puts it back on. 'I'm investigating the disappearance of a boy in Moon's class. His name is Zach Locat.'

'I see,' Stephanie says, her expression unreadable.

'Did Moon ever mention him to you?'

'No. At least, I don't think so.'

'Are you sure? Another student said they were friends.'

'I knew all Moon's friends.' Stephanie's voice is firm. 'And I didn't know Zach.'

'Hmm.' Kiara takes in the pictures on the walls. 'Perhaps I could ask your husband?'

'Perhaps you could. But he doesn't live here anymore.'

'Ah. I'm sorry.'

Stephanie bows her head slightly. It's strange that she hasn't asked for more details about the disappearance, or expressed concern. Kiara gets the feeling that nothing she's said so far has surprised Stephanie.

'I wish I could be of more help,' the woman says, moving to herd Kiara back towards the door.

She stands her ground. 'Do you know Indica Aigner?'

'Not well. She visited my old house from time to time. I suppose I was fairly friendly with her mother, Olive. But we've lost touch.'

'How about William Yu?'

'No, I'm sorry.'

Now that she's seen actual ignorance on Stephanie's face, Kiara is sure she lied about not knowing Zach.

'Are you sure you haven't heard anything?' Kiara asks. 'Zach's been missing for almost two months. His parents are very worried.'

'What are they like?' Stephanie asks. 'The parents.'

It's an unexpected question. Kiara remembers the couple, hovering in the kitchen of a big, bright house that resembled an art gallery, their faces twisted by pre-emptive grief.

She clears her throat. 'I never meet people on their best day. I don't really know what they're like—just that they miss their son.'

She hoped Stephanie would empathise with this, but instead the woman seems annoyed. 'Oh, do they?'

'I'm sorry. I know you lost your daughter, too.'

Stephanie's mouth pinches in a silent expression of righteous anger. She reminds Kiara of a man she arrested last year—he'd bashed a gay couple after following them home. In the back of the paddy wagon, his face still bleeding from the asphalt, he just sneered at her, like he could tell. And like he was sure others would finish what he had started.

A clock ticks somewhere.

Stephanie folds her arms. 'If this boy vanished months ago, why are you asking me now?'

'A witness has recently come forward,' Kiara says carefully. 'Their statement suggests that Zach and Moon had exchanged messages shortly before her death.'

Stephanie doesn't ask what was in the messages. 'Well, I wish you could talk to Moon about that,' she says instead. 'But you're about five months too late.'

Kiara flinches. 'How about Callum Glyk?'

Something flashes across Stephanie's face, too quick to identify. 'The drug addict?'

'The physical education teacher.'

'Yes. But you found ecstasy in his house, didn't you?'

'Not me personally. How did you hear about that?'

'It's a very small town.'

She's right. But she doesn't seem very connected to Warrigal anymore. It's hard to guess where she might have picked up that bit of gossip, now she's a recluse.

'What about him?' Stephanie asks.

'He would have known both Moon and Zach,' Kiara says. 'And he's missing.'

Again, Stephanie doesn't seem surprised. 'Well, if the police found drugs in his house, it wouldn't make much sense to stick around, would it?'

'Did you ever meet him?'

'Can't recall.'

'Did you see any signs that Moon was pregnant?'

The question gets the desired result. Stephanie's guardedness disappears, replaced by horror. 'What?'

'I heard a rumour from someone at her school. One of her friends says it wasn't true, and the ME's report is consistent with that. But I'd like to know for sure.'

Stephanie clamps down on her bottom lip, holding something in.

'Did you see any evidence that Moon terminated a pregnancy, sometime in the past year?' Kiara prompts.

'No. I—' Stephanie's eyes well up.

'If she did, do you have any idea who the father might have been?'

Stephanie just shakes her head. Her face has crumpled. Her shoulders are trembling.

'Are you sure?' Kiara mentioned Callum only seconds ago. The bridge is obvious, but Stephanie doesn't step across it.

'My poor baby.' She can hardly get the words out.

Police officers are allowed to pat someone down or wrestle them to the ground, but they're not supposed to hug people. Feeling guilty for causing Stephanie's anguish, Kiara hugs her anyway. Stephanie's whole body slackens.

'She must have been so scared.' She lets out a sob.

'I know. It's okay.' Kiara pats her back and releases her. 'How about I make you a cup of tea?'

Stephanie draws herself upright. She wipes her eyes on her sleeve and takes a deep breath. 'No, it's all right.'

'Are you sure? I—'

'Thank you, but I have . . . a telehealth appointment. In ten minutes. I need to get my documents ready. It's hard to reschedule those.'

The hug took only a few seconds, but it feels like they've been through something together.

Kiara takes a card out of her wallet. 'Look, this is me. My mobile and email. And this . . .' She quickly scribbles another number on the back of the card. 'That's for anonymous tips. The identity of the caller isn't recorded. You understand?'

Stephanie accepts the card reluctantly. 'I really don't know anything.'

'Well, it's there if something jogs your memory. Thanks for your time.'

It's not until Kiara steps back into the sunshine that she realises how dark it was in Stephanie's house, how cold. She takes a deep breath, as though emerging from a swimming pool.

There are no solar lights out here, broken or otherwise. They must be around the back.

Kiara walks towards her car but stops when she reaches the Barina. 'I almost forgot.' She turns around just as Stephanie is about to close the door. 'Do you know Elise Glyk?'

Stephanie looks quizzical. 'Who?'

'Callum Glyk's sister,' Kiara says. 'Elise.'

'Elise Glyk,' Stephanie says slowly. 'Wait. The sprinter, right? Banned for using performance-enhancing drugs?'

Elise was a hurdler, and the ban was for illegal blood transfusions, but Kiara doesn't correct her. She's suddenly very tired. 'That's her. Sometimes people around town give her a hard time, because of what happened at the Commonwealth Games.' Kiara gives Stephanie a stern look. She thinks of this as her *I'll be watching you* look.

'I didn't recognise her,' Stephanie says, with an air of wonder. 'She's changed her hair since she was on the news. It's red now. And she has tattoos.'

The woman looks truly astonished. Retrospectively star-struck, Kiara supposes. 'So you've seen her? How long ago?'

'I thought she looked familiar, but couldn't place her.' Stephanie rests her hand on the door. 'She drove past me in an old Suzuki, on the highway. She looked like she was on her way out of town.'

'When was this?' Kiara presses.

Stephanie thinks about it. 'Tuesday? Maybe?'

Elise called Kiara about the Barina on Monday after-noon. So either Stephanie is wrong about the day, or they crossed paths twice. Stephanie, lacking Elise's paranoia, may not have noticed the first meeting.

'Well,' Kiara says, 'if you see her again, leave her alone, okay? She likes her privacy.'

'I will, Officer,' Stephanie says. 'Good day.'

'Thanks for your time.' Kiara walks back to the patrol car and gets in. As she rolls down the driveway, she checks her mirror and sees Stephanie still standing in the doorway, watching.

CHAPTER 36

'There!' A spark flashes in the dark. But it winks out as soon as it lands on the cardboard flap, just like the last seven sparks did.

Elise is exhausted, balancing on the ladder, one hand braced against the ceiling as the other scrapes endlessly with Callum's belt buckle. She's starting to think this was a stupid idea. But she refuses to stop until she has a better one.

When she was nine, she went on a camping trip at the coast. On the first night, while she and Callum raced around the campground on their bikes, Dad was scrunching up balls of newspaper and balancing kindling carefully on top of them. He had a couple of logs ready to throw on the fire once it got hot enough.

He didn't need the logs. The newspapers dissolved into clumps of ash without ever seeming to burn, and the sticks were barely charred. After an hour or so, Mum offered to help, and someone in a neighbouring tent snickered. That was when Dad lost it. Enraged and humiliated—imagine a *man* who needs help from his *wife* to start a fire—he grabbed Elise by the back of her shirt as she whizzed past, pulling her off her bike, and announced they were all going home.

Elise whined the whole way back. She hadn't even tried on her new swimmers. But now she understands her father's fury. All the ingredients are here—heat, oxygen, fuel. Yet the only thing burning is her muscles, particularly her arms.

Callum is dragging fertiliser bags away from the other end of the tank, since the plan is to take cover over there once the fire starts. 'Any luck?' he asks, for what must be the fiftieth time.

Scrape, scrape, scrape. 'You want to try?'

'Not especially.'

'Well, shut up then.'

In Warrigal, fire is the enemy. Everyone is always watching the horizon and sniffing the air. Any sign of smoke, and they all rush home to switch on their sprinklers and pack their bags. There's a satellite monitoring system designed to detect fires and predict their movement. Elise has been warned over and over how easy it is to start a fire, even accidentally. It's infuriating, not being able to make one on purpose. *Scrape, scrape, scrape.* Much of the buckle has worn away. There's metal dust all over her clothes.

The cereal box is balanced on the top rung of the ladder, packed with fertiliser. It certainly smells flammable. The stench, blended with body odour and the smell of the toilet buckets, is giving her a hell of a headache. Maybe they don't even need to start a fire. Maybe next time Stephanie opens the hatch, the stink might kill her stone dead.

Out of the corner of her eye, Elise sees Callum edging away from her, like he thinks the bomb might go off early.

'What?' *Scrape. Scrape. Scrape.*

'Nothing,' he says.

'*What?*'

'Remember that trip to Jervis Bay?'

She snorts. 'I was just thinking about that.'

'I was so mad at Mum. She always hated camping, and I thought she'd pissed Dad off on purpose.'

Typical of Callum, to blame Mum for Dad's crabbiness. Callum usually sided with Dad, and vice versa. But this is an empty story, like he's trying to distract Elise. She glances over and sees that he wasn't edging away from her—he was edging towards the bracket on the floor. Sharp at one end, easy to grip at the other.

He must still think she's considering killing him. Maybe he's going to hide the weapon from her.

'What are you doing?' she asks.

He starts. 'What do you mean?'

'With that bracket.'

'Oh. I thought I'd try it against the wall. Make a spark that way. I might be able to use more force than you.'

'I doubt that.' She's a former athlete, and he's been starved half to death.

'Worth a shot, isn't it?' He sounds innocent. Just like he did when he claimed he didn't have sex with Moon.

'If you think you're stronger, you can use the belt instead.' Elise climbs down the ladder and gives Callum his belt back.

He hesitates.

'Go on,' she says.

Reluctantly, he climbs the ladder. Elise can feel him observing her from the corner of his eye. She makes no move towards the bracket. She wonders where he was planning to hide it—the room is so small and bare.

He scrapes the belt against the concrete. He looks surprisingly strong, even after what he's been through. No sparks, though.

As she watches, a dark thought strikes her. Maybe Callum wasn't planning to hide the bracket at all.

The kind of man who rapes a fifteen-year-old is surely capable of other things. If Callum still thinks she's planning to kill him . . .

. . . he might decide to kill her first.

CHAPTER 37

Elise cleared the last hurdle and hit the ribbon. There had never been a ribbon at any other race—just cameras and lasers. She had expected the paper to provide some resistance, to tug at her belly, but it slithered away immediately to be trampled by the runners behind her.

Behind her, all of them. She had won. She had won!

As she slowed to a canter, Elise raised a wobbly arm to wave at the twenty thousand people in the stands. She looked for her parents and brother, but couldn't see them. They had VIP seats, somewhere near the top. All three of them.

'I want to be there, just in case,' Mum had said.

'In case what?' Elise had asked.

'You know, just . . . just in case.'

At the time, Elise had thought she meant, *Just in case you get injured, or die*. But now she realised Mum had meant, *Just in case you win*.

And she had! She felt superhuman. Invincible. She was the fastest woman in Australia. The fastest in all the Commonwealth nations. She could do anything.

As she beamed up into the floodlights, strangers hurried towards her. Paramedics. Photographers. Mystery people with laser pointers and tape measures. A small man in a black T-shirt patted her back and said something. She understood all the individual words but didn't attach any meaning to them.

I won, she thought again, with a kind of wonder. It was like discovering that the world rotated the other way, or learning that she was part of the Royal Family.

The other runners had all passed the finish line. Narelle, then a Jamaican woman, then five other people whose names no one would ever know because they hadn't won medals. Narelle was bent over and puffing, but Elise wasn't even tired. Victory held her upright.

Some of the runners avoided Elise's gaze. Others forced congratulatory smiles at her. She stared back at them in wonderment.

The man in the black T-shirt was still talking. He had shadows under his eyes, and a bald spot so shiny he must have polished it. 'Follow me, please,' he said.

Elise nodded but didn't go with him.

'Come on.' This time he held her upper arm. She let him take her away from the track, towards the opening under the stands. Narelle was watching. The others looked beaten, but Narelle just looked tense.

Elise smiled at her as she was led away. Narelle didn't smile back.

'Elise!' someone yelled from above. She thought it might have been Callum, but when she looked up, it was just a fan—a teenage boy with a bum-fluff beard giving her two vigorous thumbs up. She gave him a wave.

In the distance, her coach was arguing with a woman from the Games Committee. He was red in the face, pointing a finger at her chest. The woman stood her ground, jaw clenched. Elise couldn't hear what they were saying.

She called out, 'Coach! I did it!'

He looked shocked rather than happy for her. But before she could even register the strangeness of his reaction, she was led away into the darkness of the concrete tunnel under the stands.

As they walked, the man in the black shirt said, 'As you can imagine, we have to take all allegations seriously.'

'Mm-hm,' Elise said, still only half listening. This wasn't just a gold medal—it could be a world record. She might go to the Olympics next. Mum and Dad would be so relieved that all the time and money they'd put in hadn't gone to waste. What would she say in the interviews? She must remember to thank everybody. *I gave 110 per cent, but so did my family, and ...*

The man pushed open a heavy fire door, revealing a windowless room with a steel table, two chairs and a single light bulb. It looked like the sort of place where spies were interrogated. It didn't look like the sort of place where officials handed out medals.

Two middle-aged men with green polo shirts and lanyards—they could have been clones—hovered in the corner. They'd been having a hushed conversation, but they stopped when they saw Elise. There was also a woman Elise recognised as a logistics coordinator for the Australian team. She was on the phone but didn't seem to be doing any talking, just listening.

Unease finally penetrated the fog of triumph. 'What is this?' Elise asked.

'Sit down,' the small man in the black shirt said. Elise finally took note of his name tag: *O'Toole*.

She found herself craving a transfusion. Not for her muscles—for her nerves. She wanted that feeling of invulnerability. 'Why?'

'Sorry to blindside you. But it's important that we clear this up immediately.'

One of the clones was setting up some kind of device on the table. A plastic cube dotted with switches and dials was connected by rubber tubes to a blood-pressure cuff and a breathing mask.

Elise had passed a rebreathing test once before, not long after she started taking the transfusions. Dr Mickleham had assured her that another of these tests wouldn't be a problem for her. But they were supposed to be done before the race, not after. And this machine looked more sophisticated than those she had seen before.

'I've already been tested,' she said.

'This shouldn't be a problem, then,' said one of the clones, as he blew dust off a plug and connected it to a power point.

'Actually, it is,' she said. 'After a run like that, I'm already low on oxygen. A rebreathing test could make me hypoxic. I'm already light-headed.'

This was a lie. She was still vibrant and energetic, and everyone in the room could tell.

'Not to worry,' the clone said. 'Re-inhaling your own carbon dioxide won't deplete your oxygen, and the concentration of CO_2 won't get higher than five per cent.

Nowhere near enough to cause hypoxia, hypercapnia or anything else.' The words were reassuring, but they were delivered in a gloomy, resigned tone. Like he already knew what the test would find.

'Give me some time to catch my breath,' she pleaded.

'That would defeat the purpose, I'm afraid.'

They knew already. Someone had sold her out. One of the other runners, maybe, hoping to move up the line of succession.

Elise thought of Narelle's tense expression. Maybe not worried that Elise would fail the test—worried that she would pass.

'You can take the test, or you can forfeit your win,' O'Toole said. 'Which will it be?'

Until this moment, Elise hadn't considered herself a cheat. She'd avoided thinking about her visits to Dr Mickleham, even while she was there. When she had thought about it, she'd found ways to rationalise the situation. All the other athletes were doping, so she wasn't getting an unfair advantage. She wasn't taking drugs—it was her own blood, taken away then given back. Reinvested into her system, like superannuation. How could that be cheating?

But now she couldn't pretend anymore. This machine didn't care about her denials or excuses. Those dials would point, like accusing fingers, to the proof of what she had done.

Unless they didn't. Unless by fluke, or divine intervention, the machine found nothing.

Tears stung the corners of her eyes. 'I'll take the test.'

Elise pounded on Narelle's door. 'I know you're in there,' she shouted.

This was a lie. There had been no sounds from inside, and no change to the light behind the peephole. But Narelle wasn't on the track, or in the gym, or the cafeteria. This was the only other place Elise could think to look.

The door to a neighbouring apartment opened. An alarmed face—forties, Asian, male—appeared in the gap. The door closed again before Elise could tell the guy to mind his own business. Had he recognised her? Probably. Four thousand people had seen her cross the finish line first, then seen her not appear on the podium. Ten million more had watched it on TV. No one knew exactly what had happened, least of all Elise. But the man would soon come back with a camera, hoping to sell the footage to a network, or rack up some retweets. Soon the Games security team would be here to take her.

She needed a transfusion—her hands were shaking. She jammed them into her pockets and kicked the door this time. 'Narelle!' She had always assumed that it would be easy to kick down a door. It looked easy on TV. But even with her powerful leg muscles, she only scuffed the wood. The hinges and the lock stayed strong.

The lift dinged. Elise turned in time to see Narelle bounce out of it, grinning, a gold medal gleaming around her neck. She stopped moving when she saw Elise. The smile froze on her face. Then she stuck her hand back out, in time to stop the lift doors from closing behind her.

'Hey!' Elise bolted towards her.

Narelle slipped between the doors and disappeared.

Elise heard the *clack-clack-clack* of buttons inside. The doors started to slide shut.

Elise might not have been a gold medallist, but she was still a champion runner. She hurtled up the corridor and got between the doors just in time for them to close on her chest. They compressed her ribcage for a frightening second, then gave up and let her in.

'Elise.' Narelle already seemed more composed. The lift started its journey downwards.

'What the hell?' Elise demanded. 'Did you tell them to test me?'

'Performance enhancement tests are random. You know that.'

'Bullshit. They don't randomly screen a single person straight after a race, especially not with a rebreathing test. They knew.'

'Knew what?' Narelle asked.

'Knew that I—' Elise stopped herself. She didn't want to say it out loud.

'I don't know what you're talking about,' Narelle said.

Elise just looked at her, open-mouthed. Did Narelle really think she could bullshit her way out of this?

'You're disappointed,' Narelle continued. 'I understand that.' She didn't sound like a country girl anymore. Was that an act she'd been putting on?

The medal around her neck was sterling silver, plated with just enough gold that you could leave tooth marks in it. It was worth almost nothing in dollars, but Elise couldn't stop staring at it.

Narelle zipped up her jacket, hiding the medal from view.

'How did you know they wouldn't test you as well?' Elise challenged. 'And all the others on the team?'

'If they had, I would have passed.'

'For God's sake, it's just us in here. Tell me the truth!'

Narelle looked her in the eye. 'I am.'

Elise faltered. Realising.

'I never doped,' Narelle said. 'To my knowledge, no one else on the team did, either. It was always just you, Elise.'

'But ... how ...?' The horror threatened to swallow her. Those other women had all seemed superhuman. Right up until Elise started cheating, and promptly overtook them. Was it really possible that no one else had broken the rules?

'They worked harder than you,' Narelle was saying. 'Trained harder. Or they wanted it more, or maybe they had natural abilities you don't have. Does it matter?'

Elise backed into the corner of the lift, as though Narelle was a spider. 'Then why did you tell me to cheat?'

'I never told you that,' Narelle said, and Elise realised it was true. Narelle had given her the name of a dodgy doctor. That was all.

'But why me?'

An answer came to her quickly. She remembered Narelle's words on the track: *You're improving faster than any of us. Three months, and you'll be the leader of the pack.* Narelle had thought Elise would win, so she'd sabotaged her. Convinced her to cheat, and then turned her in.

But the real answer was much worse.

'I talked to *all* the girls.' Narelle gave Elise a pitying look. 'I gave them all Dr Mickleham's name. You're the only one who took the bait.'

The lift doors opened. A security team was waiting outside—a forest of thick necks, bulging biceps and ear-plugs. Elise barely felt the massive hand close around her wrist and pull her out of the lift.

'Goodbye, Elise,' Narelle said.

CHAPTER 38

The private investigator is Callum's sister.

Stephanie lies on her bed, too angry to move. If she gets up, she might smash a window or kick a hole in the wardrobe door.

The silence isn't calming her down. She should be able to hear her sheep snuffling outside, her husband snoring next to her, Moon turning pages hours after she's supposed to be asleep. But Stephanie can't hear any of that, because of Callum Glyk. Who is down there right now, plotting, with his sister.

A hardened PI might kill a stranger to save her own life, particularly if that stranger was a child molester. But Tina—or rather, Elise—was never going to kill Callum, or help to prove his guilt. Stephanie would be impressed by the deception if she wasn't so pissed off. This whole thing has been a waste of time.

She needs to get rid of them. Both of them. But she can't just dump them in the grave with Zach. That policewoman sounded nine tenths of the way to identifying Stephanie as a suspect. She'll be back soon, maybe with a search warrant. Stephanie needs all three bodies gone, and fast.

But how?

The more she thinks about it, the more impossible it seems. However she kills the Glyks, it will leave a trace. However she moves the bodies off her property, it will leave a trace. However she hides them, it will leave a trace. They will eventually be found, and Stephanie will be caught.

It's so unjust. It was Callum Glyk who raped Moon, leaving her pregnant and suicidal. It was Elise Glyk who cheated her way to stardom on the track, trespassed on Stephanie's property and lied about her identity. But it's Stephanie who is going to jail.

No. She won't accept that.

Stephanie doesn't remember getting out of bed, but she finds herself pacing the house, her fists bunched, elbows tucked. There must be a way out of this.

What if she didn't kill the Glyks here? She could dope them up somehow—GHB in their food, perhaps—and get them out of the tank. She could put them in Elise's Suzuki and drive it somewhere far away. Atop a hill on a deserted stretch of highway, she could strap Callum into the driver's seat and Elise in the passenger side. She could roll the car down the slope and ram it into a tree. Then she could hike home, or hike halfway and hitch the rest. When the Glyks' bodies were found, party drugs in their bloodstream, the police would stop looking at Stephanie as a suspect. Zach's grave would remain undisturbed.

There are plenty of holes in this plan, but she's desperate. She hurries over to her laptop. She should have enough bitcoin left over from the last transaction to buy some more pills.

Opening the Tor browser, she starts making her way through the dark web, link by link. The seller who helped her frame Callum is gone, but plenty of others are flogging drugs. Stephanie scrolls through the forums, trying to work out who is reliable.

Then she sees something else on the same message board.

I need to get rid of my partner. I'm not looking for judgement. You don't know my life. Does anyone have a name? Discretion is a must.

Stephanie scrolls through the responses, mesmerised. Some people are warning the OP—original poster—that all dark web hit men are scammers or undercover cops. Other commenters are straight-facedly suggesting couples counselling. But a few are providing links for people who claim to be assassins.

And people who say they can get rid of bodies.

Stephanie hadn't considered getting professional help. But the more she thinks about it, the more appealing the idea is. Could she just pay a few thousand dollars to make her problem vanish? Could it really be that simple?

Apparently it is. Soon she's astonished to find a review site, like *Choice* magazine for hit men. It ranks killers on price, speed, number of confirmed kills and customer service.

Wondering if she might be dreaming, Stephanie clicks on the top-rated murderer in her area. As with every other kind of online shopping, there doesn't seem to be any point going past number one.

The guy does look good. For starters, his prices are prominently displayed. Stephanie always appreciates this when she's browsing. Most dark web sites are ugly, but this one is slick and functional. The testimonials could be fake, but they sound convincing. *You got me out of a really tough situation, and so quickly! I'll always be grateful.* To reassure visitors that he's not a police officer, the hit man—who calls himself Vermilion—has provided sections of the criminal code that deal with entrapment. He claims it would be illegal for the police to run a site like this, and if they did, a judge would dismiss any charges against the would-be client. Links to news articles seem to confirm this.

To prove he's not a scammer, Vermilion points out that he takes no money upfront. The funds are transferred afterwards. Stephanie wonders how he makes sure that he gets paid, then decides she doesn't want to know.

The services listed include murder, crime scene cleaning/staging and—there it is: corpse disposal. If Stephanie kills the Glyks herself, she'll only have to pay for the bodies to be removed. Fifteen thousand dollars in total.

A chat window pops up.

I see you're having a look around! Let me know if you have any questions.

Stephanie almost leaps out of her chair. The hit man can't know who she is—the web browser has routed her data through so many different servers around the world that her location should be impossible to track. But still, the realisation that she's already connected to this man, albeit digitally, is unnerving.

A second message: *But if you're just happy having a browse, that's fine, too. :)*

Could Vermilion really get her out of this mess?

Her fingers hover over the keyboard.

CHAPTER 39

The phone chimes.

Vermilion opens his eyes.

He mostly ignores these midnight messages. He gets plenty of enquiries during the daylight hours—no need to work all night, too. But he's more refreshed than usual. He must have woken up in the shallowest part of his sleep cycle. No point turning down a potential client, when it will be a while before he's ready to nod off again.

He rolls off his yoga mat and crawls over to the charger, where his phone is plugged in, a notification light blinking. There's nothing else in the room—just the mat and the phone on a hardwood floor. Vermilion lives like a monk. This started out as a way to save money, since hired killers don't have long careers, and he was aiming for early retirement. But life with few possessions quickly became part of who he was. He's rich now, and he still hasn't bought a proper bed. Smoking is his only indulgence.

He unlocks the screen, and the glare blinds him. He rubs his eyes, trying to focus on the pixels.

The message says, *Are you real?*

The conversations often start this way. The first two messages on his website are automatic, and visitors seem to sense that. It's only if they respond that he gets a notification.

He's feeling uncharacteristically honest tonight. He types, *Those first two messages came from a bot. But I'm awake now—you've got the real me.*

The visitor types. Slowly. Maybe old, or maybe just hesitant? He shouldn't assume too much, too soon.

Sorry to wake you.

It's no trouble. What can I help you with?

There's a long pause. The visitor isn't typing. But they haven't disconnected.

Vermilion gets that tingling in his spine. Less than one in a hundred queries turns into a job, but he's pretty good at sensing which ones they will be.

He prompts: *I don't need much information. A name, a location and a photo is usually enough.*

The visitor starts typing again, then stops without sending the message. They're still connected, but saying nothing.

Vermilion adds: *We're just making conversation at this point. I won't do anything until you say so.*

This is a risk. He knows some people don't want to give the actual order. They want to be able to pretend—to law enforcement, to him, to themselves—that they didn't really expect the person to die. But he's getting a vibe, from this visitor he can't see, that they're not really committed yet. He needs to be gentle. Make it clear that it's safe to make the transaction.

Finally, the woman—Vermilion gets the feeling the visitor is a woman—types back. *I'm interested in your body disposal service. How soon are you available?*

Vermilion stretches his neck and rolls out his shoulders, already getting ready.

I'm available now, and I'm based in New South Wales. Whenever possible I travel by car.

Another long pause. Vermilion uses the time to pry the air vent off the wall and pull out a sports bag. It doesn't contain any weapons—his kill kit is elsewhere. This is the bag he takes in case something goes wrong. It holds clothes, protein bars and bottled water. Sewn into the lining is a collection of driver's licences, passports, and bundles of cash in rubber bands.

Ding. An address comes through. Only two hours away. The job is on.

Relieved, Vermilion types back: *I can be there at 5 PM tomorrow.*

You said you were available now?

I am, but I'll need some time to prepare. The car and the phone registered to him will both have to stay here, so it looks like he never left the city. He has to travel on foot to his other car and his other phone. He also wants to research the local area—he's been to Warrigal before, but not this side of it. He'll investigate the client, too. Just to make sure there are no red flags. He's wary of undercover police, and he also doesn't like working for organised crime. Those groups usually have someone in-house, meaning they usually don't intend for freelancers to survive.

He types out another message. *Name and photo?*

The visitor types: *Not necessary. I'll meet you there.*

Vermilion hesitates, the bag dangling from one shoulder. *It's safest if I don't meet the client.*

It's a complicated situation.

I hear that a lot.

He chews his lip. He doesn't want to meet the client, but he is keen on the job. It's not far to travel, it sounds like a lone client, and body disposal is easy money compared to murder.

Finally, he writes: *Okay. Have you seen the price list?*

Yes. It's fine.

Now he's thinking the client might be a man. There's a certain blunt efficiency to the messages.

A follow-up message: *How much for three?*

CHAPTER 40

'Stop,' Elise says.

'What?' Callum is still on the ladder, scraping his belt buckle above the cereal box.

'Stop! Get down.'

Apparently hearing the footsteps, Callum drops the belt and scrambles down the ladder, away from the hatch.

'The box,' Elise hisses.

They both look at the box of fertiliser. He's left it balanced on the top rung. It's dark, but Stephanie is sure to see it. Will she guess what their plan is? She'll certainly realise they're up to something.

Elise runs across the tank and jumps. She hits the ladder halfway up with a clang, then stretches out and grabs the box.

It slips out of her grip, falls, splats against the concrete. The fertiliser spills out. No time to do anything about it. Hopefully Stephanie won't notice.

Elise leaps down and backs away from the ladder, just as the lock rattles and the hatch creaks open.

Stephanie calls out, 'Callum.'

He says nothing. Elise realises this is the first time she's heard Stephanie talk to him directly. He never talks to her, either. They only communicate through her. It's like Mum and Dad all over again.

'Come on up,' Stephanie says. 'I've decided to let you go.'

Callum looks disbelieving. 'Really?'

'Yes. Hurry up, before I change my mind.'

Elise's mind is racing. Why him and not her? What's different now?

Still he hesitates. 'How do I know you won't hurt me once I'm up there?'

Stephanie sighs. 'Fine. Elise can come up first, if that helps. Move it.'

Elise starts walking cautiously towards the ladder—

Then she realises that Stephanie used her real name.

She leaps back just in time. The crack of a gunshot is deafening. The bullet hits the floor where she was just standing and ricochets, bouncing off the ceiling. Both impacts cause sparks. The hot bullet tunnels into one of the bags of highly flammable fertiliser—

But it doesn't ignite. There's a long silence.

'Did I get you?' Stephanie asks grimly.

Elise keeps quiet, her heart pounding.

Stephanie's hand reaches down into the tank holding a compact like a periscope. In the mirror, Elise gets a flash of one narrow eye lasering in on her. The hand snaps the compact shut and pulls it out of sight.

'You tried to shoot me.' It's all Elise can think to say.

'You should have told me the truth.' Stephanie sounds

unmoved. 'I wouldn't have asked you to kill him if I'd known. I would have found some other way to let you go.'

'You can't just murder us,' Elise says.

'Not with you standing all the way over there, no.'

'This is wrong. It's not justice. It's inhuman.'

'You're a liar, just like him. And a cheat. I guess I shouldn't be surprised.'

Callum shifts on the floor. Elise lowers herself behind the little wall, in case Stephanie comes down the ladder.

'My father died in a nursing home,' Stephanie begins.

'I'm sorry—'

'Shut up. He got colon cancer. The doctors removed most of his colon, and the cancer went away. He got to spend a few extra years in pain, eating mush, surrounded by people he hated. Then the cancer came back, and killed him. Towards the end, he told me I should have just shot him the first time around.'

There's a pause.

'That's what I'm offering,' Stephanie says. 'Even to you, Callum. A quick death, assuming you give me a clear shot. This is a one-time-only deal.'

'If you kill us, you won't be able to live with yourself,' Elise says.

'I killed that kid, and I sleep just fine.'

'No, you don't. I can see what this is doing to you. You need help, Stephanie. If you let us go, you'll be able to get it.'

'Oh, don't worry,' Stephanie says. 'Help is coming.'

Then she slams the hatch shut, and locks it.

Elise and Callum look at each other.

'What did she mean by that?' he asks.

'No idea.' She picks up a bag of fertiliser. 'Grab a bag.'

'Why?'

'She's going to drown us.'

CHAPTER 41

The bags are too big for the inflow pipe. Elise and Callum rip them open, push the crumpled plastic into the gap and stuff the fertiliser in after it by the handful. They work like lunatics, shoulder to shoulder, bumping and scratching each other in the darkness. There's fertiliser under Elise's nails, in the creases of her palms and on her brow where she wiped the sweat from her eyes. The stink is ghastly. The mouth of the pipe is slightly above her head—she has to reach up to push each handful in. Her skinny arms are on fire.

There's no sound from further up the pipe. Maybe Elise was wrong. She hopes so. Because the fertiliser feels too loose and crumbly to stop the water, if it comes.

They keep shoving in the dirt. Soon the job gets harder, because the fertiliser is becoming compacted against the vertical bend up ahead—or maybe because Elise's muscles are weakening. After a while it feels like pushing on a tree trunk.

Callum is panting. 'There's no more room.'

'Yeah.' She gives one final shove to check. 'Listen.'

There's a rattling sound from somewhere in the distance. She presses her ear to the wall.

'You think she's switched on the pump?' he asks.

'Shh.' Elise can hear a gurgling, glugging noise.

They both back away from the pipe. She wishes they had stuffed more plastic in first, to waterproof their wall of dirt. Too late now.

Silence falls.

Stephanie said it would take twelve hours to fill the tank. But it won't fill all the way, because there's an open drainage pipe at the other end, leading to the absorption trench outside. Even if Stephanie blocks that, there's still the ventilation tube in the ceiling.

How long can Elise and Callum tread water before their limbs freeze up and they slip under?

A creaking, groaning sound from the pipe. It's like being on the lower decks of the *Titanic*, waiting for the ocean to come pouring in.

Without speaking, she and Callum climb onto the wall that divides the room. The lowered part of the ceiling is right above it, so they have to stoop. She reaches for his hand, forgetting what he's done. He clasps it, and squeezes back.

A rumbling sound gets louder and louder.

Bang! Something explodes further up the pipe. Maybe the pump. The rumbling ends.

Because they're right under the ventilation tube, Elise hears a screech in the distance, then swearing.

After another rattle, the gurgling, glugging sounds die away. Their dam has held, for now.

Elise exhales and lets go of Callum's hand. 'I think we're okay.'

He laughs darkly. 'We're a long way from okay.'

They drag the fertiliser bags back over to the walls so Stephanie can't drop a lit match directly onto them. Not that Elise has had any luck igniting the fertiliser herself. And not that moving the bags will help, if Stephanie decides to throw in a Molotov cocktail instead. Or if she pours her jar of chloroform down the hatch and waits for her prisoners to suffocate in the fumes. Hopefully she won't think of that.

Without speaking, Elise and Callum collapse onto their fleeces, a few metres apart. It feels like that moment just after a race, when some pretty journalist is asking questions that Elise can hardly hear over her heartbeat and is too out of breath to answer. This time, there's no protein shake, no soft hotel bed, no pep talk from her coach to bring her back to life.

When she touched the fertiliser blocking the inflow pipe it was damp. The water had made it past the plastic and been absorbed by the dirt. She and Callum had come so close to drowning. They might not be so lucky next time. Stephanie has plenty of other options. If all else fails, she can simply let them die of thirst.

What did she mean, when she said help was coming?

Elise would do anything to be out of here. She'd take it all back—the doping, the lying, stealing Kiara's laptop. She would hit the reset button on her whole life and endure a quiet existence in Warrigal, unnoticed by everyone except the patients in her ambulance. When her brother disappeared, she would ignore it.

She listens to Callum's breaths. Waiting for them to slow. If she killed him, then Stephanie would probably let her go. He knows this. Therefore, Elise can't go to sleep until he does. He might murder her first, in self-defence.

She doesn't want to believe he would. He's her big brother. He's always looked out for her. He never had a go at her for cheating. He never blamed her for Mum's death.

But she didn't want to believe that he would rape a student, either. Anything seems possible down here, in the dark.

He might not even wait for her to sleep. He might stab her while she's still awake. She can barely move after the day's exertions. She wouldn't be able to fight him off. Does he know that? She needs to act strong, no matter what.

But even if she survives the night, what then? The fertiliser bomb is a failure. She's going to die down here.

A quiet snore. Callum is asleep.

At last, Elise relaxes. Her spine seems to melt, her hands unclench, her head clears. And then a thought enters her mind: *He could be faking.* Everything tenses back up again. He's such a convincing liar. He's fooled her over and over. He could be trying to trick her into sleeping, so he can plunge that sharpened bracket into her neck.

She's so tired. So sore. So hungry. So scared.

Callum is still snoring, like an old dog. He always sounded like that. So he *must* be asleep. He wouldn't be able to mimic his own snores—he wouldn't know what they sounded like.

Unless someone has told him. Unless he recorded himself. Unless every time she has ever thought he was asleep, he has been pretending. The paranoid thoughts swirl around Elise's head, like mosquitos moving too fast to swat.

She needs that bracket. She'll be able to sleep if it's tucked safely underneath her. Earlier, she saw Callum drop it in the corner of the septic tank. The corner closest to his sleeping fleece.

She rises, wincing at each rustle of her clothes, and creeps towards the corner, remembering when she played murder in the dark as a kid. Switch out the lights, tiptoe around, try not to giggle. If someone grabs you, scream and play dead.

None of her friends would play with Callum more than once. They never said why.

She reaches the corner and fumbles around on the floor.

The bracket is gone.

Her blood runs cold. He must have taken it. Maybe he *is* faking, waiting, the bracket clenched in his hand.

She has to take it from him. She's dead if she doesn't.

Elise approaches slowly. She can make out his sleeping form in a patch of moonlight, filtered through the dirty plastic window.

As she gets close to Callum, she crouches, wanting to stay out of sight in case his eyes are open. She's close enough to see his open hands by his sides.

He's not holding the bracket. But it could be under him.

As carefully as if she's disarming a bomb, she slides one hand underneath him, between the fleece and his back. He doesn't stir. If he's faking, he's decided to see how this plays out.

The bracket isn't there.

She slips a hand beneath the fleece. It's not there, either.

Reassured, she turns away. But her foot brushes against something that makes a metallic grating sound.

She freezes, her heart hammering.

Callum doesn't move. But she can't hear him snoring anymore.

Teeth clenched, she reaches down and finds the bracket, lying on the floor like half of a bear trap. She pinches it between her thumb and her index finger, wary of making any more noise, and picks it up.

He left the bracket here, within reach. So she couldn't attack him? Or so he could attack her?

She keeps the cold metal clenched in her hand, watching his prone form. If he's planning to kill her, maybe she should kill him first. Then she would be safe. She could sleep. In the morning, Stephanie would release her, she's sure of it. This whole thing would be over.

Her chest is tight. Her wounds throb—her knee, her hands, the inside of her elbow. She stands like a statue for what feels like hours, the bracket trembling in her grip. Can she really do this?

'Leesy?'

She stifles a scream.

Callum is wide awake, looking at her. 'Is that you?' he rasps.

She's outside the pool of moonlight. She can see him, but he can't see her. His eyes are wide with fear. Like she's the monster, not him.

When she was playing murder in the dark, Elise found it much more frightening to be the killer than a potential victim. She felt other people's terror more keenly than her own.

'Leesy?' Callum whispers.

She isn't sure what to say, so she says nothing. As silent as a ghost, she backs away, deeper into the shadows. He rolls over like he's looking around for her. She tucks the bracket safely beneath her fleece and lies down on top of it. Callum says nothing more.

After a minute, she pretends to snore.

CHAPTER 42

'A phoenix,' the bikie repeated. He didn't sound impressed. Elise had never been in this tattoo parlour before, but she had the sinking feeling that the guy recognised her anyway. Maybe he'd seen her on TV, escorted from the hotel in tears.

'It's a mythical bird,' she told him. 'It dies in a fire, then is reborn. Flames out, then comes back.'

'Yeah, I get it. But given who you are and what you've done, it's a bit on the nose.'

'No, I want it on the neck,' she said.

'I meant—'

'I know what you meant. Do you usually insult your clients?'

'No,' the bikie admitted. 'But my clients are usually armed and violent.'

'How do you know I'm not?'

'Fair point.' He leafed through a book of designs until he found a page filled with phoenixes. 'Which one do you like?'

As she examined the pages, she found it hard to articulate exactly what she was trying to say to the world with this tattoo—a promise that she'd redeem herself, or a warning that she wouldn't stay down, or something else. She picked the ugliest phoenix, with the sharpest beak. It looked not unlike the dead bird she'd once found under her bed.

The bikie studied the picture for a minute, scratching the back of his head, then got out an alcohol swab and started wiping her throat.

The tattoo parlour smelled like leather and cigarette smoke, but both smells came from the bikie—no one else was around. The walls were lined with photos of elaborate back tattoos, and of gruesome piercings that Elise found it hard to look at.

The bikie drew the design on her skin with texta, then rolled his stool back so she could see the mirror. She peered at the phoenix, and at herself. She'd already changed her hair and started wearing different makeup. With the tattoo, she hoped she wouldn't resemble the young woman who'd been booted out of the Games a month ago.

'How's the size?' the bikie asked, a hint of a smirk in his voice. Maybe he thought she would ask him to make it smaller.

'It's fine,' she said. 'Do it.'

'Okay. Don't talk or swallow.'

She lay back on the chair, and the bikie got out a little buzzing instrument and touched it to her skin. It hurt, but not as much as she'd expected. Perhaps not as much as she had hoped.

The bikie drew stinging lines on her in silence for a while. Then he said, 'You must be used to needles, I suppose.'

She couldn't nod or speak. She just watched him.

'I used to gamble.' He didn't look up from his work. 'Can't usually afford it anymore.'

Elise wondered if a sympathetic grunt was too risky. Something in his tone made her conscious of the fact that she was alone with this man, and that he had a tiny blade at her throat.

'I had a lot of money on you,' the bikie continued.

Elise tensed up.

'Stay still,' he warned. He kept tracing the vibrating spike across her throat, stabbing her hundreds of times per second. 'Nugget said you were a sure thing, and I knew it was probably just Warrigal pride, but I let him convince me. When you won that race, I was over the moon. Thought I'd be able to pay a chunk off my mortgage, retire early. But when I went to my bookie to collect, he wouldn't pay up. Said you'd been disqualified. I couldn't believe it.'

The saliva pooled at the back of Elise's throat. She didn't dare swallow.

'I never dreamed that someday you'd come into my shop and sit on my chair, under my needle. Thinking you could make everything right with a—what's the word?—*self-aggrandising* tattoo.'

Sweat broke out across her brow. If she pulled away from him, what would happen? Would it just ruin whatever he was drawing on her neck, or would the needle actually puncture her windpipe?

She was still thinking about it when the bikie said, 'All done, love.'

He held up a mirror. There was the phoenix, exactly as she'd requested, surrounded by a halo of angry red skin.

'Thank you,' she said.

'That'll be four hundred,' the bikie said. 'I might put it on the horses.'

It wasn't until days later, changing the plastic-wrapped dressing in her bathroom, that she saw the camouflaged message. He'd woven it into the phoenix's feathers. Predictably, it said, FUCK YOU.

She kind of liked it. It was, she realised, exactly what she'd wanted the tattoo to say.

Her phone dinged. A message from Dad:

Your mother is dead.

Dad didn't tell Elise when or where the funeral was. But Callum sent her a photo of the obituary in the paper: *Elizabeth Glyk passed away at her home in Warrigal, NSW. Much-loved wife of John and sister of Tania. The funeral will be held at St Barnabas' Church, 12 p.m., Saturday, 17 November.*

Mum's obit didn't mention her two adult children. Elise could guess why she wasn't mentioned but wasn't sure how Callum had been left out. Perhaps Dad had thought it would look odd to mention only one child, when everyone in town knew there had been two.

Even after the vandalism to her car and the jeers on the street, even after the beating behind Kingo's, Elise hadn't realised how much everyone loathed her. Not until she and Kiara walked into the church on that sweltering Saturday afternoon and an angry silence fell. It was her own mother's funeral. Couldn't people cut her a break?

She was trembling. It was just a need for red blood cells—the cravings always hit at about this time of day—but she hated how much it must have looked like fear. Dr Mickleham hadn't warned her that blood doping could become addictive. After a transfusion, she felt invincible. Without one, she felt like the walking dead.

Kiara held Elise's elbow. 'You can do this.'

Elise was conscious of being stared at. This wasn't how she'd imagined coming out to her family. But what was the point of hiding, when everyone hated her anyway?

She took a program booklet off a table. There was a photo of Mum from before she had children. She looked happier than Elise had ever seen her. Inside there was the order of ceremonies and the words to the Lord's Prayer.

They walked up the aisle. Most of the seats were empty. The family hadn't lived in Warrigal long enough to develop deep connections, and Elise's disgrace had scared off the few friends Mum had. Elise sat up the front, next to Callum. Kiara took the spot on her other side, their thighs touching.

Callum squeezed Elise's hand. His eyes were red and his cheeks were wet.

'You okay?' she asked quietly.

He nodded in silence.

Dad was sitting on the other side of Callum. He didn't look at Elise. He had paid her legal bills but hadn't spoken to her at all. Tania, an aunt that Elise hadn't seen since she was fifteen, was a few seats further up, looking shell-shocked.

Two old women were whispering up the back of the church:

'Imagine the nerve—'

'My friend is a doctor, and—'

'Under so much pressure after—'

'Bringing her girlfriend to her own mother's funeral—'

'Broken heart syndrome, the doctor called it—'

Kiara turned around. The whisperers fell silent. Kiara kept looking at them for a minute, and then swivelled back to the pulpit.

Elise didn't thank her. The words *broken heart syndrome* kept circling.

She'd studied the condition they were talking about: stress cardiomyopathy. Common after menopause—heart failure caused by divorce, overwork or anxiety.

Mum's friends thought Elise had killed her. They were wrong. They *had to* be. Heart disease ran in the family. It wasn't Elise's fault.

Was it?

The casket was plain pine, closed, unadorned but for a bouquet of white roses. Elise thought Dad should have organised something nicer, then realised he probably couldn't afford to, after supporting her athletics career for so long. Money she'd now never be able to repay.

Looking at the wooden box, she couldn't stop picturing Mum sealed in the darkness. Elise had the stupidest thought: *But how can she breathe in there?*

———

'Didn't expect to see you here,' Rafa said, his voice as flat as a bad ECG.

Elise forced a rueful smile. 'Where else would I go?'

There were no patients in the waiting room. Typical of a country hospital. Ninety-nine per cent of the time, it was the quietest place on earth. The other one per cent, it was all blood and screaming because someone had lost an arm in a head-on collision or had their leg crushed under a tractor.

Rafa's eyes had shrunk into sultanas after years of squinting in the sun, and the sleeve tatts had faded. But he looked healthier than Elise remembered. His teeth were white, and he still stood with a straight back, like a drill sergeant.

'You look good,' she said.

His expression softened, like he'd remembered that this was a hospital, and she might actually be sick. 'Are you okay?'

She jammed her hands in her pockets to cover the trembling.

'I'm after a job,' she said.

'Oh. Good luck with that.'

'Come on, Raf, you know me.'

'I'm not so sure I do. The Elise I knew was hardworking and honest. She would never have done what you did.'

Elise clenched her jaw. She was so sick of this—everyone feeling entitled to have a go at her. She had been turned away at the pub. The post office. The taxi company. The supermarket. Her reputation preceded her everywhere. Some business owners hated her, others worried that their customers would.

She'd asked Callum for advice, but he'd been no help. He was distracted and irritable—'woman trouble', he'd said, and refused to elaborate.

The hospital was her last chance. An employer that was short-staffed, with a job that didn't involve cash handling. And customers who couldn't say no.

She licked her dry lips. 'You need my help.'

Rafa gestured around at all the empty seats. 'Does it look like I'm run off my feet?'

'Right now, no. But it must be hard, always being on call. Never drinking, keeping your phone on all the time. Wouldn't you like someone else to share the load?'

'I'm five years sober.'

Elise was surprised. In all the time she'd worked with Rafa, she'd never suspected that he was an alcoholic. Another reminder of how self-absorbed she'd been. How little she'd cared about anything other than running. She wondered if they could bond over their recovery—him from alcohol, her from transfusions.

Now didn't seem like the time to ask.

'So, I don't mind being on call,' Rafa was saying.

'Do you mind losing half your patients on the way to the hospital?'

He flinched.

'That's what's happening, right?' she pressed. 'Because you can't be behind the wheel and stabilising the patient at the same time. I assume plenty of people don't make it.'

'It's easy enough to grab a bystander,' he snapped. 'Anyone with a driver's licence can operate the ambulance.'

'Great.' She put her bag down on the triage counter. 'I can start today.'

Rafa stabbed a finger at her face. 'Wrong. I'm not riding with a liar and a cheat. If you—'

Then the alarms went off. Bright lights flashed overhead.

'Shit,' he muttered.

Elise held his gaze. 'Sounds like someone needs help. Are you going to risk their lives to save your ego?'

'Shut up, and grab the keys.'

It had been a long time since she drove an ambulance. It handled differently to a car—more weight in the back and a wider turning circle. It rode high, on over-inflated tyres.

The dark green uniform felt different, too. Looser where she'd lost fat, tighter where she'd gained muscle. The radio and the pouches on her belt seemed flimsy, weightless.

'You right?' Rafa asked from behind her. He was prepping the stretcher.

Elise swallowed. 'Fine.'

'You sure?'

'Yup.'

When she'd been using the patient's life to manipulate Rafa, she hadn't seen them as a real person—just a chip on a poker table. But now reality was speeding towards her. If she screwed up, someone might actually die. The stakes were higher than they had been at the Commonwealth Games. And this time, there was no way to cheat.

Her heart was like a bird trapped in her rib cage. She should never have quit this job. But now she had it back. That would fix everything. Right?

'I can do this,' she said, partly to herself.

It was peak hour, but no one had told the residents of Warrigal. The streets were empty. With Elise doing twenty over the limit, they should arrive in half an hour. She hoped that would be fast enough. Most medical emergencies were no longer emergencies after half an hour. A person could bleed out or suffocate in much less. Brain death started four minutes after the heart stopped.

'People around town are pretty pissed off with you,' Rafa said from the back.

'Thanks, Raf.' This had been apparent from every conversation she'd had since she came home—and every conversation she hadn't had. Yesterday she'd gone to a café where the service staff had avoided both her table and her eye, making it impossible to order. The person she was supposed to be meeting about a job hadn't showed. When she gave up and walked home, an old acquaintance from her schooldays had crossed the street to avoid her.

'I'm just saying, let me go in first, okay? It'll be best if they start engaging with me before they notice I've brought a . . . what's the bad version of a celebrity? A piranha.'

'Pariah,' Elise said.

'Right. That. Whoa, stop!'

She almost overshot the driveway, slamming on the brakes just in time. The ambulance lurched to a halt in front of a little red-brick house with lacy curtains drawn behind arched windows. An apple tree grew in a rectangle of recently mown grass.

A twenty-something woman with braided hair and a superhero T-shirt was standing in the doorway, waving and shouting. 'Here! Here!'

Rafa had already leapt out and was running up the stepping stones towards the door. Elise followed, her baseball cap pulled low over her eyes. Was she supposed to lock the ambulance? She couldn't remember. She'd discarded all her training, thinking she was leaving this life behind.

'You're Casey?' Rafa asked.

'Right,' the woman said, her sparkly earrings dangling. 'He's through here. Quick.'

Elise followed them into a stuffy, sparsely decorated lounge room, where a middle-aged man was sprawled on a shagpile rug, his flabby face as purple as a grape. There was a hard red line around his neck. His hair was scruffed up, as though he'd had a static shock. Elise was reminded of a dead cat she'd seen at one of the towns she'd lived in before Warrigal, its eyes bugged out, wire wrapped around its throat.

A spiderweb of tangled straps hung in a nearby doorway. It took a minute for Elise to recognise them as part of a home-gym set-up. You were supposed to attach them to a doorframe and then pull on the handles for resistance exercises. She'd seen the loud, hypermasculine ads on late-night TV.

'I just don't understand how this happened,' Casey said faintly. She sounded like she was going into shock.

'Quiet.' Rafa was bent over, listening to the man's mouth.

Elise took Casey into an adjacent dining room but made sure she could still see Rafa through the doorway in case he needed her.

She was pretty sure he wouldn't, though. The man was dead. A wave of disappointment washed over her. She'd wanted to save him—to *be* the one to save him. To redeem herself with a single heroic act. But she was too late, in more ways than one.

'I'm sorry,' she told Casey. 'He was your father?' She realised immediately that she shouldn't have used the past tense, not yet.

But Casey didn't seem to notice. 'I just thought I'd check on him.' The woman pulled up a chair but didn't sit down. It was as though she suddenly wasn't sure what chairs were for.

'He was like this when you found him?'

'He was hanging from the . . .' She gestured. 'Exercise thingy. I had to cut through the straps to get him down. It looks new—he must have just bought it. Didn't know how it worked, got himself tangled up. Dad's like that. He doesn't read manuals. Just have a go, he always says.'

Elise peeked through the doorway at Rafa, who was going through the dead man's pockets. Searching for a wallet and driver's licence, to get the guy's full name and date of birth—but he looked like a graverobber. Elise gently led Casey to the kitchen, so she wouldn't see.

'He owed a lot of money,' Casey said numbly. 'What am I going to do?'

Elise opened the pantry. 'Do you have a biscuit tin?'

Casey blinked. 'Biscuit tin?'

The shock of seeing your father dead was different from medical shock. It wasn't dangerous, but that didn't mean it was pleasant. Your blood vessels constricting, your extremities going numb, the creeping levels of adrenaline making you dizzy. Sugar would help.

'Never mind.' Elise pulls the tin out of the pantry. 'Found it. Here.' She hands Casey a Scotch Finger.

'Elise,' Rafa called.

'I'll be back, okay?' Elise rubbed Casey's back, then returned to the lounge room. The corpse had a dark patch on his shorts. She could smell the urine amid the stale-old-man smell of the house.

'He's gone,' Rafa said.

'No kidding.'

Rafa leaned sideways, saw Casey nibbling the biscuit in the dining room. Then he put his hands under the dead man's armpits. 'Help me get him out of here.'

'Wait.' Elise was looking at the man's neck. There was a thin red line from the cord Casey had cut away, but the bruising around it looked too wide. Like he'd been strangled with something else as well.

'What is it?' Rafa asked.

'Look at this.' Elise pointed.

Rafa looked, but he clearly didn't see what she was seeing.

'I think maybe we should call the police,' she said.

'They're on their way already.' He went to lift the corpse again. 'Come on. We have to get him out of that poor girl's sight.'

She wasn't sure if they should move the body. But she didn't want to argue with her boss—not on her first day at her last chance of employment. So she gripped the man's ankles, lifted, and walked backwards into her new life.

Months later, Elise was at a bedside in the middle of the night. The patient—a forty-something woman who worked at the chemist—was unconscious, a mask over her face. Her chest rose like a cake, then sagged as though someone had opened the oven too early. Over and over, swelling and deflating. Stable, in the medical sense.

Yet another suicide attempt. Elise and Rafa had found her on her bedroom floor, an empty pill bottle still clenched in her fist, her distraught husband screaming like a kid and squeezing her shoulder so hard Elise could still see the marks. But it looked as though they'd got to the woman in time.

Elise was exhausted. After the adrenaline-fuelled race to the woman's house, the labour of getting her into the ambulance, the urgent drive back to the hospital with Rafa yelling in the back, then the work of getting her into a bed, Elise had spent the rest of the night watching the stomach pump gurgle and suck. The rostered nurse had called in sick. Rafa was asleep. He would check on the woman at 7 a.m. Elise had to stay until then. There was nothing she could do if the patient started slipping towards death, but at least she wouldn't die alone.

Pills were a selfish way to go, Elise thought. They messed up your heart and your liver, which then couldn't be donated to those on the transplant list. Plus, they weren't reliable. You sometimes survived, like this woman might. Or, in what seemed to Elise like the worst outcome of all, you survived just long enough to change your mind, just long enough to see your family's horror and anger and shame, before your pancreas couldn't take the strain anymore and you died in agony.

If Elise were to commit suicide—and she'd thought about it—she would stick a gun in her mouth, like men did. Instant. Pain free.

There were plenty of guns in Warrigal. Why hadn't this woman used one? Then there would have been no saving her, and Elise would be at home in bed with Kiara right now.

She was so tired. Since she'd stopped doping, everything was hard. Getting up each day. Washing the dishes. Folding clothes. Life was now a cross-country event—a never-ending slog towards a finish line she couldn't see.

The woman's chest rose and fell.

Elise's eyes fell on the O-neg blood pouches. They were prepped and ready to go, thanks to a miscommunication. She and Rafa had been told that the woman had slit her wrists rather than OD'ing on paracetamol. Now that the pouches had been taken out of the fridge, they couldn't be used. Some poor blood donor had worked hard on those— got their finger pricked and their vein drained, drunk a milkshake and eaten some individually wrapped cheese and crackers. After all that, their bag of blood was going straight into the biohazard bin, where no one could ever use it.

Where no one would ever notice if it was empty.

Elise closed her eyes. *Don't even think about that*, she told herself.

The clock ticked towards seven, agonisingly slow.

Elise didn't remember standing up, but found herself walking around the room. She sat back down. Checked the ECG again. Then she was squeezing one of the pouches of blood, feeling the fluid between her fingers.

What did she have left to lose?

Her self-respect, that was what. Everyone else hating her was one thing. But if she took this last terrible step, she'd hate herself, too. And that would be too much to bear.

She put the pouch back down, then saw Rafa in the doorway, holding two takeaway coffee cups. He looked at her, and at the blood. His face darkened.

'I wasn't going to.' The shame in her voice made it sound like a lie.

Milk foam bubbled up out of the lids, like he was squeezing the cups. It was hard to meet his gaze.

'Don't come back,' he said finally.

CHAPTER 43

'Where's the water?' Callum asks.

Elise turns away from her fruitless efforts to produce a spark. She's been up the ladder, facing the window—she has to blink away the daylight. 'What water?'

As her eyes adjust to the dark, she sees his jaw clench. 'What do you mean, what water?'

She meant, *Are you talking about the water trickling down the wall from the pipe, or our dwindling supply of bottled water?* But she's too tired to say any of that, so she just looks at him.

He kicks one of the bottles. 'That was half full yesterday.'

'It's still half full.'

'Wrong. Look.' He stabs a finger a centimetre above the water line, at what he must think is the halfway mark.

She turns back and keeps scraping. She hasn't slept. She hasn't eaten. She can't handle his bullshit right now.

'I saw you creeping around last night,' he snaps. 'You were drinking, when you thought I was asleep.'

She wonders if he would be comforted to know she was just looking for a weapon to stab him with. 'Maybe it leaked, or evaporated. Maybe you didn't close the spout all the way.'

'Oh yeah? Do you see a wet patch on the floor?'

You practically are a wet patch on the floor, she thinks.

'I know what you're up to,' he says. 'You think you can outlast me.'

'Outlast you?'

'You're going to drink all the water and wait for me to die of thirst. Then your mate Stephanie will let you out.'

It's not a bad idea. 'Fuck off, Cal.'

'You fuck off.'

He storms towards her. She barely has time to let go of the ladder before he wrenches her off it.

'Hey!' She lands clumsily, putting her weight on her injured knee. It crumples under her, and suddenly she's flat on the concrete.

He pins her down by the shoulders. She struggles, but he's too heavy. It's like being held in place by a seatbelt during a car crash.

'Get off me,' she snaps.

He sneers at her. 'You've had enough. The rest of the water is mine.'

'Like hell it is!'

He doesn't seem to hear her. His eyes are roaming down her body. She's suddenly conscious of how little she's eaten this week, and how thin she's getting. How much she looks like a teenager.

She twists sideways and bites his wrist.

He yowls, letting go. She does a sit-up, slamming her forehead against his nose. Pain explodes in her skull, but it knocks him back. She scrambles out from under him, into the corner.

He touches his face. 'You broke my nose,' he snarls.

She's pretty sure she's broken her own nose, too, against his chin. 'From now on, that's your side.' She points to the other half of the tank, behind the low wall. 'And this is mine. We keep the water on the wall, and we share it.'

'You've had yours,' he insists, but with less confidence.

'Yeah?' She rises. Tells herself to act strong. 'You think?'

He stares at her, sizing her up. She stands on her tiptoes and squares her shoulders, making herself big, like she's trying to scare off a bear. Callum's taller than her, but he's been starved for longer. And she was an athlete, once. A good one, no matter what people say.

'Fine,' he says at last. Then, clutching his nose, he climbs across the low wall to the other side of the tank.

Elise sits back down, letting her heart rate drop. She checks—the sharpened bracket is on her side. She tucks it under her sleeping fleece.

No more scraping the belt against the wall. She needs to save her strength. She'll have to sleep sometime. And if she nods off before Callum does, she's sure the water will be gone when she wakes up.

If she wakes up at all.

CHAPTER 44

Moon Hartnell opened her eyes and reached for her phone. The screen said it was 6.51 a.m. on 14 February. Valentine's Day.

Most mornings, she would stay in bed until her alarm went off. Usually for a while after that, too—as long as it took for Mum to bang on her door. Not today. Moon sprang out of bed, took off her pyjamas and wriggled into her school uniform.

She had already written the card. She tucked it into the pocket of her jacket, grinning. Mr Glyk was going to lose his shit when he read it.

He had told her to call him Callum, and she had, throughout the affair. As soon as he ended it, she had gone back to thinking of him as Mr Glyk. It made him seem extra ridiculous, and a little bit pathetic.

Moon brushed her teeth, styled her hair, applied a little mascara and smeared on some lip gloss. Sometimes she liked to have a shower before school, but today she was keen to get out the door. She would have a bath later. Celebrate with some candles and Epsom salts.

When she opened her bedroom door, Mum was standing there. 'You're up early.'

'Good morning to you, too,' Moon replied. She always tried not to be adversarial, but Mum made it hard.

'Anything special happening today?'

Moon shrugged. 'Not so far as I know.'

Mum still looked suspicious, but stood aside and let her pass.

In the kitchen, Moon boiled the kettle, made a cup of peppermint tea and took it to the table. She itched to take her phone out of her pocket, but Mum was watching, so she just gazed out the window at the pomegranate tree in the front yard.

'You're not eating?' Mum asked.

Moon sipped her tea. 'I'll have a banana when I get to school.'

Mum didn't look like she believed her. 'You have to eat, Moon.'

'I will, relax. Is Dad up?'

'Not yet. Why?'

Moon shrugged again. 'I just wanted to know.'

Silence fell, broken only by the scraping of Vegemite onto toast. Eventually Mum put the knife down. 'You know I care about you, don't you?'

Moon forced a smile. 'Of course.'

'Well.' Mum squeezed Moon's shoulder and turned back to her toast. 'I wanted to say so, anyway.'

Later, when she was flying down the hill on her bike, no helmet, the wind in her hair, Moon realised she should probably have said she cared about Mum, too. She had been distracted, thinking about Mr Glyk. She told herself she'd mention it later. If she could find a way to bring it up casually. She didn't want to sound like a loser.

At 3.15 p.m. Moon was leaning against the wall outside the gym, twiddling a stick between her fingers as though it was a cigarette. She was nervous. Why was she nervous?

Maybe because it had always been Mr Glyk, not her, who organised their moments alone. He had told her where and when to meet him—in a stairwell after school, halfway up a bushwalking trail, at a toilet block next to the highway. Once he'd even given her a detention, just so they could spend a few hours together on a Friday evening. It had seemed funny, at the time.

The boys at school had never shown any interest in Moon. She'd told herself that was a good thing—they were all so immature. Loud, stupid, shoving each other and hooting like apes. She'd started dressing in punk garb, so it seemed like the pink hair and the torn leggings were putting the boys off. It worked—people thought there was something wrong with her clothes, rather than with her.

And then, suddenly, there was Mr Glyk. Who seemed to really *see* her. Who got her jokes. Who always checked if she was okay when she was sitting alone at lunch, again. Who crouched next to her desk, so close she could smell his aftershave. Whose warm smiles started to seem flirty, in a way she slowly realised wasn't her imagination.

The first time they kissed, she knew it was wrong. But she'd spent so much time wanting to be wanted. She was too scared to turn down any affection, even if it came from a teacher. She told herself this was a sign of how sophisticated she was, an older man being attracted to her. She chose to think of them as a misunderstood couple, star-crossed lovers. She had let him talk about their future—when she was eighteen and they could be together openly. She had let him do all sorts of things.

When he gave her the ecstasy and she woke up naked, she was forced to admit it had gone too far. However she'd imagined her first time over the years, it hadn't involved getting high with a teacher, who wasn't even that good-looking once you got a close-up view.

She'd been going to break off the affair—that was the word he always used. But he beat her to it. 'We can't do this anymore,' he said, acting noble. She was furious. What the hell was his problem? Was she too old for him all of a sudden? Was he only interested in virgins?

When she told him she was pregnant, he believed her, but didn't seem as scared as she'd hoped. She was shocked when he suggested an abortion, casually but firmly. It was then that she finally understood—he had never loved her, not for real. She had just been a juicy piece of jailbait to him, the fucker.

Now she wanted to hurt him. And refusing to have the fake abortion seemed like the best way to do it.

The door creaked open next to her, and Mr Glyk walked out of the gym. It was the end of the day, and he'd changed into a suit and tie. Not his normal casual clothes. She remembered—he'd organised some kind of singles dinner for Valentine's Day. Hoping to pick up, probably. Now that he was done with her, or so he thought.

'Hi, Mr Glyk.'

He looked like he'd seen a ghost. 'Moon?'

'That's me.' She tried to look vulnerable. 'I know you said you didn't want to see me anymore—'

'Get in here, before someone spots you.' He pulled her into the gym.

It was empty at this hour. The equipment had all been packed away, the wooden floor mopped, the basketball hoops taken off the backboards and locked away so no one could steal them.

'I have something for you.' She reached into her jacket and gave him the Valentine's Day card.

'You can't keep doing this, Moon,' he said.

'Just read it.'

Grimacing, he tore open the pink envelope and scanned the handwritten message inside. Moon had made it as over-the-top and sickly sweet as possible. It was the message of a girl who was *definitely* keeping his baby.

But again, he didn't look as frightened as he should have. 'It's over, Moon. I'm sorry.'

'I know.' She forced a sniff. 'But I wanted to tell you how I felt.'

'Of course. I get it, I do. But you—' He broke off, as if something else had occurred to him. 'Maybe we could talk about it tomorrow.'

She was thrown. 'Talk about what?'

He smiled. 'Your feelings. And anything else you'd like to get off your chest.' He glanced down at her chest as he said this.

Moon felt a creeping sense of unease. She'd wanted to frighten him—she hadn't wanted to rekindle his lust.

'Tomorrow?' she asked.

'Right. Tomorrow.'

'Where?' Then, before he could answer, she said, 'Actually, no. Thank you, but I've said what I needed to say.'

He didn't seem disappointed by this answer, and she wondered if he'd tricked her with some kind of reverse psychology. 'Okay,' he said. 'Your choice. I'll see you around, Moon.'

She could feel his eyes on her as she walked out. It made her skin crawl. At first she'd thought he was a tragic romantic, then a desperate pervert. Now she couldn't shake the feeling that he was something else entirely.

CHAPTER 45

As the sun sets, Vermilion watches the house through binoculars. He's crouched on the dirt behind a tree in a distant paddock on the other side of the road. The hood of his overalls isn't doing much to keep his ears and scalp warm. He's seen movement behind the lacy curtains, but not much of it, and only from one room at a time. The client seems to be alone.

He's a little late. In his business, being on time is a surefire way to get nabbed by police.

He sweeps the binoculars across the surrounding paddocks. Long grass trembles. A kangaroo stares at him, chewing slowly. No one other than him seems to be out here. No planes have passed overhead. No drones either, judging by the lack of noise. The whole time he's been watching, only two vehicles have passed by on the road. Both trucks, big and hard to manoeuvre. Not undercover police.

It's time to meet his client.

He starts shuffling down the hill, pushing the long yellow grass aside, watching out for snakes. His dad got bitten by a brown snake once, while looking for Vermilion's soccer ball. Lost his leg. Vermilion vividly remembers the ride in the back of the ambulance, his dad shaking, the only time Vermilion has ever seen him scared—then furious, when he saw that his son was watching. At the time, Vermilion thought his dad was angry about the ball. Now he thinks it was about the fear. No one was allowed to see Dad looking afraid. Vulnerable.

He crosses the road, briefly exposed. His grey overalls concealed him well in the paddock, not so well against the black asphalt. Then his feet find the dirt again, and he's invisible once more, trudging alongside the road, away from the house, towards his van.

In the back, there are dozens of four-litre cans. All are filled with paint, except for one. That can, buried deep in the middle, contains his kill kit.

Vermilion pulls on some black gloves, starts the van and takes it up the road towards the house. He parks at the top of the driveway, picks up the can from the back and gets out. The day has been warm for July, but there's a sudden chill now. A wind, maybe all the way from Antarctica, sweeping away the still air.

He walks up the last few metres of the gravel driveway, still scanning the windows for signs of a trap. He has a sense of unease he can't explain. There are no other vehicles around. No tracks from police-issue boots. No sounds on the wind.

He's come this far. May as well complete the job. He walks up the steps, keeping his footfalls light, and reaches for the front door.

Someone knocks, and Stephanie's heart leaps into her throat, her mouth suddenly dry. There's a *tap-tap-tap*, then a pause, *tap-tap*, another pause, *tap*. Like *three, two, one, go*.

It's him.

She puts away the dustpan and brush. Smooths down the shirt she picked. She's oddly keen to make a good impression on the hired killer.

As she approaches the door, she sees a large, dark blur behind the frosted glass.

As a girl, Stephanie read a story in which a grieving mother used a cursed souvenir—the severed paw of a monkey—to make a wish. The woman wished her child back from the dead. That night she heard a knock at the door, but before she could open it, her wise husband used the paw to wish away the thing on the doorstep, whatever it had been.

Stephanie hesitates with her hand on the doorknob. But only for a second.

Vermilion doesn't look like a hit man. She had pictured a slick-looking bloke in a suit and tie, a mafia type. Instead he's wearing painter's overalls, with a hood, and holding a large can in one gloved hand.

He pulls back the hood and rolls up his sleeves. He's bald, with a heavy brow and hairy arms. 'I'm looking for Leah Wentworth,' he says.

Stephanie remembers the correct response. 'She doesn't live here anymore. Come in—I'll find a forwarding address for you.'

Vermilion is tall—he stoops to follow her into the warmth of the house. He puts the can on the floor. Something rattles inside.

'Thanks for coming,' she says.

'No worries.' He flicks a cigarette into his mouth. 'Is this okay?'

'Sure.'

He opens a gold lighter with a crossed swords logo.

'Can I get you a tea or coffee?' Stephanie asks.

He smiles. 'I could murder a coffee.' He looks around, taking in the house. His gaze flicks to the wet patch on the carpet in front of the bathroom door.

'A plumbing problem,' Stephanie says. 'The pump exploded, and the toilet backed up.'

'Ah. Not in my skill set, I'm afraid.'

She laughs nervously. 'This way.' She walks through the living area into the kitchen. Vermilion picks up the can and follows her. She takes two china cups off a shelf and switches on the kettle, which starts to emit a low rumble.

'I need to apologise,' she says.

'Oh?' There's a warning note in his voice.

'I brought you here to dispose of three bodies. But two of them are still alive. I couldn't do it.'

He relaxes. 'That's okay. Not everyone has the stomach for it.'

'It was a practical issue.'

'I see. They're contained?'

'Yes. One male, one female. In an empty septic tank out back. Just behind that big rock.' She points out the window.

'No problem. I can take care of that for you.' He sucks on his cigarette and blows the smoke out his nose. 'An extra four hundred each.'

That's significantly cheaper than on his website. Perhaps he feels sorry for her—or maybe he knows that if the price is too high, she might make another attempt on her own.

'Deal.' She pulls the key for the hatch out of her pocket. 'That will get you in. Do you want to know who they are?'

'No.' Vermilion takes the key and watches her put a bag of Lady Grey into one cup, the tag dangling over the rim, and spoon some Moccona into the other. 'Maybe they wronged you, or threatened to. Maybe you need a secret kept. That part's not my business.'

Stephanie nods. The conversation has a sense of unreality about it, as though the hatch out back might turn out to be a rabbit hole. 'How do we do the part that *is* your business?'

'Let's work backwards.' He crouches, then pops the lid off the can with a bottle opener. 'Payment comes last, so I like to discuss that first.'

'Bitcoin, I assume?' She tries to make this sound natural, like she's used to paying for things with cryptocurrency. In reality, she's only done it once before, and she found it baffling and fiddly.

'No. It's all out in the open. I'll call you next week and give you some account details. You'll make a regular bank transfer. Then I'll send you a painting.'

From the can he takes a handgun, a suppressor, a length of rope, a small hacksaw, a roll of tape, some garbage bags and a straight razor.

'A painting?' Stephanie asks.

'Right. If the police, or anyone else, ask why you sent the money, you'll say it was to commission a painting. You can even show it to them. I'll say the same thing.'

She remembers Elise telling her that Callum recently bought an expensive painting. She doesn't like having anything in common with him. 'Are the police likely to ask me that?'

'It's just a precaution.'

'What will the painting look like?'

'Abstract. Eighteen by twenty-four inches. You can choose the colours. We'll discuss it over the phone and via email. That way, the comms trail makes the transaction look even more legitimate.'

Stephanie nods slowly. 'Clever.'

A businesslike smile. 'Is that all okay?'

'Sure.'

'Let's talk disposal, then. You said there are three bodies?'

'Two of them are alive right now, but yes.'

'We'll get to that. Will you need proof that any of them are dead? For an inheritance, perhaps?'

'Quite the opposite. I'd rather no one ever knows what happened to them.'

'Great. Missing persons don't get as much attention as homicides. Do you have their phones or credit cards?'

'Credit cards for two,' she says. 'A phone for one.'

'The phone is switched off right now?'

'Correct.'

'Okay. I'll switch it on and leave it with the credit cards in a high-theft neighbourhood in Canberra. That way there will be some transactions and signal tower movement that suggest the targets are still alive.'

Stephanie did something similar with Callum's car—left it in a poorly lit public car park with the keys still in it. 'And the bodies?'

'There's plenty of room in the van. Are there any body parts you want to keep?'

Stephanie is shocked. 'God, no.'

'Okay. Just checking. I have access to a fertiliser factory,' Vermilion adds. 'The bodies will be turned into blood-and-bone mix and sold. No one will ever know.'

She thinks of the bags of fertiliser down in the septic tank. It's possible that she already has some of Vermilion's past victims.

'What about the killing itself?' she asks.

'You want details?'

'Yes.'

The rumbling of the kettle has turned into a roar. Vermilion raises his voice to be heard over it. 'My specialty is suicides. But in this case, that won't be necessary. Are the neighbours close enough to hear a gunshot?'

Herbert said he was going back to Wagga, but Stephanie has no proof he's actually gone. 'I'm not sure,' she says.

'No problem.' Vermilion holds up the straight razor. It's spattered with paint, but the edge is keen. 'This is just as easy, and almost as quick.'

'What do you mean, your specialty is suicides?' Stephanie asks.

'If the client needs to prove the target is dead, it's best to make it look like they ended their own life. That's not suspicious, because suicide is so common.'

Stephanie stares at the razor in his hand. She thinks about the painting Callum bought. She thinks about how easy Vermilion was to find—the number one ranked killer in her area.

'Unfortunately,' Vermilion adds gently, like he's worried he's offended her.

Her mouth is dry. 'How would you do it? If one of your clients needed a secret kept and asked for a fake suicide?'

If Vermilion hears the dawning horror in her tone, he doesn't show it. 'Again, let's work backwards. The police can't usually pinpoint the time of death exactly, so some well-chosen web searches immediately afterwards can make the scene more convincing. If someone commits suicide, they usually Google the available methods first. It's easy enough to type a goodbye note on a computer—it doesn't even need to be printed.'

'And the method?'

The kettle boils and clicks off. Silence falls. Stephanie makes no move to pour the water into the cups.

'Hanging is popular,' Vermilion says. 'A strangulation can be disguised as a hanging without too much difficulty, or even as an accident. Pills are a little harder, but still doable. And slashed wrists are a good choice.'

'Slashed wrists.' Stephanie's breaths are getting louder. Her vision is tunnelling.

'Depending on the size and strength of the target,' he says. 'They have to be held down.'

There's a pause.

'Excuse me a moment,' Stephanie says, and leaves the room.

CHAPTER 46

The woman, Stephanie, doesn't go towards the bathroom, where Vermilion saw the water leak before. Instead she ducks left, towards what looks like an office, or maybe a bedroom. There could be an ensuite through there, he supposes. One without a plumbing problem.

But she's gone a while.

He lingers in the living room, near the sofa. It's times like these he thinks about quitting. He's made enough money, supposedly from his artworks, that non-criminals are starting to notice. Recently, a rich widow enquired about buying one of his paintings and didn't ask him to kill anyone as part of the bargain. She just liked his style—or, more likely, she assumed he was talented because he was successful. Others might make the same mistake. He could go straight and just be an artist for the rest of his life.

'Drop it.'

He turns around and sees Stephanie in the doorway that separates the living area from the entryway, holding a rifle.

No one has pointed a gun at him since Afghanistan. Was it something he said?

He raises his hands, still holding the straight razor. Slowly backs away towards the kitchen. 'If you're having second thoughts . . .'

She keeps pace with him, the rifle aimed at his head. 'I said, drop it.'

He lets go of the razor, shifting his foot slightly so the blade doesn't hit it. The razor clatters to the kitchen floor.

'There's no need for threats,' he says. 'I'm here to help you, remember?'

'You killed my daughter.'

Ah. Vermilion's heart sinks, weighed down by the familiar sense that this client will be reluctant to pay.

'If that's true,' he says, 'and I'm not saying it is, surely your problem would be with the person who hired me? I am an instrument of their will, nothing more.'

It's a common joke in his profession: *Hired guns don't kill people. People kill people.*

Stephanie's eyes glow with fury. 'You held her down and cut her.'

Vermilion remembers the job now. A girl about the right age, same grey-green eyes as the mother, at a house not too far from here. Teenage targets are unusual. He didn't like doing it. But he considers himself a professional.

'I could tell you who my client was. Wouldn't you rather shoot them?' Vermilion reaches for the kettle. 'Let's discuss this over tea, like civilised people.'

The tendons twitch in Stephanie's wrist as she puts more pressure on the trigger. 'Hey! Don't—'

Vermilion picks up the kettle and throws it at her.

The gun goes off, but he's already dropped to the floor. The bullet punches through the wall behind him. The kettle sails through the air, trailing boiling water. Stephanie darts aside, but not quickly enough. The water splashes her bare arm, and she screams.

Vermilion twists sideways, reaching into his can for the pistol. In one smooth motion he flicks off the safety and takes aim—

At an empty doorway. Stephanie is gone.

He rises to his feet and sidesteps, in case she pops out for another shot. He keeps the pistol trained on the doorway, but she doesn't reappear.

'You missed me,' he calls. 'No harm, no foul. I'll just go, all right?'

He won't. Stephanie has seen his face, and it's possible she told her two captives he was coming. He can't leave anyone alive. But she might not have figured that out.

He listens for a moment longer, then moves through the living area towards the doorway as fast as he dares. He swivels left and right. Clear.

She can't have gone out the front door—he'd have heard. She's still in the house, somewhere. She has a home court advantage, but his reflexes are probably quicker, and it's easier to shoot someone at close range with a pistol than with a rifle.

He steps over the water leaking from the bathroom and turns left, retracing Stephanie's steps from earlier. It's a small study, tidy. He quickly checks behind the door and under the desk. He's box-breathing—inhale for four, hold for four, exhale for four, rest for four. It keeps his hands steady.

As he turns to leave the room, he hears a soft scuffle from back the way he came. She's slipped past him. The lock clicks in the front door.

He can't let her get away. He turns and runs out of the study, back down the hallway to the front door, finding it closed and deadlocked. She hasn't escaped. She's locked him in.

He sees her reflection in the frosted glass, taking aim behind him. He ducks. The glass shatters at the same moment. Vermilion swivels, shifting one knee to the ground and raising the gun with both hands. As the falling glass jingles, he fires three times, the gun kicking in his hands.

The first shot thuds into the brickwork next to Stephanie. The second one punches through the muscle between her neck and shoulder. The third one goes over her head as she scrambles back, gasping.

Vermilion moves after her, pulling the trigger over and over, but she's out of sight again. It's like hunting Houdini.

He has to keep going. He's seen people die from wounds like that, but he's seen them survive, too.

The back door bangs. He takes the corner in time to see her out the window, sprinting away through the garden in the failing light.

He wrenches open the door and steps onto the porch. He can't run and shoot straight at the same time. He has to choose. *Chase or fire?*

He plants his feet, lines up a shot, takes it. *Blam.*

A miss. Stephanie disappears into the trees.

She definitely has the advantage now. She's out there in the dark with a long-range weapon. He's up here, lit by the house, with a pistol.

Cursing, Vermilion goes back and grabs a spare clip from the paint can. Then he's outside again, trotting down the steps into the garden. He hurries towards the boulder he saw earlier. He can take cover behind that, and regroup.

Mentally he's already staging the scene. He's been wearing gloves since he got here, and the pistol is a ghost-gun—assembled from a kit, with no serial numbers on any of the pieces, and a new barrel for this job. It can't be traced to him or to any of his previous crimes. Once Stephanie is dead, he can collect his razor, clean her computer and search the house for other traces. But there's no way to make her death look like a suicide, not now he's clipped her, and not now that there are bullet holes in the walls. The cops will sniff around for months. He needs at least one more body. That way he can make it look like they killed each other. Case closed.

He crouches behind the boulder. A plan is forming, based on something his lieutenant once said—*We're outnumbered, fellas, so let's create a distraction.* Two of Stephanie's captives are still alive. Vermilion can make the male put on his painter's overalls, then let him make a run for it. While Stephanie is hunting the male, Vermilion can get the drop on her. The tricky part will be making sure the male doesn't make it off the property. Killing the female won't be a problem.

The hatch is right where Stephanie said it would be. He takes out the key she gave him, opens the padlock, pockets it and lifts the lid.

CHAPTER 47

Clang, clang, clang. The sound of boots on the ladder wakes Elise. She's slept deeply, exhausted—but now gets the sense there have been strange noises for a while. Popping sounds in the distance.

She sits up in a panic. She fell asleep. She wasn't supposed to fall asleep. Where's Callum? Where's the bracket? Where's the water?

Somebody steps off the ladder onto the concrete floor. Elise scrambles to her feet, still dizzy and confused.

A cigarette lighter clicks. A flame appears. She's so used to the dim chamber that it seems painfully bright, casting a flickering glow over the whole tank.

The person isn't Callum or Stephanie. Someone much bigger—he has to stoop to fit. As he holds up the lighter to better illuminate the tank, his face is revealed.

It's Aiden Deere, the painter. He's wearing gloves and holding a pistol.

He sees her at the same moment. Recognises the red hair, the phoenix tattoo. His mouth twists like he's just bitten something with an unexpected flavour, neither pleasant nor unpleasant. 'You're the PI,' he says. 'Tina.'

Elise doesn't correct him. 'How did you find us?'

'Who are you?' Callum asks from behind her.

She feels like she's dreaming. Maybe she is. 'This is Aiden Deere. The guy you bought the painting off.'

Deere shifts his gaze to Callum. 'Mr Callum Glyk,' he says, like he's just figured something out.

'What are you doing here?' Elise asks.

'I'm here to rescue you both—but the woman isn't far away. Callum, you'll need a disguise. If she recognises you, she might shoot.' Deere starts peeling off his overalls, exposing a shirt and trousers that look cheap—the kind he might throw away if any paint got through. 'Keep the hood on, to hide your hair. Tina, I'm sorry, I don't have anything that will fit you. You'll just have to stay close to me.'

Callum seems wary. Frightened, even. Elise has no idea why. The hatch is open. Why isn't he already halfway up the ladder?

Deere holds the overalls out to Callum.

He doesn't move. 'I'll take my chances,' he says.

'Don't be a moron.' Deere sounds angry. He throws the clothes at Callum.

Elise is still catching up. 'Why don't you just call the police?'

'I already did,' Deere says. 'But apparently something is happening on the other side of town. All the cops are dealing with it. It'll take at least an hour for them to show up. The woman will have found us by then, and I don't want to get trapped down here with you two.' He gives Callum a strangely threatening look. 'Put those on.'

Reluctantly, Callum steps into the overalls and pulls them up.

'How did you find us?' Elise asks again. It seems so implausible, being rescued by a painter from Canberra.

'I'll explain on the way,' Deere says. He steps aside so they can get to the ladder.

Callum clambers over the low wall. The overalls are too big for him, and he's moving stiffly.

'No. You first, Tina.' Deere gestures with the gun to the ladder. Something about that movement, almost like he's sending them up there at gunpoint, makes Elise hesitate.

The gloves. The gun. Stephanie's voice: *Oh, don't worry. Help is coming.*

Callum doesn't seem to hear him. He puts one foot on the ladder, but Elise grabs him. 'Wait. It's a trap.'

'What?' Callum tries to struggle out of her grip, suddenly keen to be first out.

Deere levels the gun at him. 'Don't listen to her.'

'You're some kind of hired killer.' Elise lets go of Callum and backs away. She's unarmed, but not for long. 'No wonder your paintings are rubbish. Stephanie brought you here to get rid of us.'

'Oh, *shit*,' Callum says.

'If that were true, you'd be dead already,' Deere snaps. 'Up the ladder, both of you. Tina first.'

'Why?' Elise crouches, keeping one hand behind her back. Reaching towards her sleeping fleece, where she hid the sharpened bracket. 'So you can shoot us when we get to the top? Makes sense. You don't want to carry our bodies up the ladder—'

'That's enough,' Deere shouts. The gun is pointed at her, now. 'I don't have time for this. Get moving.'

Elise pushes her hand under her fleece to grab the bracket—

But it's gone. *Fuck!*

'Get moving!' Deere stomps towards her.

She turns to stand up, then keeps turning, faster, shifting her weight onto one foot. As he closes in, she turns the spin into a kick, knocking the cigarette lighter out of his hand.

He fires twice, the noise deafening in the enclosed space. But he's blind without the lighter. Elise isn't. She has evolved, the days and nights down here turning her into some kind of nocturnal creature. As the ricochets buzz overhead and the burning lighter sails away through the air, she uses her other leg to kick Deere square in the chest. Her legs are still the strongest part of her body. Even a big man like Deere is knocked backwards, slipping on a crushed cereal box and landing on the fertiliser bags, next to his lighter.

The little flame is still burning—and starting to grow. Melting through the plastic, devouring the fertiliser beneath.

Elise snatches up the woollen fleece with one hand and grabs Callum with the other. She elbows the water bottle off the low wall as she drags him over it, putting the concrete between them and the gun.

Deere is back on his feet. 'Get back here!'

As they hit the ground on the other side of the wall, Elise grabs the water bottle and twists off the lid. Then she pulls the fleece over them both like a blanket.

Just in time. There's no kaboom, but a tremendous *whumpf*, like an approaching hurricane, and the whistle from the ventilation tube becomes a shriek.

The fertiliser explodes with a flash, making the septic tank as bright as the surface of the sun. It's blinding even through the fleece, even through her closed eyelids.

She's trying to pour the water onto their bodies, but it seems to evaporate before it reaches them. The steam is suffocating. Her skin sizzles all over, like she's being microwaved. Every time she thinks the fire has reached its zenith, it grows even more. She's finally here—in hell, with flames that just keep getting bigger and louder for all eternity, so hot they burn the screams right out of her lungs.

Then there's a dip in the temperature. The fire hasn't gone out, but it's coming back down from its peak after consuming most of its fuel. They can't wait for it to die completely, though. There's no air.

'Come on!' She shouts the words, but they come out as a whisper. With no clue if Callum heard her, she drags him back over the low wall—touching the concrete is like putting her hand on a pizza stone—and they stumble towards the ladder together. Her nostrils sting. Her eyes are streaming.

Then a monster made of fire rears up at them. Elise shrieks. Aiden Deere is still alive, his clothes ablaze, his flesh peeling off in charred strips. The gun is gone—his burning claws clench and unclench, empty. She doesn't know if he can see her or if he still has eyes. As he lunges forward, she goes to punch him, forgetting that the hard plastic bottle is still in her hand. She clobbers him with it.

Sparks burst from his ruined face and he goes down, squirming like a snake.

Elise stumbles around him, then realises she's lost her grip on Callum. She turns but can't see anything through the smoke. When she tries to call his name, it comes out as a coughing fit.

She doesn't want to leave her brother. But she refuses to die for him.

Staggering through the heat and the smoke, she bumps into something made of metal. The ladder! It must be. The steel is scorching. She grabs it anyway, the skin of her palms frying like bacon. A river of cold night air pours down on her from above. It's keeping her alive, but also feeding the flames below. She climbs. The ladder seems to have hundreds of rungs.

Suddenly she can see again. She's surrounded by melted plastic—the hatch has dissolved in the heat. Her plan would have worked. Her plan *did* work.

She gets her elbows up over the edge and drags herself out of the hole. As if the fire has given birth to her. She crawls away and collapses onto the cold grass. The blaze roars behind her, smoke pouring from the hatch.

She's out. She's free.

But only for a second.

There's a faint rattle behind her. The sound of a rifle being raised.

'Where is he?' Stephanie demands.

CHAPTER 48

Elise tries to speak, but her lungs are too raw. Tries to stand, but her limbs are jelly.

Stephanie is underlit by the flickering glow of the fire. She puts the safety catch on, apparently just so she can take it off again and make that menacing click. 'I'm not going to ask twice.'

Elise finally manages to catch her breath. 'He's dead. They're both dead.'

'Don't lie to me.' Stephanie takes another step. An ammunition pouch jingles on her hip. She won't miss at this range.

'You got what you wanted!' Elise rasps. 'I burned them up! Just let me go!' She swings a fist at Stephanie's ankle, but the blow has no power. It feels like punching a table leg.

Stephanie grabs Elise by the wrist and drags her to her feet, nearly wrenching her arm out of its socket. She slams Elise against the boulder, teeth bared, eyes shining in the darkness. The smoke hides everything else from Elise's view. Stephanie is the whole world.

'Someone climbed out before you,' she snarls. She's bleeding from the neck, as though she was attacked by a vampire. 'Was it Callum, or Vermilion? Where was he going?'

Elise isn't thinking clearly enough to work out who Vermilion is. 'If you saw him, why are you ask—?'

Something erupts from Stephanie's chest. Her mouth pops open, and she makes a hard gagging sound. Horrified, Elise squirms out of her grip. Stephanie's eyes roll back and her arms slacken, then she crumples, thudding to the ground. The missing bracket protrudes from her back, quivering like a recently fired arrow.

Callum is standing over her, breathing heavily. His nose is still broken. He's pale and thin. But he saved Elise's life. To her, he's beautiful.

'Are you okay?' he asks.

She tries to say thank you. But what comes out is, 'How . . .?'

'I'm sorry. I didn't mean to leave you behind. Thought you were already out.' He nudges Stephanie's body with his foot. 'Then I couldn't find you, so I came back. Did the painter survive?'

Elise gets a flash of Deere's burning face, his hands grasping at her, the thud as she hit him with the bottle. She just shakes her head.

They're still right next to the hatch. The smoke billows out. Stephanie is done. Deere is done. They're free.

Callum covers his mouth with his elbow against the fumes. 'Come on. Let's get out of here.'

'Wait.' Elise crouches next to Stephanie. It's an old paramedic's instinct. She can't just walk away. She has to help—or, if she can't help, to bear witness. Never let a patient die alone.

She puts two fingers to Stephanie's throat. There's a flicker. Then nothing. It looks like Callum stabbed her through the heart.

Elise feels an unexpected wave of pity. Stephanie did terrible things, but it's hard to hold her responsible for them. The moment her daughter died, something in her broke.

No point giving her CPR. Chest compressions will just shred the heart further. Elise closes Stephanie's eyes. She reaches for her own phone, to note the time of death—but she still doesn't have it.

'Why was the painter here?' she wonders aloud. 'What was the plan?'

'We'll never know,' Callum says. 'No point thinking about it.'

'It seemed like Stephanie invited him here to kill us. But when I came out of the hatch, she seemed worried he might have escaped. Like she'd decided he was the enemy.'

'They were both violent criminals—I guess they betrayed each other. It doesn't matter now.'

'It's just so weird that the guy I visited while I was looking for you happened to be a hired killer—' Elise stops herself from talking, but too late. She's remembered why she visited Deere. Because Callum paid him seven thousand dollars, right around the time Moon died.

She turns back to look at Callum.

His eyes are hard. 'Goddamn it, Leesy. I told you not to think about it.'

CHAPTER 49

Elise rises slowly to her feet—and then keeps rising. It feels like she's floating away, a balloon tied around her throat. 'Oh, Callum.'

'It wasn't my fault,' he says flatly.

Nothing ever is, Elise thinks. 'You killed Moon.'

'She killed herself.'

'No.' Her guts are churning. 'The suicide was—'

'She killed herself the moment she decided to lie to me.'

Even though Elise has already figured it out, the admission is shocking. Her brother isn't just a rapist. He's a murderer, too.

She's edging away from him, but it's too late to run. He's untangling the rifle from Stephanie's corpse. She'll never get out of range.

'Moon said she was pregnant. I told her to have an abortion.' His voice is reasonable, exasperated. He's always been a talker, always sounded so convincing. 'I even said I'd come with her, like I did with Ophelia.'

314

Elise remembers the frightened-looking girl from the Catholic school, curled up in the hospital waiting room.

'But she refused,' Callum says. 'She said we had to raise the baby together, as a family. I asked her, what kind of fucking family would that be? Me in jail, her on her own, the baby taken away because she's only fifteen? But she didn't care. It was like the whole thing was a game to her.'

Elise wishes he looked different, sounded different. Like a mask had fallen away, revealing the psychopath beneath. But he's acting just like he always did. Like her brother. This is who he has been all along.

'She was a child, Cal,' Elise says. 'Children play games.'

'I kept waiting to hear that the medical examiner had identified pregnancy hormones in her blood, or cut her open and found a foetus.' His mouth is a grim line. 'But there was nothing. Eventually I realised what she'd done.'

'What *you* had done.' His monstrousness keeps growing. He didn't just murder Moon. He tried to murder his own child, too.

'And worse than that, she'd told her friends. How could she be so irresponsible?'

'She—was—a—child,' Elise shouts. He's going to kill her either way. She's not going to pretend to forgive him.

'Yeah, well. I've learned from the experience. I'll do better from now on.'

From now on. Like he already has another victim in mind.

Elise is sickened. 'Did you think I'd never figure it out? We'd just walk away, and I'd never notice the coincidence that it was your painter who showed up to kill us?'

'I hoped. You missed plenty of other things over the years.' He points the rifle at her. 'I'm sorry about this, Leesy.

Really, I am. But I know you. You'll tell your cop girlfriend everything, if I let you go.'

He pulls the trigger.

Click.

They stare at each other for a moment.

Elise turns and bolts.

'Leesy, wait!'

As if she would, after he just tried to shoot her. She runs and runs, her feet pounding the uneven ground. She's been starved, bled, burned. But she's always been faster than him. She just has to get to the road.

She expects Callum to give chase, but he doesn't. Instead she hears the clacking of bullets being loaded into the rifle. He must have found some ammunition on Stephanie's corpse.

Elise swerves, heading for the trees. On the open plain, he might be able to hit her. In the forest, he might not.

A bullet whines over her head, too close for comfort. She hears the bang a split second later. She ducks, and keeps running. Her lungs ache. There's still smoke trapped in them, shredding the cells like steel wool. But she's almost at the tree line. Shelter. *Just keep running.*

Something stabs her in the arm.

She screams. The shot has hit her triceps, maybe the bone, too. The wound is hot and bloody. Nausea rushes up her throat.

There's another bang as she stumbles into the trees and leans against one of them, protected by the trunk. She clamps a hand across the gunshot wound. The blood squirts onto her palm.

There are no more shots. But over her thumping heart, she can hear Callum coming after her.

Run, she tells herself. *If you stop, you're dead.*

She lurches away from the tree trunk and races through the bush towards the road. But she can't go as fast, now—the ground is strewn with rocks, fallen branches and hidden roots. She can't stop the bleeding from her arm. The blood loss makes it feel like she's in moon gravity, bouncing rather than running. He may not be able to shoot her through the trees, but he'll catch up long before she gets to the road.

Think, think! She looks around. There's nowhere to hide. The undergrowth is too thin, and she's too weak to climb a tree.

The grave. She can lie on top of Zach's corpse, or even under it. The thought is chilling, but it's her only chance. If she drags some branches over the hole, Callum may even forget it's there. He'll think she's escaped. To the road, or back to the house.

She changes direction again, running through the maze of trunks. She's trying to be quiet, but she's too dizzy. She used to compete with too much blood—now she doesn't have enough. One foot thuds barely in front of the other. She feels like a marathon runner, not a hurdler, on the last of the forty-two kilometres.

She risks a glance back, checking that she's alone—

But there's a dark blur between the trees.

Because Callum's face is hidden by the shadows, she can see him as a man, big and dangerous, rather than as the boy she used to love.

She can't hide now. He's seen her. She's doomed. But she keeps running, harder than when she qualified for the Games, harder than when she won gold, harder than anywhere.

'I can't let you go,' he shouts. Justifying it to himself. Like she did, when she took the transfusions. 'Don't you see that?'

She chokes back a sob as she runs.

His voice echoes. 'There's no other way, Elise.'

Her head is killing her. Her vision wobbles. She's not even sure what's keeping her upright.

The grave is just ahead. Stephanie has hidden it again, dragging branches over the hole.

A spark ignites in her brain. One last idea.

She slows. Wanting Callum to gain some ground.

'Leesy,' he calls, 'don't make this harder than it needs to be.'

She edges closer to the grave.

'What's the point of this?' He's right behind her now. 'Just give up. Aren't you tired?'

Fuck you, she thinks. She puts on a sudden burst of speed. As Callum charges out of the trees, Elise takes three final steps and then leaps.

She hurtles forward, just like in her last race. Hardly any vertical movement, just forward, lifting her feet but not her body—

And it's as if she never bombed out, as if she suddenly is the athlete she could have been. She lands perfectly on the other side of the grave, first one foot, then the other, and keeps running. An imagined crowd cheering in her head.

Maybe Callum can't jump far enough, or maybe he forgets the hole is there. She'll never know and doesn't care. She doesn't even look back as she hears the crash of branches, a startled curse, then a thud and the wet snap of a bone. Callum screams. The gun goes off.

Elise throws herself to the ground. But there are no more shots. Just more clicking. He must have only loaded four bullets. Now he's defenceless.

She climbs to her feet, shaking like a newborn sheep. She's badly burned, and she's still losing blood. She needs to get to a hospital.

Looking back, she sees Callum in the grave up to his chest. The hole isn't that deep—his legs must be bent beneath him. At least one is broken, maybe both.

He struggles but can't free himself. 'Oh God.' His flesh is pale, his eyes hollow. 'Help me!'

She watches him for a moment, catching her breath. She should run. But that's what she's always done, instead of facing him. Instead of seeing the clues. Instead of admitting there were clues to see.

She picks up a crooked stick, about half a metre long, jagged at one end.

'Please,' he says.

After snapping off some of the twigs that protrude from the sides, she approaches the hole. 'You tried to kill me.'

'I'm so sorry, Leesy.' Tears stream down Callum's cheeks. Real, or fake? Does it matter?

She says nothing. The stick feels heavy in her grip.

'I wasn't thinking straight. These last few weeks—it's all been too much.'

She keeps staggering towards the grave. Towards her brother, who always looked out for her.

Towards a killer, who only ever looked out for himself.

Which man is squirming in that open grave? Both? Neither?

'Please,' he whimpers. 'I didn't mean any of it. I'm sick in the head. You deserve better, I know that.'

Maybe his remorse is real. Maybe not.

Elise looks down at him. Tells herself to walk away.

'Just help me.' He reaches out with a trembling hand.

She takes one last step forward. Testing him.

He lunges for her ankle.

Elise tries to snatch her foot back, but she's too slow. Her leg is wrenched out from under her, and she slams down onto the dirt. Even as she screams, she's swinging the stick like a dagger, stabbing the air. Callum manages to avoid it, clawing at her head with grubby fingers. Like he's trying to blind her. She squeezes her eyes shut, twisting her face away as she keeps jabbing with the stick, over and over.

Finally it punctures something and sinks in deep. Callum goes still, but his weight holds her in place. She's wrapped up in him as though he's a mass of seaweed, drowning her. She has less and less strength to get free. She's lost her grip on the gunshot wound, and the struggle has reopened the cut to her inner elbow. She's so tired, slipping down, down, into a place deeper than sleep.

She's dying. But she's taken two monsters with her. It's not much consolation. But as the stars are snuffed out above her and true night floods in, she tells herself it's enough.

CHAPTER 50

The phone is ringing. Kiara snorts awake and fumbles around the bedside table, knocking off a book and a water bottle before putting her hand on the buzzing rectangle. Her eyes are too blurry to read the name on the screen. She pushes the green button and puts the phone to her ear. 'Yeah?'

'Grab your things and get in the car.' It's her sergeant.

Instantly she's wide awake. 'You got the warrant?'

She's surprised. When she made her case, the magistrate didn't seem convinced. Yes, Stephanie Hartnell could be connected to three missing people. But Warrigal was a small town—everybody was connected to everybody. Where was the material evidence? Where were the witnesses? The magistrate had agreed to deliberate, but Kiara hadn't expected the search warrant to come through.

'No,' Rohan said. 'But there's a fire. State early warning system picked up the smoke two minutes ago.'

'What? Where?'

'Exactly where you wanted to search. Burunda Road, number one-fifty.'

Kiara's blood runs cold. Has Stephanie torched her own house, rather than let it be searched?

'You got all that?' Rohan asks.

'Yeah. On my way.' Kiara isn't a firefighter, but she can help if someone needs rescuing—or arresting.

'Put your sprinklers on before you leave,' Rohan says. 'I don't know how bad this will get.'

By the time Kiara arrives, there's steam rather than smoke in the air. No signs that the house or the trees bordering the property have been burned. The satellite warning system did its job—the fire department reached the blaze before it could spread.

She parks a few car lengths back from the fire truck in case it has to move, then hurries up the driveway on foot. She can hear firefighters around the back of the house, shredding her crime scene with jets of water. Hi-vis shapes are moving behind the windows. They're searching the house. No sign of the ambulance yet, but she's heard there's one en route.

The garage door is open. She's horrified to see Elise's Suzuki there, her worst nightmare come to life.

The glass in the front door of the house has been smashed, but not by the fireys. The broken glass is mostly on the outside. Kiara opens the security door with a gloved hand and steps through the empty frame, bowing to avoid the remaining stalactites.

She thinks she's figured out the broad strokes of the case. Callum molested Moon, and Zach bullied her. Stephanie killed them both. Elise's relentless search led her here.

322

But then what? Kiara doesn't know the most important thing: is she too late?

'Please don't be here,' she mutters. 'Please.'

The formerly composed living area is in disarray. There's blood on the floor, and water, along with a straight razor and an electric kettle. Bullet holes in the walls, of two different sizes. Feeling sick, Kiara snaps some pictures with her phone. Who did this?

'Don't touch anything,' she tells a passing firefighter.

'Yeah, right,' he replies. Fireys save lives and homes—they think they're more important than police. Kiara wonders how much busier they would be if there were no cops to round up the pyromaniacs.

The back garden has been trampled. She finds the rest of the firefighters blasting their hoses into a steaming hole in the ground. Like a portal to another dimension.

There's a body nearby. A woman. Kiara gets a flash of terror, but it's not Elise.

Stephanie Hartnell is pale, her eyes closed, a sharpened piece of metal wedged through her heart. When Kiara touches her, her flesh is cool but not cold. She's been dead at least twenty minutes, though not more than two hours.

Kiara crouches to take some more photos, then stands up. 'What do we have here?'

'Ammonium nitrate, I reckon,' one firefighter says without looking away from the flames. Her chin is marked by old burns. 'A cheap way to boost the nitrogen content in soil, but very flammable. Anything else would be out by now.'

'You think it was a bomb?'

'Not my department. You smell that?'

Kiara can only smell smoke and steam. 'Smell what?'

'There's another body down there,' the firefighter says. 'Mark my words.'

Shell casings are sprinkled on the ground. Kiara takes a picture, then picks them up. A hunting rifle, judging by the calibre. A possible match for one of the two guns fired in the house. So where is it now?

Looking at this side of the house, she can't see any broken windows or holes in the exterior walls. She rotates a full three-sixty. The shooter could have been aiming into the trees—some grass is trampled in that direction.

'Anyone searched over there?' she asks the firefighter.

'No fire over there,' the woman says curtly. 'It's a big property. We'll search in the morning.'

'The morning might be too late.'

'Too late for what?'

Kiara can't explain. But she knows—or perhaps just hopes—that Elise is out there somewhere. That the body roasting in the hole isn't hers.

The search can't wait until Rohan gets here. 'I'm going to take a look,' Kiara says. 'If you hear gunshots, don't follow me. Wait for the other police.'

The woman gives her a look, like that was the most obvious piece of advice she's ever heard.

Kiara quickly bags Stephanie's hands so they can be tested for gunshot residue, then runs to the tree line. She clicks on her torch and sweeps it across the trunks. 'Elise?' she calls.

No answer.

Sirens. The ambulance must be almost here. Too late for Stephanie.

When Kiara enters the forest, some more casings glint in the torchlight. She can make out broken branches and spots of blood. She follows the trail deeper and deeper into the trees. Eventually she sees it. A pit, narrow and deep—with two bodies in it.

Her breaths shallow, she sweeps her torch across the tableau. One body is frozen halfway out of the hole, a stick wedged upwards into the brain via the mouth. Like a traitor's head mounted on a pike outside the queen's castle. A rifle strap is tangled around the chest. When the torch beam reaches the face, Kiara sees that it's Callum Glyk, his eyes wide and staring, his jaw slack, drooling blood.

The other body is—

'Elise!' she cries, racing over to the hole.

Elise is slumped crookedly next to her brother, one leg twisted beneath her. Her skin is charred, her hair and clothes dusted with ash. A gunshot wound to her arm. Her eyes are closed.

'No!' Kiara reaches down, grabbing Elise's wrist. She can't find a pulse. She tries the neck instead. *Please, please . . .*

A faint throb under her fingertips. Elise is alive.

Kiara puts her hands under Elise's armpits and drags her from the pit. Thorny branches and leaf matter come out with her. Now Kiara can see another body at the bottom of the pit—a teenage boy. Zach Locat, found at last.

She holds down the button on her radio. Fighting to keep her voice steady, she says, 'This is Senior Constable Kiara Lui, I'm at one-fifty Buranda Road. I have an injured adult female in the trees about a hundred metres north-east of the house. I need the ambos here, ASAP. I also have two deceased—'

Elise's eyelids flutter. 'Kiara?'

Kiara almost sobs with relief. She lets go of the radio and hugs Elise. 'I'm here.'

Elise seems too weak to hug back. 'I'm sorry about your laptop,' she whispers.

Tears sting Kiara's eyes. To think they split up over such a little thing. 'Don't worry about that. I'm going to get you out of here.' The gunshot wound is still oozing blood. Elise needs medical attention, as soon as possible.

'I had to do it,' she whispers.

For a second, Kiara thinks she's still talking about the laptop. But when Kiara releases her, she's staring at Callum's body.

A stone of fear grows in Kiara's stomach. 'Stop talking, okay?' A lawyer can't do much after a confession.

'He did something. He . . .' Elise trails off.

Kiara pulls Elise's uninjured arm over her shoulder, supporting her. 'There's an ambulance coming. We just have to get to the driveway. Can you walk?'

'I killed him,' Elise says, like Kiara didn't get it the first time.

'It doesn't matter,' she says, and it doesn't. Not to her.

In a moment of consciousness so brief it might be a dream, Elise grabs the sleeve of a paramedic she doesn't recognise. 'I'm a Jehovah's Witness,' she croaks.

'She's conscious,' the paramedic says, to someone out of view.

The lights inside the ambulance stab her eyeballs. The bed bounces under her. Something is coiled around her forearm.

'No blood products,' Elise says, and passes out again.

She dreams she's sitting in the stands, hard metal under her bum, watching a younger version of herself hurtle along the track. Her head is down, but her eyes are straight ahead. Jaw set. She's exhilaration in human form, too happy to show it.

'That's my daughter,' a voice says.

Elise turns and sees Mum sitting next to her, face shadowed by a huge sunhat.

Elise's arms are throbbing. She looks down and sees that they're covered in pinpricks. 'Everything hurts, Mum.'

'Yes,' Mum says simply. There's a great sadness in her eyes. She reaches over and squeezes Elise's hand. Together, they watch the girl sprint away into the sunshine.

CHAPTER 51

Dad answers the door on the fourth knock. It's only been four months since Elise infiltrated his practice to ask him for money, but he looks much older—his eyes pink-rimmed, his skin blotchy. He's shaved and put some mousse in his thinning hair, something he only does when he needs to feel like he's in control.

People have probably been giving him a hard time about Callum. Elise doesn't really give a shit.

'Hello, Elise,' he says, his face neutral. Like he wants to hug his daughter but also wants to punch his son's killer, and the two instincts have cancelled each other out.

'Hello, Dad.'

After a moment, he opens the door wider. 'Come in.'

'No thanks.'

They look at each other for a while. Elise's major injuries have healed, though with Gelofusine instead of blood transfusions it took a long time. The muscles of her right arm, the one Callum shot, are still weak. Her burned hands sometimes itch. The antibiotics wiped out her gut flora, so she has to eat carefully. She wears a brace under her clothes to support the knee Stephanie kicked. Despite this, she feels stronger than before. The tremors have gone. She no longer craves red blood cells, and can't quite remember why they ever held any appeal.

Everything came out in court. Ophelia testified that Callum had molested her. Computer forensics recovered deleted messages from his phone that confirmed his relationship with Moon. The propellant residue on his hands showed that he'd fired a gun, and the rifle found near his corpse bore his fingerprints. The locations of the bullets and cartridges were consistent with Elise's statement, and with her wounds. The magistrate accepted her plea of self-defence for his killing, and Deere's. Zach Locat's parents were in the courtroom, weeping. There was no posthumous trial for Stephanie; no one would ever be convicted of their son's murder.

The police made a list of several dozen people who had transferred money to Deere over the years. Each of them could be connected to a suicide, a missing persons case, an unsolved murder or, in one case, a mishap with some exercise equipment. They all claimed they just liked his art. The first of those trials was scheduled for next year.

She forces herself to hold Dad's gaze. 'Callum was the reason we moved, wasn't he?'

Dad says nothing.

'He did something to his girlfriend,' Elise continues. 'Gave her drugs? Raped her? We came to Warrigal so he didn't have to face the music.'

Dad is still silent.

'And the move before that,' Elise says, 'after all those animals turned up dead. My lizard, the bird I found, that cat that got strangled. Was that because of him, too?'

Dad clears his throat. 'Elise—'

She talks over the top of him. 'Poor Mum. Dragged from town to town, knowing her son was a psychopath. Always worried about what he might do next.' She raises her voice. 'You let me think *I* killed her. That the stress of me cheating—'

'I didn't know that Callum was—'

'I don't think you *wanted* to know. I think you were willing to turn a blind eye to anything and everything, no matter how bad it got.'

Dad looks angry now. 'If you had children of your own, you'd understand. Callum was my blood. Nothing's more important than that.'

Elise thinks of Moon, and Stephanie, and the trail of misery Callum left in his wake.

'Isn't it?' she says.

'You gave me plenty of headaches as well. But you're still my daughter. Will you just come in?'

He goes to grab Elise's arm, but she steps out of reach. 'No,' she says. 'Goodbye, Dad.'

In the process of moving all her belongings to Kiara's house, Elise finds herself looking at the boxes of Mum's stuff. She's never opened them. Now she feels like she's ready.

She had no idea Mum was so sentimental. There are VHS tapes, decorative plates, royal wedding commemorative tea towels, half-finished crochet patterns, endless books, and two jars that turn out to contain baby teeth. Photo albums are filled with pictures from Mum's uni days—she's laughing and drinking, surrounded by friends Elise never met. People from the town Mum was forced to leave. There are drawings, the scribbled subjects unrecognisable, with captions like, ELISE G, AGE 6.

There's a letter addressed to the editor of *The Warrigal Times*, sealed and stamped. Maybe Mum was about to send it before her heart attack. Elise opens it.

Her mother's handwriting is precise, which probably means this is a second or third draft. Another, scribblier version may be in this same box.

> *In response to your article on 9 September:*
> *Knock it off.*
> *Elise Glyk is not just a cheat. She is hardworking, smart, funny, kind. While volunteering with St John Ambulance and in her later work as a paramedic, she saved many of your lives.*
> *I'm proud of her, no matter how many people tell me not to be. You can all get stuffed.*

Elise smiles through the tears. Mum didn't often get angry. But when she did, it was a sight to see.

CHAPTER 52

The grass is painfully green. The flowers clenched in Elise's hand—wattle and kangaroo paw—are too vivid. The sun is out, and it's turned all the colours way up. Sweat is trapped under the brim of her hat. She finds herself walking carefully, as though the ground might not be solid.

Kiara squeezes her hand. 'You okay?'

'Yeah.' She squeezes back.

Guppy is having the time of his life, jerking the lead this way and that, sniffing like a coke-head. She doesn't have the heart to pull him closer. He deserves a little freedom. His ordeal was not unlike hers—maybe worse. At least Elise didn't have to drink out of a toilet.

There's someone up ahead. A man with hardly any chin, wearing a white polo shirt and shielding himself from the sun with an umbrella. He notices them and does a double take, recognising her.

Elise feels Kiara stiffen. But the man doesn't approach. He gives Elise a respectful little nod and hurries away, perhaps so they can have some privacy.

It's unsettling how quickly Elise's reputation has changed. She isn't a disgraced athlete anymore—she's the one who survived a terrible ordeal. The one who was right all along, saying that Callum hadn't fled. And the one who gave him and another monster what they deserved.

For a few people, Elise is tainted by Callum's crimes, being his sister. But not for most. The same folks who once berated her in the street are mostly quiet. Some want to hug her and to hear the story firsthand. Elise can't always avoid them. She's in public a lot, driving the ambulance.

Cards keep turning up at her house, but she's not there. The mail goes soggy and rots on her doorstep. She sleeps at Kiara's place most nights, Guppy curled at their feet.

Elise and Kiara soon find what they're looking for. There's no grave. Just a stone, round and natural looking. Two dates are carved into it, and a message:

MOON AMELIA HARTNELL

YOU WERE LOVED

Elise crouches down and rests the flowers against the stone. She places her palm flat on the grass, even though there's no body under there. Moon was cremated.

I'm sorry, Elise thinks. *Sorry I didn't let myself see what he was. Sorry I couldn't save you. Sorry about your mum.*

She presses her hand harder against the ground, as though she can push her thoughts down through the dirt into the next world. She takes a deep breath, and lets it go.

When she stands up, Kiara puts an arm around her. They are still for a long moment, in the sunshine.

'Want to go for a run?' Kiara asks finally. She's trying to cheer Elise up, and Elise is warmed by the effort.

But she's all done running. 'I think a walk will do.'

ACKNOWLEDGEMENTS

Thanks to all my friends at Allen & Unwin, especially Jane Palfreyman, Angela Handley, Elizabeth Cowell, Kate Goldsworthy and Janine Flew. Thanks also to my mates at Curtis Brown, especially Clare Forster and Benjamin Stevenson, who championed this book from the very beginning.

None of the characters are based on real people, but I need to acknowledge a few experts who were generous with their time, including Detective Sergeant Emily McCallum, private investigation consultant and former ambulance officer Amber Barber, Dr Maria Bernardi, twelve-time Australian national 400-metre hurdles champion Lauren Boden, and my well-read friend Isobelle Evans. Mistakes are my own.

Special thanks to Hannah Monson, for breathing life into the (fictional) town of Warrigal and its people, and to Sheelagh Noonan, for lending me the beautiful, isolated cottage in Braidwood where much of this book was written. Have you considered installing a septic tank in the back-yard, Sheelagh?

As always, thanks to my family, especially Venetia, who read several versions of this book and helped fix problems large and small. To Mum and Dad, who caught the last few typos. And my brother, Tom, who always sees the twists coming. If we weren't such good mates, I never would have dared to publish a book with this title, let alone this plot.

ABOUT THE AUTHOR

Jack Heath is the award-winning author of forty books, translated into nine languages. He lives on the land of the Ngunnawal and Ngambri people in Canberra, Australia. He is claustrophobic and faints at the sight of blood.

Read on for a preview of Jack's new book,
Kill Your Husbands

'A twisted and
devious ride.'
HAYLEY
SCRIVENOR

'Don't expect
to go to sleep.'
RAE
CAIRNS

JACK HEATH

SOME PEOPLE WOULD KILL FOR A WEEKEND AWAY

KILL *YOUR* HUSBANDS

'There are two brain-teasing mysteries
at play here: One, an expertly crafted
locked room puzzle to solve. Two ...
how is Jack Heath just so damn good?'
BENJAMIN STEVENSON

AVAILABLE FROM DECEMBER 2023

PROLOGUE

She stumbles downhill through the bush in the pouring rain, dressing-gown flapping, puddles splashing under her slippers. The beam of the torch is thin—she can point it at the trail before her feet or the branches in front of her face, but not both. The terrain is dangerous, sharp sticks and slippery rocks hidden just under the mud. She should have snatched up her walking shoes before she fled, but she hadn't wanted to stay in that house a second longer. Another mistake to add to the list.

The cold scorches her lungs. Her cheeks are numb. Her toes ache; she can already picture them turning black and popping off. The mountain is 130 kilometres from Warrigal, and most of the journey is dense bushland. If the weather stays this bad, she'll soon join the dead she's left behind. The voice in her head, which started as a whisper, has become a scream: *What if you're going around in circles?* At any moment, she could break into a clearing and find herself facing the house: those two big windows like glowing eyes, the twin chimneys like horns.

Her thoughts no longer make sense—probably a bad sign. She's been running downhill this whole time, so she can't be back at the top of the mountain. *Unless you're in hell already. Running for eternity, ending where you began.* She's never been very religious, but in her delirium, anything seems possible. The house on the mountaintop had felt safe when she was one of six. Then there had been five, and then four, then three. Now it's just her and God, out here in the dark.

She hears a creak behind her and whirls around. The trees watch her, as silent as jurors.

Has she been followed? She's left behind a trail of muddy footprints and blood-smeared leaves, but that wouldn't be obvious in the dark.

She chews her chapped lips. If she moves, she might be spotted; if she doesn't, she might be caught—

A sound like a gunshot rings out from above. She looks up. A bough has broken off one of the gum trees and is tumbling towards her, crashing through other branches on the way down. She throws herself aside, leaving a slipper behind, as the slab of wood hits the ground with a mighty crash.

That limb probably held on to the trunk for fifty years or more. Was she unlucky to be underneath when it finally snapped, or lucky that it didn't pulverise her? Is she being punished, or conspicuously forgiven?

Suddenly she feels wet tarmac under her feet. She looks around. The trees are gone. She's reached the road, flanked by paddocks. It's not midnight anymore—dawn is spreading from the horizon. Shivering, she tries to remember how she got to the bottom of the mountain, but her mind is quicksand, the memories already submerged.

Her phone chimes in her pocket—a sound she hasn't heard in three days. It keeps chiming as the backlog of messages comes through. She struggles to get her frozen hand into her pocket. When she pulls out the phone, it slips from her fingers, hitting the road with a metallic *splink*. 'No!' She scoops it up, frantically prodding the fractured glass. The lock screen glows, but she can't type in her pin. When she tries to swipe up, the image—her husband, smiling crookedly, his arms around her—keeps bouncing back.

Headlights wash over her. She whirls around, holding up a palm against the glare. Tyres squeal against the wet asphalt, drowning out her scream.

KIARA

The body lies in the middle of Victoria Street, knees folded backwards, arms splayed. At first it looks like the victim's jaw has fallen off, but as Senior Constable Kiara Lui leaps out of the car and sprints over, she sees the jaw has actually been smashed upward, flattened against the palate.

Kiara reaches for her radio, but she's off-duty, dressed in a denim jacket over a flower-patterned dress: no equipment belt.

The man lying on the road makes eye contact with her.

'Stay in the car,' she shouts over her shoulder, not wanting Elise to see.

Undeterred, Elise unfolds her long legs from the passenger seat and jogs over, carrying the first-aid kit from the glove box. Brushing her fringe out of her eyes, she stares down at the dying man. 'Well,' she says, 'we can't exactly give him mouth-to-mouth.'

It's the sort of joke Elise has been making a lot. Gallows humour is common among paramedics, but after the trauma Elise endured last year, Kiara is worried the nihilism runs deeper.

Kiara looks around. No pedestrians. No sign of the car that ran this man over. Just a flickering streetlight and a row of shuttered shops—a cafe, a real estate agency, a jeweller's. Only the King George pub on the corner is still open. The chalkboard out the front says, GET SCHNIT-FACED! CHICKEN SCHNITZEL AND BEER $10.

'Call an ambulance,' Kiara says.

Elise is crouched over the man, feeling for a pulse. 'You better do it.'

Kiara grabs her phone and dials Rafa.

The dying man is in his fifties, white, beanpole thin, with a sharp widow's peak and sad grey eyes. Elise starts chest compressions. Blood squirts from the gaping neck onto her silk skirt. She clamps one hand over the wound.

As the phone rings in her ear, Kiara looks down at the ruined fabric. Elise hardly ever gets dressed up. Tonight was supposed to be special—a chance to hit the reset button. Kiara can't afford to take her partner to a decent restaurant, but she thought a picnic dinner next to the Murrumbidgee River would be nice: a secluded spot where no one would be around to stare at them; a small bottle of sparkling, a tube of mozzie repellent, cheese and salad sandwiches with mud cake for dessert. Kiara imagined kissing Elise on the picnic rug, rolling around like teenagers. She'd hoped Elise might finally tell her what's been going on these past few weeks.

As usual, things haven't gone to plan.

Kiara scans the empty street. She can see the whole thing in her mind's eye: someone walks out the back door of the pub, spinning a car key on one finger, telling themselves they have no choice but to drive. It's too far to walk, they can't afford a cab, and anyway, how would they retrieve their car tomorrow? So they get behind the wheel and zoom around the corner, just as this unlucky guy happens to be crossing the road, camouflaged in his grey jumper and black jeans. The driver hits the brakes, but the alcohol has dulled their reaction time. The pedestrian disappears under the vehicle. The driver looks at the body and pronounces him dead, or as good as. Now they ask themselves, what's the point of sticking around? If they go to jail, their kids will starve, their business will go under, whatever—there's always some excuse. So they drive home, wipe the blood off the bull bar, and go to bed. Maybe they feel guilty, like that counts for something.

Kiara will do her job. She'll photograph the tyre tracks. She'll see if the security camera in front of the pub has finally been fixed, and request the footage if so. She'll ask the owner who was in tonight, and check if they saw the accident. She'll tell Bill at the local garage to report any suspicious damage to the front of a vehicle. But in all likelihood, she'll never find out who did this. Even if she does, and can prove it, a sympathetic magistrate will let the driver out in a year or two—and in the meantime, the bodies will keep piling up. Around here, drink-driving is the rule, not the exception.

Once, Kiara spent all weekend in a patrol car on this very corner, breath-testing people. Some of them said she was 'cheating' by doing it so close to the pub.

Rafa finally answers the phone. 'G'day, Detective.'

'Got a hit-and-run on the corner of Victoria and Phillip streets,' Kiara says, without preamble. 'By the time you get here, I think you'll be picking up a body.'

In the background of the call, she can hear several shouted conversations, clinking glasses and the tootling of poker machines. She realises he's in the pub just behind her. It would have been quicker to walk in and grab him.

'Be right out,' Rafa says, and the line goes dead.

Elise is still doing the chest compressions. But the man's skin has gone grey. His eyes are no longer focused; the pupils dilated. Soon the cloudy film will form over them. He's gone.

While Elise works, Kiara goes to the other side of the body to search his pockets. Phone, keys and a receipt from the pub: chicken Caesar salad and a Cascade Premium Light, order number thirty-nine. When she flips open the leather phone case, she finds a pair of twenties and a selection of cards: driver's licence, Medicare, a couple of bank cards. Anton Rabbek, born 3 February 1971, lives at 15/3 Barton Street, banks with Macquarie. Apparently he wears glasses; Kiara spots them a few metres away, an arm bent and a lens cracked. The photo on the driver's licence is a good match for the corpse, at least from the nose up.

She pushes a button on his car key: no reaction from any of the vehicles nearby. Barton Street is about a kilometre away and perhaps the only area of Warrigal you could describe as 'upmarket'—a lot of fancy townhouses. The guy was probably doing the right thing and walking home from the pub after his light beer. Another good bloke killed by a bad one who Kiara will try and fail to catch, while the rest of the town keeps drinking itself to death.

She has long since resigned herself to care for this place, however little it cares for her. Her family has been here for tens of thousands of years. She endures the violence, the racism and the homophobia. But Elise has been through so much already. Doesn't *she* deserve better?

It's not the time to discuss this. But it never is. On those rare afternoons when neither of them is working and they're sharing the hammock under the pergola, Kiara never wants to spoil the present by mentioning the future.

She squeezes Elise's shoulder. 'Do you want to get out of here?'

Elise is still doing compressions. 'Should wait for Rafa,' she puffs.

'I mean, we could move.' Kiara tries to keep the desperation out of her voice. 'To a different town.'

They can't afford to go anywhere. But the thought of staying is unbearable.

Elise takes a break, sagging back onto her knees. She wipes some sweat off her brow and looks up. Her grim smile chills Kiara to the bone.

'What?' Elise gestures at the pub, the blood-spattered road, the dead man. 'And leave all this behind?'

ONE MONTH LATER

KIARA

The house has a rustic look, with a weathered brick exterior and dark wood trim. There's a low-maintenance garden out the front, typical of short-term rentals: no lawn to mow, no veggie patch to water, just rose bushes herding visitors onto the path with their thorns.

The building is two storeys high, which is unusual way out here, where land is plentiful and it's cheaper to build out than up. Kiara supposes that if you're going to put a house on a mountaintop, you may as well go a couple of metres higher so the upper windows have a view over the tree canopy. Part of the roof has been damaged, perhaps by hail. A brown tarpaulin covers the hole, billowing in the breeze.

If anyone has been in the upstairs bedroom over the past several minutes, they might have seen the Tactical Response Group driving up the hill. If so, they've had some time to prepare for the raid.

Kiara adjusts her stab vest. She's gained some weight since she was fitted for it, creating gaps in front of her armpits. She's also very aware that it doesn't protect her arms or throat.

'I'm going to knock on the front door,' she says.

The commander looks at her like that's the dumbest idea he's ever heard. He's dressed more like a soldier than a police officer, with knee and elbow pads, and various tools dangling from a chest rig. Behind the visor of his riot helmet, his nose is crooked and his grey-flecked beard is patchy.

Kiara first met him at a critical incident eight years ago. A terrified teenage girl had called triple zero because her drugged-up boyfriend was threatening her with a samurai sword, which he'd duct-taped to his own hand so he couldn't be disarmed. When the response group broke into the townhouse, the boy whirled to face them, and the squad commander blasted him with a shotgun. He died, never having to explain his actions or reveal who'd sold him the meth and the sword. The group commander didn't care about any of that, but Kiara did.

She hasn't met the rest of the team: three other men and one woman, huddled around the commander. He says, 'You want to give them *even more* warning?'

'I want to give them the chance to surrender peacefully,' Kiara says.

'According to your witness, they're armed and dangerous.'

Early this morning, a woman stumbled down the mountain in a dressing-gown, and was nearly hit by a car on the highway. The driver took her to hospital, where she babbled about knives and killers but also about God and falling branches. She's still recovering from hypothermia.

'My witness is barely coherent,' Kiara says. 'Let me try to talk them down before you go in, guns blazing.'

'Listen to me. You've been a detective for what, a month?'

It's actually been less than three weeks. This is Kiara's first case since her promotion, and she's only leading because it's a public holiday, and Rohan, her sergeant, is visiting his parents in Queensland. If he'd been the one to interview Ms Dubois, she's sure he would have sent a more senior officer.

'What's your point?' she asks.

'They might kill you.'

Usually this idea wouldn't rattle Kiara. It's a risk every time she puts on the uniform—and even when she doesn't. She once spent four nights hanging around a Wagga Wagga car park in fishnets, trying to catch a rapist who'd targeted sex workers in the area.

But Elise is already fragile. What will happen to her if Kiara doesn't come home?

Kiara swallows the thought. 'I'm more concerned about *you* killing *them*,' she says.

The commander jabs a stubby finger at her chest. 'You're making this operation unnecessarily difficult and danger-ous for me and my men.'

Kiara's gaze flicks to the only woman on his team, who doesn't seem offended. She looks like she's in her fifties, with cracks around her mouth and greying curls. Kiara is thirty-three and has learned not to expect support from older women in the job. Having put up with worse sexism in decades past, they expect her to *suck it up, princess*.

'Noted,' Kiara says, and walks towards the front door, hands up.

It's finally stopped sprinkling, but the cobblestones are still slick. The afternoon sun isn't warm enough to dry them. Ahead of her, a wind-chime dangles from a rain gutter, wooden tubes clacking in the breeze.

Kiara edges around the front veranda, with its bench seat on the left, a door on the right, and muddy footprints everywhere. The boards squeak under her feet. The doormat is printed with banksia flowers and a slogan: *Bless this mess!*

After knocking on the door, she steps to one side out of habit, even though Ms Dubois told her no one in the house had a gun. 'My name's Kiara,' she calls. 'I'm a police officer. You okay in there?'

No answer.

'I just want to make sure everyone's safe. Do you need first aid? Water? Something to eat, maybe?'

The classic siege strategy is to offer pizza, but the nearest pizza place is in Warrigal, more than an hour away. Kiara is pretty sure she has a banana in her patrol car, though; it wasn't too spotty last time she looked.

'You know what always helps me get some perspective . . .? Fruit.'

Still no sound from inside. She pulls on a pair of latex gloves and tries the handle. It turns—Ms Dubois must not have locked it when she fled.

Kiara looks back at the commander. He glares at her, warning her not to do what she's thinking about doing.

She calls out, 'I'm coming in, okay?' Then she opens the door and steps inside.

Kiara finds herself in a narrow hallway. There's a window on her right, along with some coat hooks and a spot to hang skis, even though Kiara thinks there's not enough snow and too many trees for skiing. A few suitcases and saggy backpacks are lined up against the opposite wall, open as if their owners only got halfway through packing them.

Kiara walks to the end of the hall, where there's a framed poster with a collage of comforting words—*holiday, family, home, love, happy*, et cetera—and turns left.

In the living and dining area, two cream couches sit near a modern-looking fireplace. A glass dining table is surrounded by high-backed chairs. Big windows look out into the bush, and there's a giant TV for those who don't like the view. Only two Blu-rays occupy the shelf: *The Silver Brumby* and *The Man from Snowy River*.

A copperish scent lingers in the air. Blood and urine.

Still turning left, Kiara takes in the kitchen, separated from the dining area by an island bench made of white granite, dirty plates stacked on one corner. Wineglasses are everywhere, puddles of red at the bottom. There's a brushed-steel fridge with a built-in ice machine, an oven big enough to roast a whole pig in, and a body on the floor. Face up, throat slit.

Kiara says into her lapel mic, 'Got a body here.'

The commander comes on the radio immediately. 'Time to go.'

He's right. She's confirmed the house is a crime scene—now it's her job to walk back out the door without touching anything, then summon forensics. But there could still be someone alive in here, meaning the Tactical Response Group will have to clear the building first. They'll trample all over the bloody footprints around the body, and probably shoot any witnesses they find. Then Kiara will never figure out what happened.

Praise for Jack Heath's Hangman series

'Jack Heath's writing grabs you by the throat, gnaws on your bones and washes it all down with a hefty dose of funny. Sick, twisted, violent and oh so good. In Timothy Blake, Heath has created a one-of-a-kind character. I hope.'—Emma Viskic, internationally bestselling author of *And Fire Came Down*

'Blake is a brilliant, complex character . . . this quiet and unassuming figure might just be the most dangerous man in the room. *Hangman* is cinematic and grubby, brimming with pulpy noir.'—Michael Offer, producer, *How to Get Away with Murder* and *Homeland*

'Wild and original, *Hangman* stamps a high and bloodied mark on this dark genre. Hannibal Lecter will be adding Jack Heath to his reading list.'—Ben Sanders, internationally bestselling author of *American Blood*

'Let's cut to the chase: *Hangman* is a great read! Jack Heath's boundless imagination and singular voice have produced a truly unique thriller. By turns psychologically insightful, wonderfully disturbed and even darkly comedic, *Hangman* will keep you coursing through the pages at a lightning pace. Brilliant! (Probably best read with lights on and doors locked. I'm just saying.)'—Jeffery Deaver, No. 1 international bestselling author

'*Hangman* is ghoulish fun, and fills the Dexter- and Hannibal-shaped holes in our lives.'—*Books + Publishing*

'A grisly, efficiently written nail-biter packed with riddles and suspense, *Hangman* has bestseller written all over it. It's a dark book, but one with plenty of humour, and a twisty plot that keeps you guessing to the very end.'
—*Sydney Morning Herald*

'Compelling . . . Heath keeps the suspense at a high level through to its stunning conclusion. An addictive and suspenseful thriller that will keep you reading well into the night.'—*Canberra Weekly*

'Blake is a classic kind of hard-boiled hero, mixing cynicism and honour, brutality and sentimentality . . . he's a chivalrous knight of the kind we have never seen before.'
—*Weekend Australian Review*

'A cracking read full of well-crafted twists and turns . . . Heath manages to bring Blake out from behind the shadow of his predecessors and stand on his own.'
—*Australian Crime Fiction*

'Heath has given the crime world an anti-hero for this century. Gifted and flawed, Blake will horrify and entrance readers, quite often at the same time. An exceptionally taut novel both in action and execution, this sledge-hammer story is sure to entice fans of serial crime fiction, taking readers into the dark and dirty recesses of Blake's mind.'
—*Good Reading*

'*Hangman* is a pulpy and perverse delight . . . Heath makes Blake young, rough, streetwise, and precisely the sort of person Dr Lecter would avoid in the street. This is a gobsmackingly (or lip-smackingly) violent tale, but it is also bizarre, hilarious, and a stealthily astute commentary on post-financial crisis America. Give me more.'—Christopher Richardson (blog)

'Richer than Reacher . . . *Hangman* literally tingles with tension, and Heath injects a healthy dose of dark humour.'—*Sydney Arts Guide*

'*Hangman* is cheerful in its gore, with a knack for unexpected violence that'll leave even the most jaded crime readers at least a little bit impressed . . . It's all the best parts of noir fiction, all the spatter pattern ghoulishness of forensics-focused dramas, and so much fun it might just concern you a little bit.'—Hush Hush Biz (blog)

'Gloriously messed up, with a protagonist who manages to be likeable, reprehensible and totally singular all at once. A crime series like no other.'—Gabriel Bergmoser, author of *The Hunted*

'Thrilling, grisly and inventive: Jack Heath has single-handedly increased my carbon footprint through lights left on.'—Benjamin Stevenson, author of *Either Side of Midnight*

'Heath will make your spine tingle and your fingers flip pages.'—Candice Fox, author of *Crimson Lake*